The Cellar

By Katherine Lo

ISBN 978-0-9904806-0-0 (ebook)
ISBN 978-0-9904806-1-7 (paperback)
ISBN: 0990480615

Contents

For my mother, Virginia Mae Lo,
and for all my students who have lost someone dear to them

Chapter 1

IT SEEMS LIKE there ought to be some kind of warning before something terrible happens, something that is going to change your life forever. But there isn't. The most awful things can happen on the most beautiful days, like a plane crashing into Tower One of the World Trade Center where my uncle worked. On that sunny day, when the sky was a perfect blue, the world was watching a terrible, large-scale tragedy on their television screens. I was watching my uncle die.

Some of my earliest memories are of my Uncle Denny—vivid swirls of color and sensation, like most early memories. I remember the green of the grass in Central Park where he'd take me in the summertime. I remember the soft, moist feel of the bread mashed in my hands that he'd give me to throw to the pigeons. I remember the deep-barreled boom of his laugh and the sudden tilt of earth and sky when he'd sweep me off the ground and onto his shoulders. I remember the sticky slurp of the ice-creams he would buy me, which ended up all over my face and shirt and hair. When we'd get home, my mother's expression would start in a scold, but after just seconds of looking at Uncle Denny, something silent passing between them, she always ended up laughing instead.

My father used to call my mother and Uncle Denny *Yin* and *Yang*. It wasn't until I was in the third grade that I finally discovered he hadn't made those names up himself and they actually meant something. We were learning about China at school, and I came home with a picture of a Yin and Yang symbol one day and asked my father which was which when it came to my mother and Uncle Denny. With a sly glance across the room at my mother, he pointed at the black half and said, "Your mother is the dark half and Denny is the light."

"What a thing to tell your daughter, John!" she exclaimed, swinging a pillow from the couch at his head. My father ducked sideways and laughed.

"Well, it's true."

My mother stilled. "I suppose it is," she said after a moment. She'd explained the concept of twins to me the year before, and that combined with the symbol I now had made me visualize my mother and Uncle Denny as babies curled in their mother's womb, nestled together toe to head like two commas, each one containing a speck of the other. Now one of the halves had been torn away, and eleven months later I found myself sitting in a car next to my mother somewhere in northern Virginia instead of our Brooklyn apartment where we belonged.

"Here we are," she said, turning off the engine. We listened to it tick and settle as we stared through the windshield at the house in front of us. It was a white, wooden structure with black shutters and a porch that ran around the front all the way down the left side, overlooking a wide field of grass bordered by a split rail fence and a thicket of trees. It looked like something out of a movie, only less polished. The white was dingy and peeling, and the grass was on the scraggly side.

I waited for her to turn the car back on. To laugh and ask *What was I thinking?* But instead she said, "Let's get this car unloaded," and opened her door, admitting a wave of August heat. I let out a sigh and slowly opened my own door. The summers in Virginia didn't seem to be any less hot and humid than they were in New York. In fact, it felt a lot worse as I climbed out of my seat, my body stiff from the day's drive.

My mother stopped at the edge of the porch and looked up at the house again. I could see her shoulder blades through her t-shirt. She'd lost so much weight in the past year, it seemed like bones were sticking out everywhere. They shifted as she squared her shoulders and headed up the steps. "Come on, Julia," she called. "Grab a box."

I slid a box of books from the back seat and followed her inside, which was only slightly cooler. "Please tell me there's air-conditioning," I said. My mother turned, grimacing.

"Sorry, but I think it's just fans for us." She headed back out and I stood in the hallway for a moment, surveying the rooms on either side, trying to determine the best location for the box I was holding. Both rooms were only sparsely furnished, but it looked like the room on my left was once a library or study of some kind. Built-in shelves lined the upper half of the back and side walls, and there was a desk and chair positioned between the two front windows. Beyond that, the room was empty of furniture. I dropped my box in front of the shelves. Its loud *thump* had a sound of permanence that made my stomach twist. *This is only temporary*, I reminded myself. *A change of scene so Mom can focus on getting better.* She appeared in the hallway, pulling a suitcase behind her, and paused in the doorway.

"Susan said there wouldn't be much here, but I told her we only need the basics." My mother glanced at the room to her right. "Looks like there's a decent couch in there, and Susan said the bedrooms are ready for us." Her inflection went up at the end, like she was asking a question. It was like that the whole drive. *This hotel looks pretty nice? It's going to be beautiful up there? Your brother will probably enjoy the time alone with Dad?* Her doubt and frailty poking out as clearly as her shoulder blades. I watched the flicker of shadows cast against the wall by the trees outside for a moment. *Let's go home. Let's go back to Dad and Matty.* But I couldn't say those things. Not when I could feel her sadness creeping toward me like a thick fog.

"It's fine," I said instead, turning to face her. Wisps of hair stuck to her flushed face, and her mouth began to tremble. I shouldn't have hesitated. "It's fine," I repeated, walking over and looping my arms over her shoulders. Her own arms circled my waist and squeezed tightly.

"Thanks," she whispered. I held her for another moment then pulled away.

"I'm gonna go get some more stuff out of the car, okay?"

"Okay, yeah." She brushed at her eyes and smiled at me, her face still blurry with emotion. I walked out to the car and took my time unloading my own suitcase. Being here, hundreds of miles away from my father and brother, was the exact opposite of fine. But it was what my mother needed, so I was going to have to at least pretend. Worrying about me was the last thing she needed.

By the time we finished unloading the car, sweat dripped from my forehead and plastered my shirt to my back. The bedroom I chose was partially shaded by a huge oak tree growing at the back of the house, but the heat was still miserable. I was dumping clothes into the dresser when my mother poked her head in.

"I'm going to the store to get a few fans and some groceries. Want to come with me?"

I shook my head. "No, I'm just going to finish this and take a look around, if that's okay."

"Of course. Explore all you want." My mother ran her hand along the doorframe. "This is quite a historic house, you know. Susan said it was built before the Civil War and that the same family lived in it until she and Carl bought it." Susan was an old friend of my mother's who was into buying and renovating old houses.

"Wow, the same family? Weren't they, like, super old?" Dumb, but my mother smiled anyway.

"You know what I mean."

"Seriously, though, that's kind of crazy." I couldn't think of anyone in New York who lived in the same apartment their parents grew up in, much less their grandparents. "Why did they sell it after all that time?"

"Oh, I don't know. We didn't get into that."

I swiped a hand across my damp forehead. "Maybe they moved into a house with air-conditioning, like every other sane family in the 21st century."

My mother gave me an exasperated look. "Maybe so." She turned and headed for the stairs. "I'll be back in an hour or so."

I finished unpacking my suitcase and shoved an additional box with odds and ends into a corner with my foot. An old mirror was mounted on the wall above the box, and I studied my reflection in its weathered surface. My cheeks were bright red and my hair was alternately plastered to my skull and shoved up in damp spikes, which made me grin in spite of my misery. After dealing with the hassle of long, girly blond hair since elementary school, I'd shocked my family by coming home last year on my sixteenth birthday with all of it cut off. My mother had clutched her face and wailed, "Oh my God! Your beautiful hair! You look like a boy!" I'd enjoyed her shock until my father ruined it by saying, "No, she doesn't look like a boy. She looks like a little pixie—a little fairy girl." My own smile had faded as his grew. "You're a little Tinkerbell now. It's *adorable*," he'd added with exaggerated sarcasm, ruffling my shorn head like a puppy's. I hate Disney characters and my father knew this. He'd started calling me "Tink" from that moment on. I'd been tempted to grow it back out again just to make him stop, but I'd ended up liking the ease and comfort of my short hair too much to go through with it. And Uncle Denny had loved it.

For a brief second, I had the urge to run out to the hall and holler for my father to come take a look at me. But then I remembered where I was and that there was no one to look. I went into the bathroom and turned on the faucet over the bathtub. It was one of those old-fashioned ones, enormous and standing like some beast on four elaborate claws. I sat on the edge and pulled my cell phone out of my pocket to call home. My brother answered.

"Hey, Matty."

"What's that noise?"

"I'm filling the tub with cold water so I can take a bath. It's a million degrees here and there's no air-conditioning."

"That sucks."

"Yeah." I paused. "How's Dad?"

I heard my brother blow out a gust of air and shift position. He was probably lying on the couch. "All right. Working a lot. But he's being kind of weird. Yesterday, he just stood in the doorway watching me and Jeff playing video games, but not really watching us, you know? Just kind of...staring. I think it creeped Jeff out."

"Yeah." I sighed. "Mom's the same."

"This is dumb. You guys shouldn't—" his voice faltered. "It's dumb," he repeated.

"I know, Matty. Trust me, I know. I don't want us to be here either, but you know what Mom's been like. I couldn't let her come here by herself."

"I guess. But you should get her to come home soon."

"I'll try." My brother made it sound so easy, but what did he know? He was only thirteen. I heard the television go on in the background.

"Well, UFC's coming on now." His last few words got mangled by the crunch of potato chips. I had never been able to understand how he could switch gears like that.

"You're such a pig," I muttered. I could feel his shrug over the phone.

"Whatever." The bag crackled, and I could picture it all so clearly—him sprawled on the red couch in our living room, remote in hand and bag of chips resting on his chest, the afternoon sun filtering through the windows of our Brooklyn apartment where the A.C. was humming.

"Love you."

"Yeah, okay, bye." My brother was clearly not in the mood for anything mushy.

I put the phone on the floor and stripped off my clothes. The tub was about halfway full. I stepped in and gasped at the shock of the cool water against my overheated skin. I lowered myself slowly until I was sitting, then submerged myself fully. I closed my eyes, and with the water roaring in my ears, I let myself pretend that none of this is real. That I was floating in some cool river carrying me outside of time.

--->=◉ ◉=<---

The house was one of several my mother's friend Susan and her husband were working on renovating and selling, and they had left this one midway through to go visit their daughter, who'd just had a baby. So far, most of the work seemed to have been done on the upstairs. Everything downstairs was either bare or looked like it'd been here for ages. I let myself out the back door and went down the steps. The oak tree that shaded my room stood about a dozen feet away.

I stood in its shade for a moment, unsure of what to do. I wasn't used to this kind of space or the quiet. I was used to the constant hum of noise and flurry of activity that was typical of the city. The silence here felt as heavy as the muggy air. I turned to go back into the house when something to the left of the steps caught my eye. Lying at a diagonal slant against the back of the kitchen were two wooden doors covered in peeling white paint.

A cellar.

I'd never seen one before in real life, but I'd read about them and seen them on TV. I even used to wish when I was a kid that my family could live in a house that had one. Or an attic—some place where mysterious treasures might be hidden. I might not be a kid any more, but I couldn't help a small prick of excitement as I crouched down to take a closer look. It turned to disappointment when I saw the pull rings attached to the doors had a padlock through them.

Hearing the crunch of gravel, I hurried around the side of the house and held the car door as my mom slid out. "Mom, did Susan leave you all the keys for the house?" My mother reached for her purse and slung it over her shoulder.

"What do you mean?"

"I think there's a cellar in the back, but it has a lock on it. Are there any extra keys? I want to try to open it."

"A cellar, huh?" My mother opened the door to the back seat and pulled out a bag. "We can look after you help me unload this stuff." She pulled out a pair of black rubber flip-flops. "I got you these. Thought they'd be more comfy than those things," she said, eyeing my battered Converse sneakers. I made a face.

"You know I don't like things between my toes." Her mouth tightened and I noticed how exhausted she looked. "Fine," I said, taking them from her. I grabbed a few of the bags and followed her. I was already starting to sweat again, the plastic handles of the bags cutting into my hands as I carried them into the house. When

I dumped them on the kitchen counter, one of them made a solid *thunk*. "What did you get?" I asked, opening the bag. My mother glanced over.

"Oh, a flashlight in case the power ever goes out," she said. I pulled it out and hefted it in my hand.

"Perfect. I can use it in the cellar." I stared at her, and from the way her brows came together, I could tell she'd already forgotten. "Keys? For the lock?"

"Oh, right. Um…" My mother rummaged in her purse, then tossed a key ring at me, which I caught and examined. There were three regular-sized keys, but wedged in the middle of them was a smaller, brass-colored key. It looked old.

"I think this might be it!" I bit my lip. What was I, six? But what else was there around here to get excited about?

"Well, go check it out, and then help me finish putting this stuff away."

"Okay." I opened the back door and ran down the steps. I set the flashlight on the ground in front of the cellar doors and knelt with my knees braced against them. The key fit in the lock but wouldn't turn. I jiggled it a bit, then pushed against it harder, the edges biting into my fingers. Suddenly, the key turned and the lock popped open. I slipped it free of the rings and tossed it on the grass. Standing, I grasped one of the rings and pulled. With a slight sticking sound of old paint letting loose, the door swung toward me. I opened it until it was folded all the way back on its hinges and resting against the ground.

The sunshine revealed concrete steps fading into darkness. Picking up the flashlight, I shone it into the space below. There were only a few wispy cobwebs and a slight haze of dust, but not much else. I descended slowly, turning the beam from side to side. I would have thought a cellar dating back to the Civil War would just be made of dirt, but someone had lined this one with concrete. At the bottom of the steps, I saw a cord hanging from a bare light bulb. I pulled it, and to my surprise, the light turned on. It was a low-wattage bulb and only brought the cellar from dark to dim, but it made the flashlight unnecessary. I turned it off and looked around, but it was bare. No secret treasure. Not even some old junk. I felt let down and stupid for feeling let down. What had I expected?

The cellar was about ten feet wide and seven or eight feet deep, and I could touch the ceiling with my fingertips. I liked that. At five-foot-two, there wasn't much I could reach that easily. And then I realized something else that made me even happier. For the first time since driving into this godforsaken place, the air around me was cool. "Hallelujah," I breathed. I leaned against one of the walls and closed my eyes. Finally, something about this house I could like—a place that wasn't a thousand sticky degrees. A place where the quiet felt right.

A sudden noise popped my eyes back open. It was a raspy, scratching sound, like something heavy being dragged on the floor. I pushed away from the wall and turned the flashlight back on, but there was nothing around me that could have possibly made that noise. I waited for several more minutes, listening intently, but there was only silence. Maybe my mother was moving boxes in the kitchen and somehow the sound had traveled down here into the cellar. But how was that possible through all the layers of dirt and concrete separating the two?

I headed back up, and as I stepped through the back door I saw my mother. The question I was about to ask stopped in my throat. She was standing in the middle of the kitchen, shoulders hunched. A box sat open on the counter next to her.

"Mom?"

I walked over and saw what she was cradling against her stomach. It was a Yankees mug. Uncle Denny's mug. The one he'd always drunk his coffee out of whenever he came over to our apartment, which had been nearly every Saturday morning of my life. A mug I'd put in the box at the last minute, wanting to bring some small part of him with us.

"Mom," I said again, touching her hand. She raised her head, and as her eyes met mine, her face collapsed inward and she began to sob. I wrapped my arms around her and held her as tightly as I could, the mug still between us digging into my ribs.

Chapter 2

BY THE END of our first week in Virginia, my mother and I had already established a kind of routine, which seemed to be built around her avoiding me. We ate dinner together, but the rest of the time, she shut herself in the library. One of the things she talked about when she first brought up the idea of coming to Virginia was painting again. She'd been working as a fashion buyer for Macy's in New York, but she'd been an art major in college. She found an art supply store our second day here, and now there was an easel set up in the library and the desk was covered with a tarp and various art books and supplies.

I didn't know what she was working on. She always shut the door and I wasn't invited in. When I knocked a few days earlier and asked what she was up to, she answered, "I'm working, Julia. Mind if we do our own thing in the mornings?" Of course I said that was fine, *fine* being the go-to answer lately, but I couldn't help wondering why she brought me with her if she didn't want to talk to me. And if she wasn't not talking to me, how I was supposed to help her get better enough to go home?

My phone buzzed in my pocket. It was my friend Sarah, who'd already left me three messages.

"Julia! Oh my gosh, it's about time!"

"Sorry. Things have been kind of busy here."

"That's okay. So what's it like?"

"All right, I guess. It's a really old house. Creaky floorboards and all that, which is kind of cool, but no air-conditioning."

"Ugh. You poor thing. I'd die without air-conditioning. So," she said, her voice turning tentative, "how's your mom? Is she doing better?"

"Sarah, it's only been a few days."

"Right." I tensed at the disappointment in her voice. "But I'm sure she'll be doing better soon. I mean, without having everything around her, you know. And some space and all that beautiful countryside. I'm sure it will be very healing for her."

"Yeah. I hope so." Sarah didn't seem to hear the doubt in my voice, because she started talking about Jacob, the boy she was dating, and how he was starting to blow her off. Hanging up an hour later, after we'd analyzed everything he said to her in the last two weeks, I realized that I was a little bit glad to be away from my friends. They kept wanting me to be happy and my mother to be better, and it felt like I kept letting them down by still being sad and not having better news about my mom. So I faked being okay and faked being interested in all the same things I used to be interested in, and it had started to get exhausting. Down here, at least I'd only have to fake it once in awhile.

I headed down to the cellar, where I'd spent most of the hot, mid-afternoon hours the last several days. I'd set up a chair and a tray table I'd found, where I could set a glass of iced tea. Not exactly plush, but a good enough place to sit for an hour or more, listening to music, my eyes closed, memories flickering in my mind like pieces of film. Family dinners, wrestling with Matty for the remote control, my mother putting her feet on my dad's lap and rubbing my head while we watched a movie. How had that all changed so quickly? How was it that when Uncle Denny died, we didn't just lose him but our whole way of being a family together? But that was just it. Uncle Denny *was* part of our family being together. He had no wife or kids of his own and was over at our place all the time.

When I was in the fourth grade, I was actually shocked to find out that most of my classmates saw their aunts and uncles only a few times a year and considered them virtual strangers who had no real part in their immediate families. I'd even gotten in an argument with a classmate about it, and two nights later, when Uncle Denny was over for dinner, I asked him about it.

"You're part of our real family, aren't you?" He raised his eyebrows at my question and leaned back in his chair.

"Of course I am, baby girl. Why do you ask?"

"Jenny Hawkins says you're not. She says aunts and uncles and grandparents are only extended family."

"Is that so?" My uncle took a swig of his beer. "Well, Jenny Hawkins sounds like a little bitch. I wouldn't pay any attention to what she says."

"Dennis Shaw, I would ask you not to use that kind of language around my nine-year-old daughter," said my mother primly, but my uncle and I just grinned at each other.

Today I had a stack of magazines from my mother's bedroom. Even though she quit her job at Macy's a few weeks after Uncle Denny's memorial service, she still had a habit of buying fashion magazines every time she was at the store—*Cosmopolitan, Vogue, Glamour*. Much to her disappointment, I'd never developed much interest in fashion. But today, glossy pictures and celebrity gossip were just the kind of distraction I needed.

Settling into my chair in the cellar, I propped the flashlight against my shoulder and began thumbing through the first magazine. After about twenty pages of ads, I got to the first article, which was about the must-have handbag for the fall. I skipped ahead to the one on "How to Please Your Man." Never mind the fact that I still didn't know how to even *get* a man. It couldn't hurt to be prepared.

I was only one paragraph in when a faint noise caught my attention. I straightened up in my chair. There it was again—a faint rustling. I shone the flashlight in the direction the sound seemed to be coming from, but there was nothing there. *I must be imagining things.*

Nothing else happened for several minutes, so I relaxed and went back to the magazine. Just as I reached for my iced tea, a sudden flash of white flickered in my peripheral vision. My hand jerked, knocking the glass over. Definitely *not* my imagination. Heart pounding, I stood up and did another sweep of the cellar with my flashlight, but it was still empty. My mind raced with possibilities. *Maybe it's just those color spots you get when you move your head too quickly. Maybe this is some type of delayed heatstroke.* And then I heard it—the faint tapping of footsteps going up the cellar stairs.

⇥═◉ ◉═⇤

"Did Susan mention anything strange about this house?" I asked my mother as we made dinner that night.

"What do you mean?"

"Like, I don't know, any ghost stories or anything?" It sounded ridiculous out loud, but I couldn't take it back. My mother looked up from the tomato she was slicing.

"She didn't, but you can call her and ask her yourself if you want. Why, did you see a ghost?" My mother's skepticism was obvious.

"No, of course not." I didn't believe in ghosts any more than the Tooth Fairy. But I needed something to explain what happened in the cellar other than early signs of insanity. "I'll call her. It'd be cool to learn more about the house's history. Might break up the monotony a little," I added without thinking. I winced as soon as the words came out. Maybe she hadn't noticed. But of course she had. There was a pause in the sound of the knife against the cutting board.

"I'm sorry you find living here such a drag." Her tone was frosty, full of hurt. "You know you can leave any time."

"Mom," I started, but she cut me off.

"I know you and your father and Matty all think I'm being selfish, that I'm going off and leaving everything like this is some kind of, I don't know, *vacation* or something." Her voice rose and she threw the knife down with a clatter. "I hate this too. I hate being away from your brother and dad. But I can't live in that city right now. I can't keep waiting for Denny to walk in the door. I asked, you know. I asked your father to come with us, for this to be a family thing, and he said no. So this," she waved her hand in the air, "is both of us—not just me." She leaned against the counter and her shoulders slumped.

"I know, Mom." I folded my arms across my chest and stared at the floor. I thought of all the fights I heard between my parents in the weeks before we came out here, the accusations of denial and selfishness. Neither of them was right, but neither of them was wrong either. And that was what made this all so hard. I could understand why she needed to be here even while I believed we both needed to be home. And that was why I was here. I had watched her drift farther from us with every week that passed while we were in New York, and that was with all of us in the same apartment. How far would she go without any connection at all? I rubbed my face at the thought.

"Look," I said as the silence between us lengthened. "Let's just finish the salad, okay?" My mother's lips twitched and she made a sound somewhere between a sob and a laugh.

"You sound just like your uncle." She swiped her eyes, then opened the cupboard and pulled out a bottle of wine.

"What's that?"

"I'm just having a glass of wine with dinner, okay? Relax." Another thing my parents fought about constantly in the month before we left—how much she was drinking. My mother changed the subject. "I called the school this morning and tomorrow's registration for the seniors. Make sure you're up in time. We need to head over about nine."

"Okay." I carried the salad into the dining room and set it on the table. My mother followed with the plates. I tried not to, but I couldn't help noticing that instead of just bringing in a glass of wine, she'd brought the whole bottle.

When my alarm first went off the next morning, it took me a minute to figure out why I'd set it. I groaned when I finally remembered and pulled my pillow over my head. Seconds later, my mother was banging on the door.

"Get up, Julia. We leave in half an hour."

"Okay," I said into my pillow.

"Julia, did you hear me?"

"I said okay," I repeated, throwing the pillow to the side. I sat up and leaned over to open my dresser. The room was so small I could reach it from the edge of my bed. I pulled out some clothes at random and headed into the bathroom, where I did a quick version of my morning routine. When I entered the kitchen, my mother was rinsing out a mug.

"You'd better hustle," she said. "I don't want to end up at the back of the line."

"I'm hustling." I poured myself a bowl of cereal and looked up to see my mother eyeing my outfit critically. "What?" I asked, looking down at myself. I was wearing a pair of cut-offs and a faded Blondie t-shirt I'd found at a thrift store.

"Couldn't you have put on something a little nicer?"

"Why?"

"It's your first time at this school."

"We're just filling out some forms."

"I know, but I don't want people getting the wrong impression about you. You're such a nice, pretty girl. You look borderline homeless in that outfit." She brushed some of my hair to the side and picked a piece of lint off my shirt. Her movements were shaky, almost agitated. "I just want things to go well for you here, Julia."

"I promise I'll look nicer on the first day, okay?" Not that I really cared what kind of impression I made. What did it matter when we were only going to be here a month or two? But I kept those thoughts to myself. My mother didn't look like she could handle much this morning. Her white dress was stylish and fresh, but her face was grey. She noticed me studying her and turned away.

"Just make sure you're ready to go."

I went over to the trash can to throw out the rest of my cereal and saw the wine bottle from last night, empty. *So much for fresh starts.*

On the drive to school, I made a mental note of the route. A few turns brought us out of the residential area onto the highway, where we passed a row of shops, a steakhouse, and a gas station before things opened up into a large, grassy field. It was dotted with football players in blue jerseys running laps and high-stepping their way through tires.

"That's not so bad," my mother said as we pull into the parking lot. "It will probably only take you about fifteen or twenty minutes to walk."

"I guess." Seeing all the students arriving in their own cars, I had a feeling I'd be one of the only ones walking to and from school. In New York, hardly anyone drove a car, or at least not in the city. My mom already had to buy a used Camry for our trip up here, so I knew asking for a car of my own wasn't an option. Plus there was the small fact that I didn't know how to drive.

I tried to remind myself that it didn't matter, but I couldn't help feeling a little like some transplant weirdo walking to the main office with my mom in the middle of what seemed like hordes of preppy teens in khaki shorts and pastel polo shirts, all squealing with delight at the sight of each other if they were girls, or hand slapping and fist bumping each other if they were boys. Apparently, everyone at this school was best friends.

The plus side of everyone being so occupied greeting each other was that there was hardly any line at the registration table. When we got to the front, a heavyset woman with tight grey curls asked, "New or returning?"

"New," my mother answered, and the woman handed her a large envelope.

"Fill these out and return them by Friday," she said. "Next!" My mother and I scooted out of the way.

"That's it?" I asked.

"Here." My mother thrust the envelope at me. "You can carry this." As we headed back to the parking lot, a group of boys started jostling each other, and one staggered into me as I walked past.

"Sorry about that," he said, grinning at me as he punched the boy who pushed him in the shoulder.

"That's okay." I kept walking.

"He was cute," my mom said a few seconds later.

"What?"

"That boy who ran into you. He was cute. You should have introduced yourself."

"You're kidding, right?" We climbed into the car and she turned the ignition.

"No, I'm not. It'd be nice for you to have some friends. Maybe go out on a date or two."

"What's the point of that? I've got friends."

My mother's mouth pinched as she shifted gears to reverse. "I'm just making a suggestion. I want you to be okay here. Because I can't..." She stopped and tried again. "I can't..." But her voice failed again. *I can't take care of you*, was what she seemed to be trying to say.

"Mom." I touched her hand and she turned to face me. "I am okay here. You don't need to worry. Just focus on yourself and, you know, whatever you need." My mother's eyes skittered away and we were both silent on the drive home.

When we got to the house, my mother paused only long enough to toss the keys on the hallway table before heading upstairs. "I'm going to lie down for a little while," she said. She went into her room and shut the door. I probably wouldn't see her again until dinner. A year ago it was the other way around. Me going into my room and closing the door but knowing I could come out any time and talk to her. Knowing that she wanted to spend time with me. There were still glimpses of that, the old mom, the Mom Before Denny Died, but they were becoming fewer and fewer. A brief concern about my clothes or a comment about a boy, and then the door shut. I thought with just the two of us here, she'd talk to me more, that she'd open up about what she was thinking and feeling and we could finally grieve Uncle Denny together. But instead she seemed to find it harder.

Almost a year had gone by since he died, and I was still waiting for things to go back to normal. The urge to call him was overwhelming. I could even imagine the conversation.

What's up?

Mom's being difficult.

Yeah, she does that sometimes. I'll talk to her. Want to get out of there and go see a movie?

Yes. Come get me.

Pulling my cell phone out, I went into the library and shut the door. There were only two rings before my father picked up.

"John McKinley." The clipped tone of his voice told me he was in full work mode, but I didn't care. I needed to talk to someone.

"Hi, Dad."

"Julia." His voice softened. "How are you?"

"Fine." The answer came automatically. "I got my registration forms for school this morning."

"Huh." My father cleared his throat. "How's your mom?"

"Not so great. She spends a lot of time alone in her room or her studio. Sometimes she just goes off driving for a long time. She doesn't tell me where she's going. She just leaves." I paused to make sure my voice was steady. "And she's drinking, Dad. A whole bottle of wine last night." My father sighed and I heard the faint squeak of his chair. I could picture him leaning back, pinching the bridge of his nose like he always did when he was frustrated or upset. I could tell what was coming, and it made me wish I hadn't been so desperate to talk to someone. Or at least that I hadn't told him all the bad stuff right away.

"Julia, come home." The gentle tone was gone. My father was all business again, firm and direct.

"Dad, I can't. I can't leave her here alone."

"You are not responsible for your mother, Julia. You just turned seventeen. Come home," he repeated. I began to pace back and forth across the room.

"I'm not trying to be responsible for her. I'm just trying to be with her and support her." *The way you should be*, I added in my head.

"I know you are. But your mother could have all the love and support she wants right here. She chose to leave and it's not your responsibility to deal with that."

"Oh, come on, Dad. Like that makes it any easier."

"What do you think is going to happen with you there? How do you think you're helping the situation?"

"I don't know. Keeping her connected to family." My frustration at his response began to build. "Helping her not be so alone."

"I should have never let you go."

"You told me I was old enough to make up my own mind."

"Well, maybe that wasn't such a good idea. Look, I was willing to let you try it out. I guess I was hoping things would be better there too. But from what you're telling me they're not, so I think it's best if you come home."

"I can't," I whispered. I wasn't ready to give up yet. Not so quickly and easily. Not when there was a chance we could still be a family. Hadn't we lost enough already?

"I know it's hard. I love your mother too, you know. But at a certain point we just have to let go and give someone the freedom to grieve however they're going to grieve." It was like he could read my thoughts. "You can't make her feel better. She has to get there on her own. You know that, Tink," he said, his voice softening again. *No, I don't*, I thought. *It's just your way of handling things.* I knew my father was hurting too. Uncle Denny had been his best friend. But his way of coping seemed to be powering forward no matter what.

"It seems wrong to just leave her. When you're a family, doesn't that mean you hang onto each other no matter what?" It was the closest I'd come to criticizing him. My father exhaled sharply.

"You know what I think. You should come home. But if you feel you can't, that's your decision, and I'll abide by it as long as it's not harming you or your academics."

"Okay." The grief rock, as I'd come to think of it, rolled onto my chest, pressing down with its unbearable weight, making it difficult to breathe.

"I've got to get back to work. I love you, Tink."

"I love you too." He hung up. *I love you, but you're on your own*, was what he really seemed to be saying. I found myself staring at the canvas propped up in front of me, unseeing until I finally focused and realized something. It was completely blank. I scanned the room, thinking maybe there were other canvases my mother worked on stacked somewhere, but there weren't. This was the only canvas in the room. And the paintbrushes were still clean. In the week we'd been here, in all the hours she spent shut away in this room, my mother hadn't painted a single thing.

I crept back into the hallway, closing the door so carefully there was only the faintest click. I felt like violated her privacy somehow, regretting what I saw only after it was too late to un-see it. Another piece of knowledge to keep to myself. That space in my head was getting more and more stuffed, and I wasn't sure how much more could go in before I burst.

I found myself heading to the back door, fingering the cellar key that now rested under my shirt, hanging from a thin chain. I drew it over my head as I walked down the back steps. I opened the lock and descended into the familiar, dim coolness. At that moment, I didn't care if there was a stupid ghost. I slumped against the wall and pressed my forearm against my eyes, trying to stop the tears already leaking out. *What if things never get better? What am I supposed to do?*

The leak became a flood, and the sobs tore through me, jagged and ugly. I'd never let myself cry like this back in our apartment. It was too easy for others to hear. But no one could hear me now, and for the first time in months, I cried until my throat was raw and I felt empty and limp. I leaned into the wall, exhausted but lighter. I could breathe again.

I wiped my face, opened my eyes, and froze. The light shining around me was brighter than the usual dull glow of the bulb overhead. Every limp muscle in my body went rigid, and my heart raced with a surge of adrenaline.

Something or someone was in the cellar with me.

Chapter 3

I FORCED MYSELF to turn around, the breath whooshing out of me like I'd been punched in the stomach. Standing in front of me, just a few feet away, was the image of a boy holding a lantern. He was dressed in a white shirt and dark pants with suspenders—clothes from an earlier era. And he was transparent. To distract myself from the fact that I could see through him, I focused on his dark, shaggy hair and square jaw and estimated that he was somewhere around my own age. He was tall enough that he had to stoop under the low ceiling of the cellar. He peered intently into the space around him, his gaze passing over me several times as I pressed myself against the wall, breathing as shallowly as I could. He didn't look like a murderous or vengeful ghost. In fact, it seemed like he couldn't even see me. I took a deep breath and cleared my throat.

"H-hello?" I stammered. At the sound of my voice, he reared back, then winced and rubbed his head as though he'd bumped it on the ceiling. *What kind of ghost bumps his head?* He swung his lantern around, his face reflecting the same fear I'd felt when I first heard noises down here. I wasn't expecting that. Just as I was working up the courage to speak again, he suddenly turned and looks up at the doors, as though something else had gotten his attention. Before I could make another sound, he hurried up the stairs and disappeared.

"Holy shit," I breathed, sliding down the wall until I was sitting on the floor, my legs splayed in front of me. I stayed there for several minutes, waiting for my racing heart to calm down. Once I felt capable of it, I stood and headed up the stairs myself. The sudden brightness of the afternoon sunshine made me squint, and my hands shook as I closed the doors and threaded the lock back through the rings. It was time to get some answers.

I found my mother's purse in the front hall and fished out her cell phone. Even though Susan was pleased to hear from me, I could tell she was disappointed it wasn't my mother calling. Apparently, my mother wasn't talking to her either, but I pushed that concern aside.

"There's not all that much to tell you," Susan said when I asked about the house. "It was built in 1850 by a doctor for his family and most of the existing structure is part of the original house. That's why I snapped it up. You don't see many of those anymore. But this one passed on through the same family through the generations, so they didn't change much."

"Why did they sell after all that time?"

"The last owner had some health issues and moved in with his son's family across town. I guess none of the younger generation wanted to take the house."

"So my mom and I are the first people who aren't family to live here?"

"Pretty much."

I paused for a moment to think about how to phrase my next question. "Are there any stories about the house or family? You know, any legends or anything like that?"

"Not that I'm aware of. It's obviously got a lot of history, though. The Civil War practically happened in their back yard."

"Oh, right." I hadn't thought of that. I wasn't used to thinking much about the Civil War, but it occurred to me that this was probably the kind of place where they dressed up and acted out the battles.

"Why all the interest?" Susan asked.

"Oh, I don't know." *There's a ghost in the cellar and I want to find out who it could be.* "I've just never lived in a place like this before."

"Well, I don't know if this will have anything in it I haven't already told you, but I think I left the file with the info I got from the realtor in one of the kitchen drawers."

"Okay, thanks."

After promising her I'd tell my mother to call, I rummaged around the kitchen and found the file. There were only a couple sheets of paper in it. One of them was a family tree of sorts, listing every family member who took ownership of the house through the decades. I skipped over the most recent entries at the bottom and scanned the names at the top. Joseph Gardner was the original owner, and he had three sons: Thomson, Samuel, and Elias. The youngest, Elias, inherited and in turn passed the house on to his eldest son Andrew.

I stopped reading. Assuming the ghost was a past resident of the house from at least a hundred years ago or more, which was my best guess given his appearance, those were my most likely candidates. Still, that didn't really tell me much. I put the file back in the drawer, disappointed there wasn't more. What I needed was stories—family history, tragedies, and that sort of thing. Something that might explain why some guy's ghost was hanging out in the cellar. And whether I was the first one to see him.

–→▸■◉ ◉■◂←–

My attempts to get another glimpse of the ghost in the cellar were interrupted by the start of school. After going to private schools my whole life and wearing a uniform every day, it was strange having to decide what to wear. I settled on a pair of grey pants with a subtle plaid pattern and a bright green t-shirt. And, of course, my battered Converse. My only other accessory was the braided leather cuff my friend Sarah bought from a street vendor in Soho for my birthday last year. I wasn't going to set any fashion trends, but at least I was comfortable.

My mother's door was shut, which surprised me since she offered to drive me on the first day. "Mom?" I knocked lightly. No response. I knocked again, harder. "Mom!" I heard a small groan and opened the door. She was still in bed, and from her stiff, pained movements sitting up, I could tell she was hung over.

"What is it, Julia?" she asked, her voice hoarse.

"I thought you were taking me to school today." I tried to keep my voice neutral, but some of my disappointment seeped in anyway.

My mother rubbed a hand over her face. "Oh, that's right."

"You don't have to." She didn't look like she could make it down the stairs much less drive a car.

"Just start me some coffee, okay? I'll be okay after a shower."

"Okay." Heading downstairs, I couldn't help thinking about how my mother and father always used to make pancakes for me and Matty on the first day of school. I wondered if my father was making them for Matty.

My mother came into the kitchen and drank her coffee without saying a word. Her skin looked pasty and her hair was a mess. "I'm really okay with walking, Mom."

"No." She set her mug on the counter. "I'm driving you. Let's go." She said it like we were going into battle, her face determined and grim. Just how everyone wanted to start their day.

The drive to school was a silent one, partly because it looked like it was taking everything my mother had to focus on driving, and partly because what I wanted to say was the last thing I *could* say. Which was to comment on her drinking. To tell her how worried I was. To ask her why she wouldn't spend any time with me when I came out here to be with her.

"You can drop me there," I said, pointing to the curb across the street from the school.

"Are you sure?" my mother asked, but it sounded more like a statement of relief as she peered at the logjam ahead of us.

"Yeah, it's fine."

She nosed the car over to the right. "Well, have a good day." I leaned over to kiss her cheek, and her hand lifted and fell again, as if it was too hard to actually make contact. I blinked away the small prick of tears and slid quickly out of the car.

"See you later." I slammed the door shut and turn to face the campus, which seemed massive compared to the small school I attended at home. According to my registration packet, my new school served a wide section of the county, many of whom were bused in. Watching the stream of students swarming onto campus, I had the sudden urge to bolt. But where would I go? I couldn't exactly hang out at the gas station or the hardware store for the rest of the day, and if my father found out I was ditching, he'd make me go back to New York for sure.

I took a deep breath and crossed the street. As I walked through the front gate, a girl in denim capris and a white polo shirt with the school insignia thrust a paper at me. "School map?"

"Sure, thanks." I studied it for a moment before getting in line for my schedule. First stop was homeroom. After that, I had economics, Spanish, chemistry, and English, followed by European history and P.E. That last one made me wince. My former school only tortured us for one year, but apparently this school required two.

When I got to my homeroom, I found a desk in the back and sat down. The room filled up in the last two minutes before the bell. Most of the students coming in didn't even look in my direction, but a few did. One was a girl with long, wavy brown hair. She was wearing a pink tank top and a swishy skirt and looked like she'd just stepped out of the pages of *Seventeen*. All she needed was a fan to blow her tresses into an artful lift. She seemed to know just how pretty she was, scanning the room with a confident gaze. Her eyes flicked over me assessingly, and she gave a smug half-smile before turning her back and squealing at another girl who walked in. I rolled my eyes as they hugged. Honestly, didn't bitchy high school girls know what a cliché they were? Had they never seen any teen movie ever made?

The other students to look my way were a few of the boys who sauntered in just as the bell rang. I guess it was some kind of automatic response for guys to check out any new female in the vicinity, although I didn't seem to impress them very much. Their gazes all slid coolly over me. Except for one boy. His glance lingered a moment, and I recognized him as the one who bumped into me on registration day. He gave a faint jerk of his head in recognition before turning to take a seat next to *Seventeen* girl. Of course.

I fingered my leather cuff and make a mental note to call Sarah later. I'd been avoiding her calls the last couple days, and I knew it was only a matter of time before she stopped calling. I tried to imagine what she and my other friends were doing right now. Not that I had a ton of friends back home. I'd always been more comfortable with just a few. But it was still two or three more than I had here.

The intercom beeped and we all stood for the pledge. After that, we were bombarded by a string of upbeat voices welcoming us to the new school year, announcing the Back-To-School Dance in the gym, and reminding us to get involved in some club activities. The principal finished things off with the thought of the day that "if you love life, life will love you back." I tried not to vomit.

The teacher in front got up from her desk in the corner and walked over to the podium. Her hair frizzed out in a dark cloud, and she wore glasses that hung from a chain. She pushed back her sleeves and said, "Good morning, ladies and gentlemen. For those who don't know me, I'm Mrs. Davenport, and I'll be your homeroom teacher this year. I teach social studies, but I am here to help you with whatever you might need this year, from the personal to the academic." She paused to peer at us over the top of her glasses.

"I realize most of you are familiar with the school's policies by now since you're all seniors, but I thought I'd go over them anyway since this will be new information to some." She looked directly at me, and I slumped in my seat as most of the class turned to look at me as well. *Great.* With that one glance, Mrs. Davenport had managed to make me responsible for everyone having to sit through rules on tardies, dress code, and gum chewing.

The rest of the morning was pretty much the same thing—teachers checking books out to us and telling us their rules. I stopped listening about the middle of third period and began to think about what I'd seen in cellar instead. At lunch, I made a beeline for the library, which had a row of computers available to students. I did a search on "types of ghosts" and ended up with a long list of sites. I glanced through the first couple on the list and sent the ones that seem to have the most information to the printer before starting a fresh search. This time I typed in "why ghosts haunt" and skimmed through several more sites before choosing one to print. I wanted to print them all, but the library charged ten cents per page and I only had a dollar crumpled at the bottom of my bag. While I was paying for my pages, I asked the librarian if she could recommend any books on local history.

"Hmmm," she said in a way that made me think she was going to take a really long time on this. I glanced at the clock. There were only six minutes of lunch time left. She typed on her computer for several seconds, then said, "Well, we don't really have anything about our immediate area, but we do have several on Virginia history in general."

"Okay, great."

She wrote the numbers on a paper. "You'll find these in the second to last row by the windows over there," she said, pointing behind me. I took the slip and jogged over to the shelves. I grabbed one titled *Virginia!* (I failed to see the excitement) and another on the state's involvement in the Civil War. I jogged back to the counter, checked them out, and headed outside.

I was squinting in the bright sunshine, trying to look over the table of contents in one of the books, when my right foot snagged on someone else's. I pitched forward, my armload of books and papers flying out in front of me. Cursing under my breath with embarrassment, I squatted down to pick them up, struggling to keep my balance as kids hurrying past bumped against me. Some of them seemed to be doing it deliberately, and it was pissing me off. Suddenly, another set of hands appeared, picking up a book that had slid just out of reach, and a voice said, "Planning on doing some reading, huh?"

"No shit, Sherlock," I snapped. I looked up and saw the boy from my homeroom rock back on his heels. His eyebrows went up.

"Wow. That's a little...hostile."

I stood up and pushed my hair back from my face, which I could feel turning red. "No, no, I didn't mean...I mean, I'm sorry," I stammered. "I was just concentrating." I couldn't believe how stupid I was sounding, but the boy grinned, a dimple flashing in his left cheek.

"Oh, in that case, no apology needed. I mean, total concentration is responsible for all kinds of bad stuff. Cursing. Aggression. Petty theft. It's the plague of scientists everywhere." A smile of my own slipped out and I started to relax.

"Well, I really am sorry. I'm not usually that rude."

"That's okay. I mean, that was a pretty dumb thing for me to say, but you have to admit, it's hard to talk to someone for the first time without sounding like an ass."

"True," I laughed. He pushed dark hair longer than my own back from his forehead and opened his mouth to say something else, but we were interrupted.

"Derek!" The wavy-haired girl who sat next to him in home-room appeared at his side and slid her arm around his waist. "There you are! I was waiting for you upstairs." Her voice was light and sweet, but the slit-eyed look she shot me was anything but friendly. "Hurry up or we'll be late," she said, tugging him away from me. He rolled his eyes.

"Right. Well, see you later…?" He paused and his eyebrows went up again.

"Julia."

"Julia," he repeated. "I'm Derek," he said over his shoulder.

"Yeah, I kind of got that," I said, but I didn't know if he heard me. His escort had him firmly by the arm and was walking purpose-fully down the hall. The bell rang and I jumped. *Damn.* I was going to be late for history.

I managed to slip into my seat without the teacher noticing, and when he started droning on about his curriculum letter, I unfolded the printouts from the library. According to the articles, there were several types of ghosts and haunting. The first type, called residual haunting, was a sort of playback of tragic events like a tape looping over and over instead of an actual entity that was present and able to interact. *Nope.* My guy definitely wasn't that. The next type, interactive spirits, sounded more like it. They often appeared as a partial or full-bodied apparition, which fit what I'd seen. But, the article continued, these were extremely rare and were typically only visible to those who were gifted mediums. Which I was definitely not.

I shoved the papers into my bag, frustrated and discouraged. I skimmed through the books' contents, but they were even less helpful. The only way I was going to know more was if could find out more about the actual family history. Or talk to the ghost directly. I shivered at the thought and couldn't tell whether it was from fear or excitement. Maybe both.

Chapter 4

EVEN THOUGH I hadn't done anything but sit all day, I felt leaden when I started the walk home. As always, there was the heat with its damp oppressiveness, but I was also tired from figuring out where to go every period and from seeing so many unfamiliar faces everywhere. As exciting and distracting as it was to think about the ghost, the whole not-talking-to-anyone-all-day thing had definitely gotten to me.

I pulled out my cell phone and called Sarah.

"Hey, Julia!" She sounded out of breath. "Did you get my message?"

"I did. Sorry I haven't called before now. How are things? Did I miss anything good today?"

"Not really. Kemper's just as boring as always," she said, referring to the headmaster at our school. "And for some reason they're being super strict about the uniforms this year. I mean, how much difference does it really make to our education whether our shirts are tucked in or not? Anyway, what's the school down there like? Is it awful?"

"It's not awful, but it's not great. I mean, it's so big. And they're making me take P.E."

"No way. That's ridiculous! Like you really need to wear tacky gym clothes and play volleyball with a bunch of girls who suck at it to be educated." The disgust in her voice made me laugh, and I felt a sudden longing to climb through the phone to see her. I heard muffled voices in the background, and Sarah said, "Tim and Leila say hi."

"Tell them hi back."

"I will. Listen, I've gotta go. We're heading down to the subway. Going to eat at Dahlia's. I wish you could come with us."

"Me too." We always went to Dahlia's after school. I could picture my friends in their uniforms and the flow of noisy traffic and people around them. I could even smell the subway.

"'kay, bye!"

"Bye," I said, but Sarah had already hung up. I slid the phone back in my pocket. I couldn't expect them to stop going just because I wasn't there. That would be silly. But it still felt like they were leaving me behind. Like another part of my life changing that I couldn't stop.

I pushed those thoughts away and focused instead on deciding whether I really wanted to meet up with a ghost in a dark cellar again. I thought of all those stupid characters in horror movies who, in spite of how obvious it is that they should *not open that door!* still did anyway and died some kind of bloody, horrible death. Apparently, I was one of those stupid characters, because I had to know what was down there. Although, there really wasn't anything threatening about what I'd seen. It was a guy holding a lantern and wearing suspenders. Plus, when I'd spoken aloud, he'd looked as spooked as I'd felt. Maybe he didn't even know he was a ghost.

At home, I heard my mother's voice as soon as I opened the front door. She was in her bedroom, and it was clear from her tone that she was upset. I put my bag down and crept partway up the stairs.

"I know that, John." I froze. She was talking to my father. There was a pause and then, "We've only been here a couple weeks. I know it's been hard—for all of us—but I need more time." Another pause, and her voice sharpened. "I don't know how much, and it's not helping to have you keep asking me for some kind of deadline. You have to consider that I might, well," her voice faltered and then she finished, "that I might not ever be ready."

I crept back down the stairs, not wanting to hear any more. What did she mean, she might never be ready? This was only supposed to be for a little while. Temporary. Back to my old school by second quarter. But that was the agreement I made with my father before we left. Has my mother ever actually said so? I couldn't remember.

I stood in the kitchen for a minute, then grabbed the flashlight and went out the back door. Going down into the cellar and possibly seeing a ghost was a way better option than sitting in the house and stewing, wanting to ask my mother about what she said and knowing that I couldn't. No, it wasn't even that. *It's not helping to have you keep asking me for some kind of deadline.* It was knowing that she wouldn't answer me even if I did ask.

I slammed the cellar doors closed behind me and barreled down stairs I now knew by heart. I pulled the chain on the bulb and froze, my heart jumping into triple time. A figure huddled on the floor a foot away from my chair, clearly visible even in the dim light. He seemed oblivious to my presence, his head resting on his forearms, which were propped against his drawn-up knees. I couldn't tell for sure, but it seemed like he was crying. He was dressed as before, in dark pants and a white shirt that was now rolled up at the sleeves.

Now what? I wondered, wishing I'd looked up how you were supposed to actually talk to a ghost. My heart still raced, but I found I wasn't afraid. It was hard to be afraid of someone huddled on the floor crying. I took a small step forward and crouched down. "Hello?" My timid greeting provoked an immediate response. His head jerked up and he looked directly at me, an expression of pure shock on his face. He scrabbled back until he was pressed against the wall and raised an arm in a protective gesture.

"God in Heaven, protect me!" His exclamation startled me, and I fell back myself. Then I realized he was calling out to God for protection against *me*.

"Hey, it's okay. I'm not a...demon or whatever." What *did* I look like to him? I leaned forward, and my movement made him press himself against the wall even more firmly. In fact, he seemed to fade into it. I tried to look as calm and non-threatening as I could and almost ruined it by giggling. Part of it was nerves, but part of it was how ludicrous it was that anyone could ever find me threatening. I stifled the laugh and cleared my throat. "Look, I don't know who or what *you* are, but my name is Julia, and I'm just a normal, living, breathing girl." This did not seem to reassure him. His continued look of terror was starting to irritate me just a little. "If anyone should be freaking out, it should be me. *You're* the ghost here, buddy, not me."

The boy lowered his arm and stared at me in amazement, his eyes wide and his mouth hanging open. He seemed to notice this the same moment I did because he snapped it shut.

"You're...you're a girl?"

I was a little insulted he found it so hard to tell until I realized how I must look to him with my short hair and pants. "Yeah," I answered, "I'm a girl." I smiled and he relaxed a fraction, though he still seemed ready to bolt out of there at any moment.

"I don't...I'm sorry, but I don't understand." He closed his eyes and rubbed them.

"I know. This is a little crazy. I'm sorry if I scared you, but you really don't need to be afraid of me. I'm not going to do anything to you. In fact, I *can't* do anything to you, so you're perfectly safe." I tried to make my voice as gentle and reassuring as I could. He stared at me for several seconds, frowning, then tensed again.

"Just now, did you say that *I* am the ghost?"

"Yes," I said. He shook his head.

"I'm afraid you are confused. My name is Elias Gardner and I live in this house. This is my family's cellar," he said, rising and gesturing around him. "I hope this brings you no distress," he continued, his own voice gentling, "but *you* are the one who does not belong here. Although I will do my best to assist you if you are in need." I felt a jolt of excitement when he said his name, followed by a rush of sympathy. The poor guy really had no idea he was a ghost, and I was touched by his offer to help me.

"Nice to meet you, Elias," I said, also standing. "Look, I'm not sure how to tell you this, but you lived in this house over a century ago. I live here with my mother now. It's the year 2002. I'm afraid you really are a ghost and just don't know it. I've done some research," I added hastily when I saw him open his mouth to protest, "and it said that sometimes ghosts don't move on because they died tragically or have some unfinished business. Maybe that's something I could help you with." But even as I said this, I realized something wasn't adding up. According to the records, Elias lived to old age. So why would his ghost appear as a teenager?

Elias was frowning and shaking his head again. "I am sorry to contradict you," he said in a courteous Southern drawl, "but this is just not possible. What you're saying isn't possible," he repeated. "I am very much alive," he added, thumping his hand against a chest and legs that still appeared somewhat faint to me. "I am solid and real, as are the things all around us." He pointed to my left. "Those bags of flour. The jars of vegetables on the shelves. You're practically sitting on a case of my father's favorite wine. I know I'm alive because when I go up those stairs, my mother will be in the kitchen and my father will be reading in his library, and I will eat my supper with them in the same manner we do every evening. There may be times I wish my life weren't real," he said, his voice dropping as he looked away, "but that doesn't make it so. And what you're saying about...the future. That cannot be."

I was reminded that he was hunched over and crying when I came in, but now didn't seem like a good time to go into that. He was studying me closely. "You are the one looks like a ghost," he said after a moment. "I can almost see through you, and you just appeared in here a few moments ago without opening and closing the cellar doors. And," he added, his voice getting a little shaky, "you're floating several inches off the ground."

What? I looked down instinctively, but of course there was no need to check. I was planted firmly on solid concrete. No floating. So why was he seeing me that way? Why did *I* look like a ghost to him? My brain swirled with questions. Nothing about him matched what I'd read about ghosts on the internet, and it didn't make any kind of sense that he saw *me* as a ghost. This guy was not a figment of my imagination, nor was I one of his. I knew *I* wasn't a ghost, and he seemed pretty convinced he wasn't either. So what was this?

I thought of a science fiction story my father had read me and Matty years ago about a boy who could step through different dimensions of time. Was it possible *neither* of us was a ghost? What if, somehow, Elias and I were both in the same place in our own times, and they were somehow…intersecting? My brain cramped at the thought, but now that I'd thought it, I couldn't let it go. And then there was the whole floating thing.

"Do you have concrete on your floor?" I asked him.

"What?" His face showed his confusion.

"Concrete. Cement. What is the floor of the cellar made of?"

"It's dirt, of course. Why do you ask?" He was looking at me like I might be something to be worried about after all, but things were beginning to make a kind of weird sense to me now. Just as I couldn't see the things he was pointing to in his time, he couldn't see the layer of concrete I was standing on. This would also explain why he was able to disappear a few inches into the wall earlier. He was backing up against *his* wall, which was behind the concrete. I closed my eyes and took a deep breath, my head spinning.

"Are you all right, uh, miss?"

I opened my eyes. "Elias, I am not a ghost and I am not floating. I'm standing on several inches of concrete. In my time, the cellar is empty except for the chair I brought down. Over there." I pointed to his left. He turned and looked.

"There are only shelves there."

"I know, in *your* time there are. But in my time, there's just the chair. Look, I know this sounds crazy—I'm not even sure I believe it myself—but I think you're alive in your time and I'm alive here in mine. Neither of us is a ghost. We're both alive and here. It's just…" My voice trailed off. It was hard to explain something I didn't quite understand myself.

"Your time. You said it was 2002?" I nodded and he covered his face for a moment. "I can't…I don't…" Words failed him. He dropped his hand and looked me up and down, then glanced quickly away when he caught my eye. He cleared his throat. "I apologize. I don't mean to be impertinent. It's just that your appearance, and what you're telling me—I'm afraid I can't quite take it in."

"I know. I can't believe it myself. But think about it. Have you ever seen a girl in your time or any time in the past who looks or dresses like me?" His eyes flicked toward me and away again.

"No, miss. I don't suppose so." His mouth twitched, and it felt for a second like he was laughing at me. I guess that was better than terror.

"So I'm not a ghost, and you're sure you're not—"

"I most definitely am not," he interrupted me.

"Okay," I said, taking another stab at an explanation. "Then that means our two times, our two lives, are somehow intersecting." I tried to remember if they had anything resembling science fiction in the 1800s. Probably not, and probably no string theory or the concept of different dimensions, or whatever it was that could explain this. Elias was pacing back and forth, his head and shoulders stooped under the low ceiling. He finally stopped and rubbed his eyes again.

"I'm sorry, but this is…I can't really grasp that you are living in…" he stopped and swallowed hard, then finished, "the future. But if you really are, it would explain your appearance."

"What?" I asked, unable to resist. "Because I look like a boy?"

"Yes. I mean, no," he stammered. He dropped his head, then raised it to look me squarely in the face. "To be perfectly frank, your hair and clothing *are* more in keeping with what boys around here wear. Though I must say your face is far too pretty to be a boy's." He smiled, and I found myself wanting to duck my own head. He tensed suddenly.

"I think I hear my mother. She sent me down here to get her some butter. I must go." He walked past me toward the stairs.

"Wait a minute!" I blurted. "Can we, I don't know, try meeting up again?" It sounded like I was asking him on a date, but I pushed through my embarrassment. This was too amazing not to happen again.

"Well," he hesitated at the base of the stairs, "I suppose we might."

"What time is it for you?"

"I don't know, exactly. Somewhere between three and four in the afternoon."

"It's the same for me," I said, my heart rate picking up with excitement. "Can you try to come down here again tomorrow about the same time? I get home from school about 3:15. I'll make sure I'm down here from then until at least 4:00. Please," I added when he didn't answer right away. I didn't care anymore if I sounded desperate. I was.

"I'll do my best. That is, if I don't wake up in a moment and find that this has all been some kind of strange dream," he added.

"I know. It is strange. But isn't it also pretty cool?" He looked confused. "I mean, isn't it amazing?"

He rubbed his head and nodded slowly. "Amazement certainly describes what I'm feeling right now."

"So you'll come tomorrow?"

"I'll come tomorrow," he said with a small, hesitant smile. I let out the breath I was holding.

"Great," I said, smiling back. "See you then."

⊷═◉ ◉═⊶

My mother was in the kitchen starting dinner when I came in the back door. "Finally," she said. "Wash these carrots, will you?" All I wanted to do was go up to my room, shut the door, and think about what just happened, but instead I found myself opening the bag of carrots and turning on the faucet. A minute later my mother said, "I spoke with your father today."

"Really?" I'd almost forgotten about that.

"I know you probably heard us fighting. I saw your bag when I came downstairs, so I know you came in while I was talking to him."

"Yeah, I heard a little. I didn't listen for long."

"That's probably a good thing. Your father is being completely unreasonable. He wants to set a specific deadline for when we'll be home, and I can't give him one. It's too soon."

I thought about Elias and our plans to meet tomorrow. Would it work again? "Uh huh, I know. It's okay." I shut the faucet off and turned to find my mother studying me.

"Well, good," she said, and I could tell she was surprised. "I appreciate your support. Your dad wants you back in New York, of course. And if you want to go, I'll understand." Her voice wavered at the end and she looked away. It was my turn to be surprised. To realize that some part of her really did want me here.

"No, I'm all right," I said.

"Okay, good." She reached over to squeeze my arm.

"I mean, I miss Dad and Matty like crazy," I added, and she drew back.

"I do too," she interjected.

"But I'm starting to like it here," I finished. "It's getting, well, interesting." I couldn't help a small smile at what a massive under-statement that was.

"Have you met a boy at school?"

"No." This time I laughed. "That's not it at all." She frowned and started to say something, but I handed her the carrots. "Here. I'm going upstairs. I'll be down to eat later." I wanted to replay what happened in the cellar. I wanted to think, and for once it was not going to be about Uncle Denny or my parents.

Chapter 5

THE NEXT MORNING, Derek smiled and gave me one of his head jerks when he came into homeroom. I raised my hand in a small salute back, earning me a glare from wavy-haired girl. Natalie, I should say. That was her name. I wanted to go up to her and tell her to stop giving me dirty looks, that she had nothing to worry about, but my real-life self wasn't nearly as brave as the self in my head.

I fidgeted my way through all my classes, willing the minutes to go by faster. As soon as I heard the whistle signaling the end of P.E., I ran back to the locker room and threw on my clothes. I was already halfway across the field, heading toward home, when I heard the bell marking the end of the school day. At the house, I went upstairs to check how I looked in the mirror. My face was red and shiny from the run home. I splashed it with some cold water, patted it dry, and dug a compact out of the drawer to put on some powder. I added some lip gloss and was in the middle of smoothing a few of the wilder pieces of my hair when I stopped. What was I doing? Getting ready for a date?

I checked my watch. It was just a few minutes after three. I went downstairs, barely registering the closed door to the library, and grabbed my usual glass of iced tea.

"Elias?" I called softly when I was halfway down the cellar stairs. I turned on the overhead light. I was alone. I shrugged and sat down in my chair. There was still plenty of time for him to show. I tried to think of what I'd say to him if and when he did, but my mind went blank. It was still hard to believe that yesterday had been real and that it could be happening again in a matter of minutes.

Half an hour went by, and just as I was debating whether or not to give up, I heard a faint scuffling noise, and then Elias was at the bottom of the stairs. I stood up, and we stared at each other in silence for several seconds. *This is really happening.*

"Hello, miss. I mean, Julia," he said finally.

"Hi, Elias." I was so happy to see him again, I couldn't stop a huge smile from taking over my face. He smiled in return, somewhat shyly, and gestured toward me.

"Please, sit down."

"Okay." I lowered myself back onto my chair and saw him perch against something and set his lantern on the ground. I had to strain my eyes, but I could see the faint outline of a crate underneath him. "You know, I can almost see what you're leaning against." His eyes narrowed as he studied me.

"Yes, I can see a bit of the chair you're sitting on. It's much fainter than you are. But at least you're not floating," he added, his mouth turning up at the corner. I laughed.

"Well, that's good." I smoothed a hand over my hair, suddenly feeling self-conscious.

"I'm sorry I was late. I'm afraid I can't stay for very long either. I have a pile of chores waiting and my mother will notice if I'm gone for too long."

"That's all right." There was another silence as I struggled to think of what to say. The problem was that I wanted to ask him everything at once. I decided to start with what he'd said. "Do you live with just your mother?"

"No, my father also. He's a doctor."

"What about brothers or sisters?" It felt weird to ask him when I already knew, but I figured it would be even stranger if I were to bring up my knowledge of his family tree. My question seemed to hit a nerve. Elias looked down and his face was shadowed for a moment.

"I have two older brothers," he said, looking up again, "Thomson and Samuel, but they aren't here." He seemed to have difficulty saying that last part. I was dying to ask more, but I didn't want to seem too nosy, especially about something that was obviously causing him pain. As I was debating this, he spoke again. "You see, we are in the middle of a terrible war." His eyes widened. "But I suppose you must already know about that. How very strange," he whispered, almost to himself.

"Yes, I do know about it. At least, I know a little bit," I confessed, embarrassed that something of such significance to him was little more than a set of vague textbook facts to me. "Are your brothers fighting in the war?"

Elias brushed a hand across his face and was quiet for a moment. I waited, wishing I had not asked that. "They were," he said. "Thomson was killed a year ago July in the first battle at Bull Run. And we just got word that Samuel was injured badly in the second."

"That's awful. I'm so sorry." I leaned forward in my chair, squeezing the edge of it. *I know,* I wanted to say, *I know that pain.* His own hands gripped the crate under him and I could see him swallow. But then he changed the subject.

"And what about you? Have you and your family been living here for long?"

"No. My mom and I have just been here since August. We're from New York, which is where my dad and brother are." His eyebrows went up, but I guess he was too polite to ask the question he was probably thinking. I found myself blurting, "My uncle, my mother's brother, was killed last year."

Elias jerked back in surprise. "Are you also having a war in your time?"

"Oh, no. I mean, not exactly." How could I explain terrorists? "It's hard to describe, but something terrible happened. Many people died that day, and Uncle Denny was one of them. It wasn't a war. He was just going to work." I paused for a moment, struggling for control. "My mother completely fell apart afterward. I mean, she held it together for a little while, but it seemed like the more time that went by, the worse she got. She wanted to leave the city and she asked my father to leave with her, for our whole family to go, but he said no. She decided to go anyway, and I didn't want her to go alone, so I came too." I took a deep breath and added, "It sounds too simple to say it like that. There's so much more to it."

Elias nodded. "I understand. It's hard to find fitting words for some things. I am sorry about your uncle."

"I think about him all the time. It's still so hard to believe that he's gone for good. I keep feeling like when we go back home, he'll just be there again." The words came tumbling out. I tensed, waiting for him to flinch or get uncomfortable, but he only nodded.

"I know. I still have conversations with Thomson in my head all the time. I find myself trying to keep track of all the things going on here so I can tell him when he gets home. And then I remember..." His voice trailed away.

"Yeah, me too." We were both silent for a moment, thinking about that kind of remembering, which had to be done over and over and always brought so much pain. It was a comforting silence, and the knowledge that he understood exactly what I was talking about and felt the same way burrowed into me and began to loosen the tight knot that was always in the center of my chest.

Elias stood up. "I'm afraid I must go now." He picked up his lantern and hesitated, looking down at me. "I may be able to come tomorrow, if you'd like."

"I'd like that very much," I said.

"Well, then. Tomorrow." He gave me a small, courtly bow, his dark hair falling over his forehead, and then he was gone. I waited another minute, then turned out the light and headed up the stairs myself. I might have enjoyed being alone in the cellar before, but now it felt a little too empty.

→═◉ ◉═←

The next day, I spent lunch in the library trying to brush up on Civil War history and the battles Elias's brothers had fought in. I didn't have time to read much, but enough to learn that Virginia had been the last state to secede and the center of the conflict for most of the war. I found myself lingering over a blurry black-and-white photo of bodies in a field. *What if one of them was Thomson?* Of course, they were all someone's brother or son or husband. But now it was so much more real.

I thought about our conversation on the way home from school. It was hard to believe I'd told him so much. I wasn't used to talking about such personal things with someone I'd just met. But this, well, this was different. The usual rules didn't apply. Besides, while he might be living in another century, Elias was the first person I'd met who was my own age and had also lost someone so close to him. Sarah's grandfather died of a heart attack when we were in seventh grade, but she only saw him a couple times a year and he was in his seventies. Not that that made it okay, but still. It wasn't the same.

Upstairs, I found myself taking off the t-shirt I'd been wearing and putting on a blouse my mother had given me last year. It had rows of small ruffles down the front and was about the most feminine item of clothing I owned. *You're being ridiculous.* I ignored that thought and smoothed my hair in the mirror, tucking the longer pieces behind my ears. My mother would probably ask about the blouse if she saw it, but I was too excited to care.

I had just sat down on my chair in the cellar when I heard the sound of footsteps on the stairs and Elias appeared before me. His smile was less hesitant than before, and he seemed more relaxed as he sat across from me. I was glad the sight of me wasn't so disturbing to him anymore. As though he could read my mind, Elias said, "Julia, why do you think this is happening to us? Why are we able to see each other and communicate in this manner?"

I shrugged. "I have no idea. Does it matter why?"

"Don't you think there is some kind of purpose to this?"

"I don't know. Not really." The possibility had not occurred to me. "Do you?"

"Perhaps. Something like this certainly raises that question, doesn't it?"

"I guess." I felt my face flush with embarrassment and hoped he couldn't see it. I'd only thought about how exciting this was, not about any deeper philosophical significance. I cleared my throat. "So, I did some reading about the war that's going on in your time."

"Did you?"

"Yes. I read about the two battles of Bull Run. The ones your brothers were in." He tensed, and I mentally cursed myself for bringing up such a painful topic. *Although it's not like he isn't thinking about it anyway*, I reminded myself. I knew firsthand that people didn't forget their grief just because no one spoke about it out loud. When he remained quiet, I took a deep breath and dove in. "Elias, you seemed really upset the day we met. Was it because you'd just heard about Samuel?"

Elias sighed and pushed a hand through his hair. "Yes and no," he said.

"It must have been hard on your family to have both of your brothers go to war," I offered after a long pause.

"It was. But the worst of it is that they weren't even on the same side." His mouth twisted into a bitter smile at my gasp of surprise. I had read a reference or two to houses divided, but I had never thought about the literal reality of family members joining opposing armies and fighting against each other.

"I can't even imagine." And really, I couldn't. Matty and I might fight all the time, but we would never do anything that would actually harm the other. We were always united on the big stuff. *But your parents are divided.* The thought crept in, insidious and unwelcome. Elias was shaking his head.

"It's a complicated story for another time. I have only a few minutes left, and I am curious to know more about you." He smiled, and I did my best to follow his cue.

"What would you like to know?"

"You spoke of going to school. What is that like?"

"Oh, I don't know. It's all right. It's really big compared to my old school." I wondered how large it would seem to Elias. He probably attended a one-room school or something like that.

"And what do you study in your school?"

I did my best to explain my classes to Elias and how the day was structured. Elias listened with absorbed attention, a slight frown of concentration creating a line between his brows. "What about you?" I asked. "Do you go to school?"

"Not anymore. I did until last spring. I had planned to attend a college or university, but, of course, now there's the war. I've been conducting my studies with my father. He has more books in his library than possibly anyone else in the state, and he seems determined to have me read every one of them." Elias smiled wryly, then stood and picked up his lantern. "I'm afraid I must go now. Do you think we might meet again?"

"Yes! I mean," I said, trying for a calmer tone, "that would be nice." I was disappointed this meeting had been so brief. "Listen, do you think you could come back here tonight? After your parents are asleep? It would give us more time to talk."

Elias shook his head. "I'm sorry, but I don't think that would be wise. My father is a very restless sleeper and often rises. And we've had more than one deserter come through here. I'm liable to get shot if my father hears someone opening the cellar doors in the middle of the night."

"Oh. Right. Well, just say when, then."

"I am to help a neighbor repair her roof for the next few days. I'm not certain how long it will take, but I can try to be here on Saturday, perhaps mid-day. Would that suit you?"

"That would be fine. What, exactly, is mid-day for you?"

"Between one and two o'clock in the afternoon. My mother rests then, and my father is usually reading in his study."

"Okay. I'll be here."

"I shall look forward to it, Julia."

"Me too."

⋺▬◉ ◉▬⋼

As thrilling as this new development in my life was, a heavy sense of dread began to settle in the pit of my stomach as the anniversary of September 11 drew near. My mother hadn't mentioned Uncle Denny in weeks, and the less we spoke of him, the weirder it became. On the eve of the anniversary, my mother was completely silent as we ate dinner. She drank from her wine glass frequently but barely touched her food. I was finding it hard to swallow myself. I gave up after a few minutes and reached across the table to touch her hand. "Mom." She pulled her hand back and stood up.

"I can't, Julia. I'm sorry." Seconds later, I heard the sounds of the car starting and the violent spray of gravel as she peeled out of the driveway onto the road. Running away for hours as she so often did these days. I sat there for several minutes, staring at our plates of uneaten food. I wanted to leave too, to walk out the front door into the dark night and keep walking until I was too tired to walk anymore, too tired to think or feel anything. *Let her come home to an empty house. Let her worry about me for a change.*

I stood up and carried the plates into the kitchen, dumping their contents into the trash and stacking them in the sink. I stared out the window, wishing I could go down into the cellar and talk to Elias, but of course he wouldn't be there. I thought of calling my father, but he would just tell me to come home again. There was Sarah, but even though I knew she'd be sympathetic and say nice things, she really didn't understand. She was probably at home watching the commemorative footage on the news and feeling awful and sad about it the way everyone in the city did. But she was with her family. They were all still together watching what had happened around them, not directly *to* them, and the thought of trying to talk to someone who wouldn't get it felt more lonely than not talking to anyone at all. All I could do was go upstairs and curl up on my bed, hugging a pillow to my chest and its unbearable ache.

⤝▦ ▦⤞

During announcements the next morning, the principal had us all do a moment of silence. I stared at the initials carved in my desk and tried to think of anything else but the "victims and heroes of that great tragedy" that we were supposed to be remembering. *Just get through it.*

"I hope you all took that moment of silence seriously," Mrs. Davenport said, gripping her podium like she might throw it at us if she suspected we hadn't. "This day marks an event that has affected us all, and I think as such we should spend some time talking about it." She ignored the low groan that rippled through the room. "Is there anyone who'd like to share a memory or talk about how 9/11 has affected them?" As the silence began to lengthen, I slid a quick glance at the clock. Big mistake. Mrs. Davenport pounced. "Julia, you used to live in New York City. Do you mind sharing some of what it was like to actually be there?"

I felt a wave of heat sweep up my neck as all the other students turned to face me. "I, um. I'd rather not," I said, my voice coming out in a croak. I looked down at my desk again, wishing I could crawl under it.

"I realize it's probably not easy for you, but I hope you know this is a safe place. You can share whatever you want here."

"I don't want to talk about it." My voice came out flat and hard. I realized she couldn't know about Uncle Denny, but still. Could she be any more clueless? I looked up and, to my relief, found that the students were looking back at her to see how she'd react to my lack of cooperation.

"Oh, well, of course." Mrs. Davenport pushed her glasses up on her nose. "That's understandable. I'm sure it was a terrible day for you. It was a terrible day for America," she continued, her voice rising, "but it was also an event that brought out great heroism and compassion in people. We should also remember and honor that on this day—the many brave men and women who sacrificed themselves to help others. That is certainly something that can give us hope."

As Mrs. Davenport smiled at us all encouragingly, a boy sitting two seats up from me leaned over and muttered, "That, and killing all the fucking Muslims" to the boy sitting next to him, and they both laughed. Mrs. Davenport didn't notice, but I saw someone to my left flinch. It was a dark-skinned girl with a scarf over her head and her mouth pulled taut with anger. I guess I wasn't the only one having a bad day.

Fortunately, there were no other references to 9/11 for the rest of the day, and in some of my classes there were even moments I was able to forget about it and focus on my work. But it all came rushing back as soon as I started the walk home, and I couldn't suppress the memories any longer. The cloud of soot and paper raining down all over the city. The images on TV playing over and over. The frantic phone calls and scouring of all the hospitals while we looked for Uncle Denny. And the awful passing of days he didn't call or show up at our door and we became more and more certain that he never would.

When I got to our street, I could tell the moment I turned the corner that my mother was gone. The driveway was empty and I wondered how long it would be before she came back. Surprisingly, the library door had been left ajar. "Mom?" I called out, just in case. I pushed the door open further and stepped inside. The last time I had been in here, everything had been clean and blank, but now the room was a mess. Several dirty brushes and uncapped paint tubes partially squeezed lay on the tarp covering the desk. The art books were scattered across the floor as though they had been flung. But what really got my attention, what made me stiffen with shock, was the canvas propped on the easel. It wasn't a painting so much as raw emotion smeared across the surface. Swirling black bloomed outward from the center, punctuated by orange, yellow, and blood-red slashes of color. And out of the top, just barely distinguishable from the black, was a crudely outlined hand stretching upward in agony.

I gasped and found myself doubling over, trying to choke back the sobs threatening to burst out of me. "Stop it! Stop," I ordered myself. I was so sick of all the sadness, of thinking it might be getting better, only to have it clobber me again out of nowhere. I swiped the tears off my face and went to the hallway closet. I grabbed a brush and bucket and went to work on the kitchen floor, scrubbing it as hard as I could.

When it had finally gotten dark and there was nothing left to clean, I went downstairs and rummaged around in the refrigerator and cupboards, looking for the most comforting of comfort foods we had. I found a can of tomato soup, some cheese, and some semi-stale bread. I had just flipped the second grilled cheese sandwich when my mother appeared in the kitchen doorway and slumped against its frame. Her face was bare of any makeup, the dark circles beneath her eyes like black thumbprints against the paleness of her skin.

"Hi," I said. "I made dinner," I added, not sure what to say.

"Thanks. Sorry I was gone so long."

"That's okay." I scooped the sandwich onto the waiting plate.

"How was your day?" My mother's voice was hesitant.

"Not so great," I said, turning to look at her. "How about you?"

"Not so great," she echoed. We stood staring at each other for a minute. I put the spatula I was still holding on the counter.

"So can we hug or something?" I hated how wobbly my voice came out, but my mother's eyes widened.

"Of course, sweetheart," she said, pulling away from the doorframe and opening her arms to me. I was there in a flash, squeezing her tightly and feeling her squeeze me back. *I miss this*, I almost said. As though she could read my thoughts, my mother whispered, "I'm sorry I'm being such a bad mother."

"You're not," I mumbled into her shoulder. "You just miss Uncle Denny." *Say it*, I willed her. *Tell me what you feel. What you're thinking.* She shuddered against me and pulled away.

"That soup smells good," she said, brushing past me and opening a bottle of wine.

And just like that, the moment was gone.

Chapter 6

IN THE DAYS that followed, I continued to spend my lunchtime in the library, reading all I could get my hands on about the Civil War. There was so much I didn't remember or know, and this was Elias's life. I didn't want him to have to explain everything to me, especially since it was obviously painful for him to talk about.

I think I impressed the librarian with my studiousness. She hovered over me and the other stray students who spent their lunch period in the library in a kind of motherly way. These kids mostly seemed to be the outcasts—the ones who had no friends to eat with at lunch. It was strange to realize I was one of them now. I had never been that popular at my old school, but I had always had at least a small group of friends and felt like I'd belonged.

On my third day in there, I noticed the girl with the headscarf from my homeroom. I seemed to remember Mrs. Davenport calling her Samira. She sat at a table in the corner, completely absorbed in the book she was reading. Even though she was alone, she didn't have that awkward, dejected look the other kids had. In fact, she seemed to be enjoying herself. I found myself sneaking glances at her in between chapters on Civil War battles and thought about what those boys in homeroom had said about Muslims. If I was honest, I might not have the most friendly feelings toward them either if it weren't for my history teacher freshman year. Mr. Ibrahim, himself a Muslim, had led us through a unit on Islam when we were studying world religions, and he and his wife had brought dinner to our apartment a couple weeks after the attacks. Even so, I liked to think I understood the difference between crazy radicals and innocent people.

Most mornings in homeroom, I sat in my back corner desk and kept my head down, working on homework. Because they were seniors, most of the kids in my homeroom had been together for over three years, and their groups were clearly established. Just like mine had been with my friends at my old school, most of whom I'd known since seventh grade. I wasn't exactly used to making new friends, and I wasn't about to sit there looking lonely and desperate. So I looked busy instead and was left alone, although Derek did one of his small smiles and head jerks at me every day. Samira always had her nose in a book in homeroom as well, but maybe she was just doing what I was doing—looking like she had better things to do than to be sitting around talking and laughing with friends. *Maybe I should try talking to her in class one of these days*, I thought.

All that fake studying wasn't helping my grades, though. My first major chemistry test came back with a big red 'D' at the top. In my family, there was no such grade, and as if he could somehow sense my academic slippage, my father called while I was walking home.

"How are you?"

"Okay."

"How's school?"

"Um, fine."

"What does that mean?" He pounced on my hesitation. "Are you having any trouble?"

"No, everything's fine. I'm on it."

"I hope so. This isn't the time to be slacking off. How are the college applications going?"

I winced, glad he couldn't see me. I hadn't even looked at them yet. "Fine. I still have plenty of time, Dad. Most of the deadlines aren't for a couple more months."

"I know, but it's easy to lose track of time, and you don't want to be rushing and doing a sloppy job on those. NYU still your top choice?"

"Yeah, of course."

"Good. Let me know if you need help with anything. When you write your application essays, e-mail or fax them or something." I could tell he was frustrated, and I could almost hear him thinking, *you should be here where I can keep an eye on things.*

"Okay. I will. Relax, Dad," I added. "Everything will be fine."

He sighed. "I don't have any doubts about you, Tink. I just don't like this situation or the thought that it could in any way jeopardize your future." Again, I could hear the unspoken thought that came next—*I don't want your selfish mother to ruin your life.*

"It won't." My thoughts drifted to Elias. With a jolt, I realized that it was him, not my mother, that I thought about most lately.

"So how about coming home for a visit sometime soon? Maybe a long weekend?"

I stopped walking, torn between a longing to see him and Matty and be home again, and dread at the thought of missing a chance to meet up with Elias. "Maybe," I said, resuming my steps, "or you guys could come down here for a weekend instead." There was a pause.

"Sure," my dad said finally, not sounding sure at all. "We can talk about it more some other time. I've got a client coming in a few minutes."

"Okay. Love you, Dad."

"Love you too."

At home, the car was in the driveway and the library door was closed. I wondered what my mother would think about my going home for a visit and, even more, what she would think about Dad and Matty coming here. She'd been painting quite a bit, judging from the spatters on her clothes and hands at dinnertime and her frequent trips to buy more supplies. At first, I'd been glad about this, thinking maybe it was some kind of breakthrough for her. But she seemed more distracted and withdrawn than ever. Was the painting actually helping her get better or making her worse? What if she decided she was an artist and didn't want to be part of our family anymore?

All these questions seemed to make my bag heavier than usual as I hefted it onto my shoulder and headed up the stairs. Compared to everything else, chemistry seemed like a piece of cake. That, at least, was one problem I could solve. I sat down at the small desk in my room and opened my book. *Studying today, Elias tomorrow.* Just the thought of it made me shiver.

When I came downstairs the next morning, I could hear my mother talking on the phone. From her tone, I was pretty sure it was my brother, and I couldn't help grinning when I heard her say, "Take care, Matty-bear" and pictured his disgusted face. She hadn't called him that since we were little kids.

"Morning," I said.

"Morning." She tapped the phone against her chin, staring into space.

"You talked to Matty?" I asked, pouring myself some coffee.

"Yeah." Her voice sounded so wistful that the question came out before I could think.

"Why don't we go home for a visit?"

My mother turned away and busied herself with wiping the counter. "I don't think that's a good idea."

"Why not?"

"Because. It's just not."

"Then why don't we invite them to come here?"

Her shoulders stiffened. "Because they shouldn't need an invitation. If your father wants to visit or send Matty, he knows he can do that any time." I couldn't believe she was being so childish. When I opened my mouth to protest, my mother cut me off. "Just drop it, okay, Julia? If you want to go home for a visit, you are more than welcome to, but don't try to push your agenda on me."

"Fine," I muttered as she stalked down the hall and slammed the library door shut. "That's right. Run away and close the door," I said to the empty kitchen, wishing I had the guts to yell it loud enough for her to hear. *Agenda.* She made it sound like wanting my family back together was something sneaky. Like I was out to get her instead of trying to help her.

I checked the clock above the sink. I still had three hours to kill. I read the newspaper over a bowl of cereal, took a bath, and dressed in my nicest jeans and a sweater Sarah had once told me made my eyes look more green. She had called a few days before and I still hadn't called her back. I couldn't tell her about Elias, and it was hard to listen to her talk about my old school and our friends. I was living in a different world now, and while I missed Sarah, talking to her only made me miss her and my old life even more.

When it was finally a few minutes before one, I made my way down the cellar stairs and sat on the chair before standing back up again to pace. What if he couldn't come? What if he did but we just couldn't see or hear each other anymore? How would I know the difference? To distract myself, I thought about what I had read in the library. Bull Run had been the first major battle of the Civil War and had pretty much been a disaster for everyone involved. The second Bull Run had been a victory for the Confederates but caused heavy casualties on both sides.

I wondered which brother had fought for which side. More importantly, I wondered which side Elias supported. Since Virginia was technically a southern state, it was very possible that he was sympathetic to the Confederacy. If that was the case, what if he also supported slavery? I had no idea what I would say to him if that were true. I hoped not.

Just as I sat down again, I heard a faint shuffle on the stairs, and then he was in front of me, ducking under the low ceiling and holding up his lantern. I could tell he saw me as well from the smile that spread across his face.

"Julia," he said, as though confirming the reality of my presence.

"Elias," I answered. He smiled again and sat down.

"It's nice to see you. I wasn't sure if this, whatever it is, would still work."

"Me neither. Listen, before I forget, can we try something?"

He tilted his head in assent and asked, "What would you like to try?"

"Let's go up the cellar stairs together and see if we can stay visible to each other."

Elias smiled faintly. "All right." We headed for the stairs, and Elias stepped back politely to let me go ahead of him. I went up two steps and looked back. I could still see him, but he seemed somewhat fainter.

"Can you still see me?"

"I can, but not as clearly."

I went up two more steps. "How about now?" I turned around but there was no one behind me. Elias had disappeared. Panicked, I scurried back down the stairs and found myself just behind him. He was standing on the step above me peering up toward where I had been.

"Elias, I'm here." He started and turned around, then stepped down to join me. "What did you see?" I asked him.

"You were in front of me, but when you started climbing again, you disappeared. And then you were behind me."

I sighed with disappointment. "I guess this is the only place we can see each other, then. I was hoping maybe it would work other places too."

"I see," Elias said, his tone pensive.

Wanting to lighten things, I asked, "How did the roof go?" and sat down in my chair. Elias moved to sit across from me.

"Well enough, I suppose. I'm not the best at that sort of thing. Samuel would have done a better job. He can build anything." Elias looked down at his hands, frowning slightly. This seemed as good an opening as I was likely to get, so I cleared my throat and plunged in.

"What army is Samuel with, if you don't mind my asking?"

"Confederate." This meant, I realized, that the other brother—Thomson—had been a Union supporter, although that still didn't answer the question of where Elias stood. After a pause, Elias elaborated. "It all started with my parents, really. My father was born here in Virginia but went up north to study medicine in Boston. My mother used to joke that he was half Yankee. That was before, well..." He stopped for a moment, then continued. "Thing is, my father has never been comfortable with slavery. He has some Quaker in his family a ways back, and they don't hold with that sort of thing." I let out a breath of relief. "My mother, on the other hand, comes from the southern part of the state. She's part of a very traditional family, if you will." He stopped again, so I nodded encouragingly.

"Yes, I understand," I said.

"Her family was never prosperous enough to own slaves, but they, like a lot of other southerners, see it as a way of life here. It's part of who we are in the South, and it got folks pretty riled up that a bunch of Northerners were trying to tell us how to live and conduct our business. They're all factories, and we're all farmers, and each state should have the right to decide for itself which direction it wants to go. Or at least that's the general feeling around these parts, though not everyone agrees. When things were heating up, we had all kinds of discussions about it at the dinner table, and while my mother had her views, she kind of quieted down with my father and Thomson. They were…" He paused and thought for a moment. "They were two peas in a pod, I guess you could say. My father is a man of strong convictions, and Thomson was just like him. The way they'd talk, it sounded like they were arguing, but really, they were just putting forth their heated agreement on matters."

"And where did Samuel fit into all of this?" I asked.

"Well, that was the trouble. Samuel didn't really have a part. I think he was jealous of the bond between my father and Thomson, and it seemed like the more jealous he got, the more ornery he became. Whenever my father or Thomson asked his opinion, Samuel would refuse to answer or get up and leave the table. My father had no patience for that. It got so that he wouldn't even look at Samuel. He and Thomson would talk as though Samuel wasn't even there."

"That must have been hard for you and your mother."

"For my mother, yes. But I was only 14 or 15 when all of this began, and I wasn't sure what to think. I've only begun to see the truth of these things thinking on them later." Which brought up another thing I was wondering.

"How old are you?"

"Seventeen."

"And you don't have to fight in the war?" I wasn't sure how conscription worked in those days.

"Not yet, but I'll probably have to soon."

I took a breath and asked, "And which side would you fight for?"

Elias sighed. "Well, see, now that's a problem. I agree with my father and Thomson that we should remain in the Union and that slavery cannot endure, but I live in a state that says otherwise. If I wanted to join the Union army, I'd have to run away. And, depending on how things go, I might not be able to see my family again for a long time."

"You know," I said, realizing something, "I could tell you how things turn out if you want."

But apparently Elias did not want. He flinched and shook his head violently. "No, no, absolutely not."

"Why not?" I asked, surprised by his intensity.

"I can't quite say," he said, sounding surprised himself. "I just feel all the way through me that it would be wrong to know. That's not the purpose of our being able to meet like this." I frowned. *Purpose? What is he talking about?* I decided to change the subject.

"So how did your brothers end up on opposite sides? If you don't mind my asking," I added when I saw him tense.

"No. It's all right. When the lower states seceded, my father and Thomson agreed that he should go stay with family in the western part of the state, which is much more pro-Union. As soon as Fort Sumter was captured, Thomson sent word that he had enlisted. My mother was upset, but my father was so proud. He felt too duty-bound to my mother and his patients to leave himself, so it made him glad to have a son going in his place."

"And Samuel?"

"Samuel went further and further in the opposite direction. He'd go to secession rallies and come back full of anger. It's my belief, thinking back on it, that he'd finally found somewhere to belong. My father tried to speak to him about it, but he went at it all wrong. He'd talk to Samuel like he was Thomson, see, and that just angered Samuel more." Elias paused and then continued with a sad and bitter smile. "The funny thing is that when he finally ran off to join the Confederate army, it was just two days before Bull Run. He didn't know about Thomson until weeks later, but that didn't matter to my father. As far as he was concerned, Samuel joined the side that killed Thomson, and he vowed never to speak to Samuel again. In fact," Elias said, swallowing hard, "he says that Samuel is no longer part of our family and has forbidden my mother and me to have any contact with him either."

"Not even now that he's injured?"

Elias studied his hands. "I'm afraid not."

"So you haven't had any contact with Samuel? How did you learn about his injury, then?"

"I didn't have any contact at first. I must admit, I felt rather the same way as my father after Thomson died. But when he got no response from my father, Samuel finally sent a letter to me through a friend of our family. And, well, that letter made me see things differently. It was full of sorrow about Thomson and longing to be forgiven. He might be ornery, but he's not heartless. He kept writing me until I finally wrote back. I may not agree with what he did, but I understand now why he did it. He's in a makeshift hospital in Manassas in a pretty bad way. They had to cut off his leg." Elias's voice broke and he swiped a forearm across his eyes. I felt my own throat tighten.

"What are you going to do?"

"I don't know. He wants to see us. He wants to come home." We sat in silence for several minutes. Nothing I had read in my library books had prepared me for the reality of hearing it from someone living through it. If he'd wanted me to, I could have told him the outcome of the war as a whole, but all I could remember from the file was who inherited the house. I didn't know whether the family ever reunited. I was just as in the dark about that as I was about my own family's fate

Elias cleared his throat and picked up his lantern. "I apologize, Julia. I must go, and I've filled all of our time burdening you with my troubles. Truth be told, I'd rather learn more about you." His eyes met and held my own.

"No need to apologize. You were just answering my questions. I want to know about you too," I added, my face flushing. I wasn't used to such direct statements but it seemed silly not to be honest in a moment like this. "We've got a few things in common, actually. But my story can wait for next time."

"Yes, next time. I would like that. When can we meet again?"

"Well, other than school, it seems like I have a little more freedom to come and go than you do. Why don't you choose?"

"I can't stop in here for more than a few minutes on weekdays, but this time seems to work well. How about the same time next Saturday?"

"Sounds good."

Elias stood up but he hesitated before turning away. "I'm still not sure what to make of this, Julia, but one thing I am certain of is that this is one of the most wondrous things to ever happen to me. I must say, it feels good to have something special to look forward to. To have something to feel glad about, with everything else going on."

This time the warmth I felt had nothing to do with embarrassment. "I know exactly what you mean."

Chapter 7

THE BEGINNING OF October brought cooler temperatures and tor-
rential rain. On my walk to school, things didn't look so bad, but
by the time I got out of P.E., the sky was thick with dark clouds.
As I headed across the field, fat drops began hitting my face and
splotching across my shirt. "Great," I muttered, wishing I'd thought
to bring an umbrella when I left the house. I ducked under a tree
and took out my phone. My mother's phone rang and went to voice
mail. No point leaving a message. I'd be home before she ever got it.

I picked up my pace as the rain increased, and by the time I got
to the road, it was coming down so hard I could barely see. A car
honked to my left, and someone was shouting. "Hey, want a ride?"
A battered blue truck had pulled up and Derek was at the wheel.
I was suddenly conscious of my hair plastered to my skull and the
soggy droop of my clothes.

"No, I'm okay," I said, turning away. He leaned over and shoved
the passenger door open.

"Don't be an idiot. Get in."

I obeyed, hiding my embarrassment by leaning over to shove my sodden bag in the space at my feet. "I'm getting your truck all wet." He shrugged.

"It's seen worse. Where to?"

"Keep going down this road and turn right at the second light." As I fumbled with the seat belt, I registered the music playing on his stereo and my mouth dropped open. "You listen to Elliott Smith?" I blurted. I saw a flash of dimple.

"Yeah. Why so shocked?"

I snapped my mouth shut and pushed my wet hair back. "I don't know. It's just not what I would have expected."

"What would you have expected?"

"I guess classic rock or country or something like that."

"I see." He braked at the light and turned to look at me, one eyebrow raised. "So you're saying because I live in the South, you'd expect me to be blasting 'Sweet Home Alabama' or cranking me up some honky-tonk?" He laughed as my face turned red.

"Well, when you put it like that..."

"This isn't the deep South, and not everyone who lives in a southern state is a redneck stereotype, you know." The light changed. "It's not like I have a gun rack and a Confederate flag in my back window."

"Yeah, but you are driving a truck."

"True, but that doesn't mean much by itself. I thought you city folk were supposed to be more open-minded than that. You know, more sophisticated and not as judgmental as us country hicks." He said the last part with an exaggerated twang, and I laughed.

"I guess I don't fit the stereotype either." I leaned down to pick up some of the CDs on the floor by my feet and read the names aloud. "Starsailor, Jeff Buckley, Radiohead. Not bad."

"I'm glad you approve." His voice was dry, but the dimples flashed again. "Where do I go now?"

"Oh, just to the end of this street and turn left. My house is toward the end."

"Really? That's the street my grandpa used to live on." I tensed. *What were the odds of that?* He made the turn and slowed as he neared the end of the street.

"That one," I said, pointing through the windshield. My pulse fluttered as I waited for his response.

"No way! That's my grandpa's house. Or it was. We used to come visit him here all the time when I was a kid. He hung a rope swing for us from that big oak tree in the back yard." His voice dropped, and I could tell he was caught up in his memories. "We'd get all crazy with it and push each other as hard as we could. My brother ended up flying off one day and broke his arm, and my mother made my grandpa take it down."

"That's a bummer." My mind was racing. *Derek was a descendent. Elias was his great-great something.* I searched his face for any resemblance to Elias but couldn't find any other than their coloring. And maybe a little something about the jaw. "So," I said, trying to keep my voice casual. "Did you guys ever play in the cellar?" I watched him closely for any sign of reaction.

"The cellar?" Derek shook his head. "Nah, we didn't really go in there. Maybe once or twice, but it was boring. Nothing down there."

"My mom told me it's a really old house with a lot of history."

Derek shrugged. "I guess so."

"I don't suppose there are any ghost stories that have been passed down."

"Nope. That would have been pretty cool, though. Why, have you seen anything?"

"Nope," I echoed him, "no ghosts." There was no way I could tell him what was happening without sounding like a lunatic, especially since there seemed to be a strong possibility that I was the first to experience this type of thing. My brain started short-circuiting from all the implications of Elias and Derek being related. What were the odds of that? What were the odds of *any* of this?

The water evaporating from my clothes and hair was beginning to steam up the windows as his truck sat idling. I unbuckled myself and picked up my backpack, feeling a sudden need to be by myself and think this all through.

"Well, thanks for the ride."

"No problem." Derek shifted to face me. "Do you walk to school every day?"

"Yeah. We only have one car," I said, gesturing toward the driveway, "and I don't know how to drive."

"Are you serious?"

"You don't need to drive in the city. In fact, it's a major pain to drive there. We use the subway."

"Well, you're not living in the city now, and being able to drive a car comes in pretty handy around here."

"I guess." I reached for the door handle.

"I can teach you."

"What?" I turned back, surprised.

"I can teach you to drive. I mean, if you want."

"Um, sure." It would be a fun way to distract myself until Saturday. "That'd be great."

Derek smiled. "Cool. Well, I'll see you tomorrow."

"Thanks again." I climbed out and sprinted to the front door. My mother stepped out of the library as I was kicking off my wet shoes. "Hi," I said, surprised to see her emerge.

"You're soaked! Why didn't you call me to come pick you up?"

"I did."

My mother frowned and patted her pockets. "Oh, that's right. I left my phone in my purse." She looked around the hall distractedly. "Who was that bringing you home?"

"Just someone from school."

"Oh, okay." She turned to go back into the library, but I found I wasn't ready to let her go. She'd disappeared on another one of her long drives yesterday evening, and I hadn't had an actual conversation with her in days.

"Actually, it was the boy who bumped into me at registration. You know, the boy you said was cute?" I prompted.

The Mom from Before Denny Died would have immediately dragged me into the kitchen, made me hot cocoa, and prodded me for every last detail. But this one said, "Better get some dry clothes on," and left me standing alone in the hallway.

--->==⊚ ⊚==·<---

Derek came over to my desk just before the first bell for homeroom. "So how does this afternoon work for you?"

"Great."

Natalie glared back at us and leaned over to whisper something to her friend, who also turned around to glare. I flashed them my sweetest smile and looked back at Derek, who was still talking.

"Since you know what my truck looks like, let's just meet there after school. I park in the back left corner of the lot."

"Okay. Sounds good."

"See you then." He did one of his head jerks and went back to his seat. As I slumped down in my own, I caught a glimpse of Samira looking at me, but she turned away when she saw me looking back. At least she wasn't glaring.

After the last bell of the day, I headed toward the parking lot, threading my way through the masses of students going in the same direction. Derek was leaning against his truck when I finally found it.

"Ready?" He unlocked the doors and we climbed in. I started getting nervous, noticing for the first time how big the truck was. *What if I crash and wreck it?* Derek seemed perfectly relaxed, humming absently to the song playing on the stereo and tapping his hand on the steering wheel.

"So what's the deal with you and Natalie?"

"Huh?" Derek glanced over, his brows furrowed.

"Natalie," I repeated. "She seems to be around you a lot and looks like she wants to pull my hair every time you talk to me. Is there anything I should know?" I could see the dimples forming, but Derek was silent while he made a left turn through a break in traffic.

"You don't need to worry about Natalie," he said finally.

"She's not your girlfriend?" This made him laugh.

"Nah. Natalie and I have known each other since we were little kids. She's dating a guy who graduated last year and went off to the Air Force Academy. I think she just uses me as a kind of male stand-in. It doesn't mean anything."

"Does she know that?" I muttered this under my breath, but Derek still heard it.

"She should. She knows I won't put up with any of her crap. She's kind of annoying on the surface, but she's pretty decent once you know her."

"I'll take your word for it." We pulled into the parking lot of a large warehouse. A couple delivery trucks were parked along the far side, but it was otherwise empty. Derek turned off the ignition.

"You're up." We got out to trade seats, and as I climbed in behind the steering wheel, Derek said, "First thing you need to do is check your mirrors. Since you're some kind of freak midget, you're going to need to adjust them and the seat."

"Fond of hyperbole, are we?" I fished under my seat for the lever.

"Okay, now turn on the ignition." I accidentally turned the key forward a little longer and harder than necessary, and the squealing grind of the engine made Derek wince. I jerked my hand off the key.

"Sorry."

"That's okay. Now put your foot on the brake and shift to drive. When you're ready, go ahead and ease up on the brake." After the whole ignition fiasco, I raised my foot as slowly as possible. When nothing happened after several seconds, Derek said, "Are you wait-ing for something?"

"I'm trying to be careful."

"There's a good fifty yards or more of space in front of us, and the truck's not going to suddenly leap into 60 miles an hour on its own, you know."

"No, I don't know that. This is my first time in the driver's seat, remember?" I pulled my foot off the brake, and the car began to slowly glide forward.

"That's it," said Derek. "When you're ready, go ahead and give the gas pedal a little pressure." I took a deep breath and he added, "Sometime before dark would be nice."

"Shut up." I pressed my foot down gingerly, and the truck be-gan to accelerate.

"Good. Now try steering from side to side a little to get the feel of it." I relaxed the tight grip I had on the wheel and pulled it gently to the right and then the left, winding my way across the parking lot. I couldn't believe it was so easy. And exhilarating.

"I'm doing it! I'm driving!"

Derek laughed. "Sort of. This is more of a wobbly coast." As we neared the end of the lot, I took my foot off the gas pedal and brought it down on the brake. A little too hard, as it turned out. Derek and I both lurched forward in our seats like rag dolls.

"I know, I know," I said, holding up a hand. "I don't need to brake that hard. Now tell me how to turn."

"Bossy little thing, aren't you?"

"I'm efficient," I said, turning to smile at him. He rolled his eyes and proceeded to explain the art of the turn. By the end of the hour, I was comfortable driving back and forth across the parking lot at slow speeds, turning the truck, and even braking without giving us whiplash.

"That was fun," I said as we switched seats again.

"Yeah. You're catching on. Just don't get over-confident. Driving in a parking lot at 20 miles an hour is nothing like driving in traffic."

"Okay, Grandpa."

"Smartass." Derek headed out to the main highway. "So is it just you and your mom?"

"It's just us out here. My dad and younger brother are still in New York."

"Huh." Derek slowed for a turn and threw a quick glance in my direction. "So, are your parents divorced?"

"No. They're...well, I guess you could say they're taking a break. It's complicated." As if any separation weren't complicated. But I wanted him to know that it wasn't just a marriage problem, that there was something bigger going on. I tried to think of the simplest and least awkward way to explain it. We had reached my street by now, and Derek pulled into the driveway behind my mother's car. "My uncle—my mother's brother—was killed in the attacks on the World Trade Center last year," I said, trying to keep my voice matter-of-fact. "She's been having a hard time dealing with it and wanted a break from New York. So we came here." Derek's face went slack with shock, and I immediately wished I hadn't told him.

"Wow. That's terrible. I'm so sorry. I can't, I mean, I can't even imagine." He ran a hand over his face and propped his elbow against his window. In the silence that followed, the tension gripping my body became unbearable.

"Well, I'd better get inside. Thanks again for the lesson." I jumped out of the truck and slammed the door on his surprised goodbye. *Stupid, stupid. Why did you have to go and ruin the afternoon like that?* I heard his truck reverse and pull away as I went up the porch stairs, but I didn't look back. I leaned my head against the front door. It was always like this with people—shock, pity, and awkward silence.

I almost fell over when the door suddenly opened in front of me. "Where have you been?" My mother was furious.

"What do you mean?"

"I mean exactly what I said—where have you been? School ended almost two hours ago."

"If you were so worried, why didn't you just call me?" I asked. A strange expression flashed across her face—surprise? guilt? Looking at her more closely, I noticed her eyes were unfocused. She was also gripping the door tightly. *She drunk,* I realized, and it occurred to me that she probably hadn't even noticed I'd been gone or what time it was until she saw me pull up with Derek.

She pointed an angry finger at me. "That's not the point. I shouldn't have to call you. Common courtesy says that you should let me know when you're going to be out for hours with some boy I've never met."

I threw my bag on the floor and yanked off my jacket. "Does that apply to you too? Because I don't see you calling me when you decide to disappear for hours." My mother recoiled as if I had struck her, but I was too angry to care. "And if you want to know about

Derek and where I was, then maybe you should try asking me about it like a normal person instead of attacking me." Her eyes filled with tears. Unable to bear looking at her, I ran upstairs and slammed my bedroom door. *Why does everything have to go wrong?* And then I remembered. *Elias.* Saturday couldn't come fast enough.

Chapter 8

FOR THE NEXT two days, my mother and I slunk around the house like two wary cats, trying to avoid direct contact as much as possible. Weirdly, we were also going out of our way to be more considerate. I started finding notes taped to the bathroom mirror when she went out, and when Derek asked if I wanted another lesson on Thursday afternoon, I asked if we could do it the following week and went straight home. I was stretched out on my bed thinking about what I wanted to ask Elias on Saturday when there was a quiet knock on my door.

"Can I come in?"

"Sure." I sat up as my mother sat on the end of my bed.

"I wanted to apologize for the other day," she said, her hands fidgeting in her lap. "I shouldn't have snapped at you like that. And you were right that I wasn't exactly fair."

I hugged my legs and rested my chin on my knees. "I probably shouldn't have snapped at you either."

There was a pause, and she cleared her throat. "So, I know we haven't spent much time together lately, and I thought maybe we could go out to lunch and a movie or something on Saturday to celebrate…my birthday." My heart rose and then immediately sank. *Elias.* But I couldn't say no. I knew what that pause meant. She'd had to stop herself from saying *our birthday.* We had always celebrated with Uncle Denny. Always.

"Yeah, that sounds nice." I forced myself to smile.

"Okay, then." My mother stood up. "I'm pretty wiped out. Do you mind fixing yourself some supper?"

"That's fine."

"See you in the morning, then." She crossed the hallway to her room and shut the door. I pushed my own door closed, then buried my face in my pillow and groaned. Of course it would be this way, the two things I wanted most scheduled for the exact same time. What would Elias think when I didn't show up? What if I never saw him again? I tried to think of some reason I could ask my mother to go Sunday instead of Saturday, but came up blank. There was nothing I could do.

⇥▬◉ ◉▬⇤

After a restless night, I woke up on Saturday feeling gritty-eyed and groggy. My mother had left a note next to the coffee pot. *Going out for an errand. Will be back by noon.* I rushed through breakfast and went down to the cellar. Maybe Elias would come down early for some reason. Maybe I could still see him after all, at least to tell him what was going on and figure out another time to meet. But as the dial on my watch crept closer to noon, I knew it wasn't going to happen. Even though I knew it was pointless, I wrote a note for him and left it on my chair. That felt slightly better than doing nothing. *It's going to be okay*, I told myself as I climbed the cellar stairs. It had to be. Besides, I didn't want to ruin the time with my mother feeling awful about Elias if I could help it, otherwise everything was a loss. It seemed to be my fate to have to always be choosing between my mother and someone else.

She pulled into the driveway a few minutes later, and I walked around the side of the house to meet her. She had put her hair up in a French twist and was wearing lipstick, looking more like she used to other than her unnatural thinness. She hoisted a bag from the seat next to her.

"Let me just take this inside." As she went up the porch steps, I heard the clink of glass. Apparently the errand had been to the liquor store. She appeared at the front door a moment later. "Ready?" she asked, smiling.

"Yup," I said, forcing myself to smile back.

I had to admit that Virginia in October was beautiful as we drove along roads bordered by green fields and forests of trees thick with leaves ranging from golden yellow to orange and red. The Italian bistro my mother took us to in the next town over was cheery and full of noise and bustle. I gave her a card I made when we sat down, and she exclaimed about how pretty it was. My mother asked about Derek, and I told her about our driving lesson. A small frown creased her forehead, but she didn't say anything, though I could tell she wanted to. We were both doing our best to have a pleasant mother-daughter outing, but something between us still felt stretched tight. For everything we said, there were about three things we didn't. It was like we were playing that game where you have to make your team guess a word without saying any of the ones listed on your card. My mother and I seemed to have our own card with words like *Uncle Denny, Dad, Matty* and the questions *why?* and *when?* written on them. It was a relief to finally be in the theater where we could just sit and watch the movie in silence. I barely noticed what was playing. I kept picturing Elias coming down the cellar stairs and waiting for me. And waiting. And then leaving again.

When we pulled up to the house, it took all of my willpower not to jump out of the car and run straight to the cellar. Instead, I followed my mother into the front hallway. She dropped her keys on the table by the door and put a hand on the stairwell. "I think I'm going to go up and take a nap."

"Okay. Thanks for taking me out," I added. Awkward as it might have been, at least she had tried.

"Thanks for going." She gave me the bare flicker of a smile and headed up the stairs. I waited until I heard her door shut, then bolted for the back door. My hands shook as I pulled out my key and unlocked the cellar doors. I knew Elias wouldn't still be there—it was nearly three hours later than we'd agreed to meet—but I couldn't help hoping. I turned on the light and did a quick scan. Nothing. Just my note lying untouched and probably unseen on the chair where I'd left it. I crumpled it and sank into the chair, dropping my head against the wall.

"I'm so sorry, Elias," I whispered into the silence. "Please come back." I sat there for another half hour before trudging upstairs again. I would try again tomorrow, and I would wait all day, if necessary.

--≡◎ ◎≡--

I woke the next morning to the sound of the front door closing. I fumbled for my watch and saw that it was just after ten. Cursing myself for having slept so late, I grabbed my jeans off the floor and pulled a sweater out of the closet. Downstairs, I picked up my backpack and added a bottle of water and a bagel.

I saw right away that the cellar was empty. *That's okay,* I told myself. *He'll come later.* I sat in my chair and pulled out the novel I was supposed to be reading for my English class. An hour went by. I ate my bagel and drank some water. Another hour. I had given up on the novel and simply sat staring into the gloom. *What if I never see him again?* The thought made me feel sick.

A faint noise, followed by the sight of Elias's legs, torso, and face emerging as he descended the cellar steps filled me with relief. "Elias!" I sprang up from the chair to meet him in the middle of the floor. His own face spread into a wide smile.

"Julia." We were only inches apart, and I instinctively leaned in to touch his arm before I stopped and drew back. His own hand lifted toward me and dropped. He was still somewhat transparent, but as I examined him more closely, it seemed like he was more distinct than he had been before. His eyes, fringed by dark lashes, were a piercing blue. Of course, maybe I hadn't noticed them before because I had never stood so close to him. Suddenly aware of our proximity, I flushed and moved back to my chair. He also sat in his usual place and set his lantern down.

"I'm sorry I wasn't here yesterday," I said. "My mother asked me to go out with her at the last minute and I couldn't say no. I waited here yesterday morning for awhile and left a note, but of course you didn't come down early and I doubt you could see the note."

He frowned. "No, I couldn't see a note. I don't see anything differently from how it usually is unless you're here."

"Did you wait a long time?"

"I waited for close to an hour. It was the longest I could stay down here without my parents taking notice. It occurred to me that perhaps you couldn't come after all. But later, I thought that perhaps whatever this is was no longer possible. That our time together had passed." He looked down at his hands.

"I'm sorry, Elias."

"You are not at fault for anything, Julia. But perhaps we ought to have a plan for situations like this. It's not easy for me to come down here for long stretches, but I planned to keep coming whenever I was able to." He paused then said, "We have known each other such a short time, really, but when I came down yesterday and you weren't here, I must confess it was a grave disappointment."

"It was for me too. Look, how about this? If one of us doesn't show when we're supposed to, we try again at the same time the next day and keep going until we see each other again."

Elias nodded. "That sounds reasonable. And now that that's settled, I'd like to hear more about you and your life."

"Oh, well," I said, and then laughed. "You're going to have to be more specific than that."

Elias smiled in return. "All right. Did you have a pleasant time with your mother yesterday?"

"Kind of. It was all right on the surface, but we were both trying really hard, which made things tense underneath, if that makes any sense." He nodded and waited for me to continue. "The thing is, I don't think we should have ever moved out here. I don't think our family should be split up like this and I'm pretty sure she knows exactly how I feel. We just never talk about it."

"What made you decide to come here with her?"

I thought about his question for a moment before answering. I'd never explained it aloud to anyone before now. "I guess I figured if she came here by herself, there was more of a chance she'd never come back. But if I'm here, she still has a connection to home." I struggled to pinpoint my other reasons. Elias stayed quiet, which was nice. I didn't feel like I needed to rush. "I also came because I was worried about her. I still am. My mom's not doing well."

"Is she ill?"

"Not exactly. Or, at least, it's not a physical illness." I took a deep breath and let it out again. "I have to go back a bit for you to understand this. I know most sisters love their brothers, but my mom and Uncle Denny were really close. They were twins, for one thing. Their parents both died before I was born, but I've kind of picked up from things here and there that they were pretty messed up." I could see Elias's look of confusion and tried rewording things. "They had a lot of problems and weren't very nice people. So she and Denny were kind of everything to each other growing up. They even went to the same college. In fact, my parents met through Uncle Denny. He and my dad were roommates."

"They were friends?"

"Yes. Good friends. It's always been the three of them." It was one of those things that had always been so obvious that I had never really thought about it before. "He didn't have a family of his own and never dated the same woman for more than a few months. I think he spent more time with us than anyone except maybe the people he worked with, and that doesn't really count." I paused, and Elias remained silent as I gathered my thoughts. "I don't think my parents know how to be together without Uncle Denny. It's like they were a three-legged stool, and one of the legs got yanked out, so the whole thing's tipped over." I leaned forward and propped my chin in my hands. "I just understood that right now. Isn't that strange?"

"It sounds like you have had to bear a great deal. I'm sorry, Julia." His simple acknowledgment felt like a release.

"Thanks. It helps to tell you about it. I can't talk to my parents about it, obviously, and my brother is too young. My friends back home try to be supportive, but they don't really understand. But you know."

Elias nodded and his mouth creased in a wry smile. "I do."

"So has anything changed with your father and Samuel?"

Elias let out a deep sigh. "Unfortunately, no. A few nights ago, I mentioned that Samuel and I are corresponding, and my father simply changed the subject. He doesn't want to hear Samuel's name."

"That's so sad." I tried to imagine my own parents cutting off contact with me or Matty and failed. *They wouldn't.* I thought of my mother's frequent withdrawals. *At least not intentionally.* "How is Samuel doing?"

"Not very well. They're low on morphine at his hospital. Although, it's not really a hospital at all—it's a hotel they turned into a hospital. He's in a great deal of pain."

"I'm sorry, Elias." I remembered something I'd read in my research about soldiers getting addicted to morphine and said, "It might actually kind of good if he doesn't have too much of that anyway." The surprised look on Elias's face made me rush to add, "I mean, it's not good that he's in pain, but that's a dangerous medication. It caused—I mean it causes—a lot of problems for the men who take it down the road."

"Is that so?" Elias seemed uncomfortable with what I'd just told him, so I changed the subject.

"Do you think you'll ever go visit him?"

"I certainly would like to, and even though my mother's never said anything to me outright, I know she'd like me to as well. It's been an awful burden for her to think of Samuel suffering alone."

"How would your father react if you went?"

"I don't rightly know. Not well, I imagine." Elias ran a hand across his face as though to wipe those thoughts away. He stood up and reached for the lantern. "I'm sorry to say that I must go now, Julia. I've enjoyed our conversation. Do you think we might meet again during the week?"

"That'd be great. What afternoon would work for you?"

"I'm helping my father for the next few days. But I can most likely come again on Wednesday."

"I'll do my best to be here from 3:15 to at least 4:00."

"And if one of us doesn't show..."

"We try again the next day at the same time," I finished. He smiled and studied me for a moment in the dim light.

"Your hair looks different."

I pushed a hand through it. "Yeah, I need to get it cut but I don't know a good place out here. So it's just getting longer."

"I like it. It's very becoming."

"If you say so. I mean, thanks." I shoved my hands in my pockets.

"It seems receiving compliments is not your strong suit."

His bluntness made me laugh. "No, it's not."

"Perhaps you ought to learn. Unless the males in your time are either blind or foolish, I expect you'll need to get accustomed to them." I couldn't think of anything to say in return, and he smiled again as he turned to the stairs. "Goodbye for now, Julia."

"Bye." I barely got the word out before he disappeared. I sat back in my chair. *He's just being nice.* But I couldn't help smiling.

Chapter 9

MONDAY MORNING, THERE was a noticeable chill to the air as I started the walk to school, and I shoved my hands into the pockets of my jacket. Seconds later, my phone buzzed against my hand.

"Hi, Dad."

"Hey, kiddo. You on your way to school?"

"Yeah."

"How are you?"

"I'm all right."

"Good." He sounded distracted. "Listen," he said, "your mom hasn't called Matty in awhile. What's going on?"

"I don't know, Dad. She's kind of the same. Depressed. I think this week was especially hard because, well, you know. The birthday."

"Is she drinking a lot?"

"Some," I hedged.

"I don't like this situation, Julia." I was glad he couldn't see me roll my eyes. *Here we go again.*

"Dad, it's really not that bad. She's painting a lot too, you know. I think she just needs a little more time."

"Julia." The obvious skepticism in his voice filled me with anger.

"She's going to get better, Dad, and we *will* be coming home. Unlike some people, I'm not ready to give up on her." There was a short silence.

"Just see if you can give her a nudge about Matty, okay?"

"Fine."

"Have a good day at school," he said, hanging up before I could answer.

"'Bye, Dad. Nice talking to you too," I muttered, shoving the phone back in my pocket. Apparently, my parents were now back in junior high, and I was the friend stuck passing notes.

When I got to the parking lot at the end of the day for my lesson with Derek, I saw him waving at me from a different truck than usual.

"We have to make a quick stop at my house," Derek said as we climbed in. "My dad and I swapped today so he could take mine in for new tires. He's old-school and only drives stick, and I figure that would be a bit much to throw at you."

"Yeah, probably."

Derek lived in a large house in a newer part of town, where two gently sloping brick walls at the end of his block were decorated with the name "Oak Park" in elegant wrought iron lettering. He pulled into the driveway next to his own truck. "Come on in for a minute. I need to get the keys."

"Okay." I climbed out and followed him through the front door.

"Anybody home?" he hollered at large. An elderly man emerged from a doorway down the hall. "Hey, Grandpa. Did Dad leave my keys?"

"They're on the kitchen table." I could see where Derek inherited his height. His grandfather was slightly shorter, but held himself upright despite a slight tremor in his left arm. He shuffled stiffly toward us and I felt Derek's hand on my arm.

"This is Julia. She and her mom are staying in your old house. Funny, huh?" Derek's grandfather didn't seem to hear him. He was studying my face intently.

"Julia, you said?"

"Yeah, Grandpa."

"Julia what?"

"Julia McKinley," I answered. I looked over at Derek, who raised his eyebrows and shrugged.

"I'm going to grab the keys. Want anything to eat?" he asked, already at the other end of the hallway.

"No thanks." I turned and found his grandfather still staring at me. I found myself staring back. *So what can you tell me about your family history?* I was tempted to ask. But of course I couldn't. Not without sounding insane. Our staring contest was starting to get weird, so I looked away. I cleared my throat, searching for something to say, but he beat me to it.

"So you're Julia." He murmured this softly, as though musing to himself. I met his blue eyes again, slightly faded with age, and stiffened at the keen look of recognition in them.

"Do you...do you *know* something about me?" He shook his head, but I couldn't tell if it was in denial or disbelief. Derek came striding down the hall again.

"Okay, got 'em. You ready?" He looked from me to his grandfather and back again.

"Yeah, sure. It was nice meeting you," I said, but his grandfather had already turned and started shuffling away. Derek grinned and shrugged again.

"Sorry about that," he said as we went outside. "Grandpa's usually pretty sharp."

"That's okay." As we pulled out of the driveway, I saw him at the window watching us go. I knew who he was in relation to Derek and Elias, but why did it seem like he'd known something about me? I forced myself to focus as Derek drove us to the same parking lot, where he reviewed the basics again and had me practice parking.

"Shouldn't I try driving around on the streets before worrying about being able to park perfectly between the white lines?" I asked, getting impatient with all this stopping and starting. I wanted to *drive*.

"One thing at a time, Speedy. Learning to park helps you develop your sense of space and get a feel for just how big the car is. Once you've done that we'll go on the road. I want to make sure you know what it feels like to be inside the lines first."

"Oh. I hadn't thought of that."

"There's a method to my madness. I'm teaching you the way I was taught."

"Who taught you to drive?" I asked, inching my way forward and peering over the hood to gauge my progress.

"My grandpa. My parents took me out once I was up and running, but Grandpa was the one to bring me here and teach me the basics. He taught all us kids. I think my parents would have just ended up yelling at us, but Grandpa's a pretty cool customer."

"So you guys are close?"

"I guess so. Especially now that he lives with us."

"Does he ever tell you stories about your family? Like your ancestors and stuff?" I tried to keep my voice casual as I shifted into reverse and began backing up.

"Nah, not really. Grandpa's not much of a talker." I don't know what I had expected, but I felt the heavy weight of disappointment at his answer. "I think you're ready," Derek said. "Want to try a few quiet neighborhood streets?"

In spite of my earlier impatience, I suddenly felt tired and anxious to go home. "How about next time? I should get home and work on my college applications," I quickly added when I saw Derek's surprise.

"Sure, that's fine." We traded seats and Derek started the drive to my house. "I should probably work on mine too. Where are you applying?"

"NYU, Boston College, Tufts. Maybe Michigan, although I don't know if I want to go that far from home. How about you?"

"UVA, George Mason, and, um, NYU." He mumbled the last one so I could barely hear it.

"Really? NYU?"

"Yeah."

"Why do you seem embarrassed about that?"

He shrugged and rubbed the back of his head. "I don't know. I guess because no one else around here has any interest in going there. And, I guess, it's kind of because of why I want to go there."

"Why do you want to go there?"

Derek hesitated. "I want to study filmmaking, and I know they have a really good program there."

"That's great," I said. I couldn't understand why he found that so difficult to tell me. He glanced over as we pulled in front of my house.

"You're not laughing."

"Why would I laugh?"

"Because a lot of other people I know would if I told them what I just told you."

"Well, I'm not other people. I'm a New Yorker, so of course it makes sense to me that you'd want to go to NYU, and I think it's cool that you want to be a filmmaker."

"Yeah?"

"Yeah. Why do you think people you know would find it so strange?" I was genuinely puzzled. Derek fidgeted with the keys for a moment before replying.

"I just feel like it sounds kind of pretentious. I was kind of a jock for most of high school. I mean, I always got pretty good grades and everything, but that's not what I was known for. This is the first year I'm not doing sports, and telling people that I wasn't going to play football this fall because I wanted to focus on academics made them look at me funny enough without the whole filmmaker stuff. And maybe it's stupid, but I don't want to be the douchebag guy my senior year of high school."

"No, I get it."

"Well, that's a relief."

"No need to be sarcastic. You're the one confiding in me."

"True."

"Besides, I think those two idiots in our homeroom already have the role of 'douchebag guy' pretty well covered."

"Who?"

"The ones who think racist comments are hilarious."

"Oh, Phil and Donny. They've always been like that, unfortunately. Probably tortured small animals when they were kids."

"It's sweet the way you see the best in everyone."

"Now who's being sarcastic?"

"Yeah, well, if I couldn't be sarcastic, I wouldn't talk very much."

"And that's a bad thing how?"

I laughed and unbuckled myself. "Thanks for the lesson."

"No problem. When do you want the next one?"

"How about Thursday?"

"Sure. See you tomorrow." I gave him a small wave and trudged up the porch steps. The light was fading quickly and I could see that my mother had turned on a light in the library. I let out a small sigh as I opened the front door. I liked Derek and our driving lessons were fun, but it had been hard holding back all the thoughts and questions unleashed by my encounter with his grandfather. Why did he seem to recognize my name? Did he somehow know about Elias and me? And if he did, how was that possible? Elias would have—my stomach twisted at the thought—died long before Derek's grandfather was born. I had never let myself think about this before, but here in 2002, Elias had already grown old and died and was now long gone. And yet the Elias whose life was already lived out and over was completely different from the Elias in the cellar, at least in my mind. The Elias I knew was young and living, and right now that felt more real to me than any dry facts of logic.

⊶⊷

My father's phone call was a nudge toward something I'd been thinking about for the last week or two, which was trying to convince my mother that our family should be together for Thanksgiving. It was still weeks away, but I had a feeling it might take some time to convince her, so might as well start early. I offered to make dinner that evening and waited until she had eaten most of it before saying anything. She'd also drunk a couple glasses of wine, and I felt a small stab of guilt when it crossed my mind that for once this might be helpful.

"So, have you talked to Matty or Dad lately?" I asked.

My mother's eyebrows went up, but she kept her gaze focused on her plate. "I talked to Matty a few days ago. Why?"

I resisted the urge to tell her she hadn't called him for a week. "I don't know. I just wondered. I miss them."

"I do too." She sounded faintly aggressive. I shoved down my irritation and forced myself to sound cheerful and spontaneous.

"Wouldn't it be great if they came here for Thanksgiving? I bet they'd love it here, and it's not as cold as the city." I winced at how fake that sounded. My mother leaned back in her chair, her expression hard to read.

"Is it already that time?"

"Pretty soon."

"Thanksgiving here," she repeated.

"I think it would be nice." When she remained silent, I added, "We've never been apart for a holiday before." My mother crossed her arms.

"I don't know if that's such a good idea, Julia."

"Why not?"

"Because."

A small snort slipped out before I could stop it. *"Because?* That's not a reason, Mom. Look, I can understand if you're not ready to go back to New York for a visit, but what's wrong with them coming here? That's what you wanted before."

"Things change, Julia."

"They don't have to. Not the things that matter. We've got plenty of room, and I think it would be good for all of us to be together." I paused then added, "At least for Matty and me."

My mother flinched and her eyes narrowed. "And just what is that supposed to mean?"

"What it sounds like," I shot back. "Matty hasn't seen us and I haven't seen Dad in over two months."

"And that's my fault? I'm keeping you all apart, is that it?"

"I'm not saying it's anyone's fault. That's not the point. I'm just saying it would be nice to be together for Thanksgiving. Why do you have to make it so complicated?"

She shoved back her chair and stood up. "Because it *is* complicated. Don't be such a child." She grabbed our plates and stalked into the kitchen. I followed her, shaking but determined.

"But I am a child, Mom, and so is Matty. We're your children— yours and Dad's."

She set the plates in the sink with a clatter. "That's a low blow, Julia. Do you think I don't care about my children? That I'm not aware of how this is affecting you two?"

"Are you?"

"Of course I am! How can you ask that?" Her eyes filled with tears, and I felt my own throat close. "I hate this, Julia. I really do. I wish I could be this perfect mom you want and somehow make myself happy again and move on with life, but I can't. I can't," she repeated before breaking into sobs. I took a step toward her and touched her arm.

"I'm not asking you to be perfect, Mom. I just want—can't you even consider what I'm asking?"

She turned away from me, wiping her face. After a moment of tense silence, she said, "As I have always said, you are more than welcome to go home for a visit if you want. But we are not going to have Thanksgiving here."

"Mom…"

"That's enough, Julia." She turned on the faucet and began scrubbing the dishes. I turned and walked out before I could give into my urge to grab one of the plates and smash it on the floor.

→═◉ ◉═←

As I sat in the cellar waiting for Elias, I thought about my mother's response to my suggestion about Thanksgiving. I had expected some resistance, but not a flat-out refusal. Maybe I should just go back to New York. We were barely speaking to each other lately, so what was the point of my being here? *But you can't leave her here alone.* The thought was always there, along with the feeling that if I did leave, that would be it—our family would be broken forever. Elias's appearance dispelled this gloomy thought.

"Julia."

"Elias."

As always, we stood silent for the first few seconds, taking each other in. I wondered if it would ever become any less strange and wonderful. Probably not. Elias leaned in closer and held the lantern next to my face.

"Have you not been sleeping?"

I touched my eyes, self-conscious at his scrutiny. "It's been harder lately," I said. "Especially last night." I was surprised he could see me that well. Looking back at him, I realized that I could see signs of his own sleeplessness. Dark circles shadowed his eyes and there were lines marking the sides of his mouth like sad parentheses. He pulled his usual crate close to my chair and we both sat down, leaning in toward each other.

"Why couldn't you sleep?" he asked.

"Oh, the usual. Fighting with my mom. Wondering if it's ever going to be okay again or just stay awful forever." He waited for me to continue. "I asked her if we could invite my dad and brother here for Thanksgiving. We have never, ever been apart for a holiday. I've been missing my dad and Matty like crazy, and I thought this would be the perfect reason for us to be together, at least for a little while."

"And she refused?"

"Yes. She wouldn't even think about it. If she won't even bend for this, what could possibly bring her back? Why am I even here?" My worries came tumbling out.

"I can see why this would trouble your sleep." Elias's face was grave. "It's difficult, isn't it?"

"What?"

"Being the one who is responsible."

"I guess so. I used to have three adults in my life. Now, somehow, *I've* become the adult."

"I would like to tell you not to lose hope, that things might still change, but I am not so certain of that myself these days."

"What's happening with your family? You look like you haven't had much sleep yourself."

"I tried to show my father Samuel's letters yesterday. I started to read them aloud at supper, and my father was furious. I lost my temper as well, and we both ended up shouting terrible things at each other. It made my mother cry." He pushed his hair back with a trembling hand. I tried to picture him shouting at anyone and failed. He seemed so gentle and calm about everything. It made me feel a little better about my own desire to scream at my mother.

"What did you say?"

"I told him he was a cruel and heartless man to punish Samuel in this way, and that it was hurting our whole family, even the memory of Thomson." He took a shuddering breath and continued. "The worst of it is that as awful as I felt saying that to him, as much as I could see how it shocked and hurt him, I believe it is true. And it is a terrible thing to think of your father—a man you've always loved and respected—in this way."

A vision of my mother sitting across from me at the table but somewhere far away, her eyes glazed over from her third glass of wine, flashed in my mind. "Weak, selfish, disappointing," I said.

"Yes." Elias nodded. He looked so vulnerable that I reached for him without thinking. It wasn't until his own hand moved toward mine that I saw what I had done. His hand lay palm up, so solid and real that I could see the lines spidering across it. There was only the sound of our quick, shallow breaths as I moved my hand slowly over his, letting it hover for a moment before lowering it, my fingers curving. Did I feel something? A faint pressure, a hint of warmth? It was hard to tell the difference between what I wanted to be real and what was actually happening.

"Can you feel my hand?" I asked.

"I want to." Elias gave me a rueful smile, and we both gradually withdrew our hands again. "You look more clear and solid than before. It seems as though it would be possible."

"Do you think it ever will be?"

"Who can say? Every time I see you, I am reminded of how impossible all of this is. And yet how very real." He bent and picked up his lantern. "I'm afraid I must be going." He rubbed his head and smiled. "I seem to always be saying that," he said ruefully. "But with just the three of us and the state of things around here, my parents worry if I disappear for more than a bit."

"It's nice they notice."

"I suppose. Although it does chafe a little now and then." He stood up. "Saturday?"

"I'll be here." I stood as well. Elias held the lantern up to my face again, and I met his gaze.

"Sleep well, Julia." He paused, then added, "And let not your heart be troubled."

I wasn't sure if he was quoting something or it was just part of his more formal way of speaking, but either way, his words seemed to smooth some of the jagged edges in my chest.

Chapter 10

TALKING TO ELIAS about my mother made me more determined than ever to get my family together for Thanksgiving, and while Matty wasn't usually much help, it occurred to me that maybe there was something he could do this time. I headed out earlier than usual the next morning so I could call home without my mother hearing me.

"Hello?"

"Oh, good, Matty. It's you," I said.

"Who else would it be?" As usual, he was crunching on something.

"Well, Dad, idiot. But I want to talk to you without him hearing. Is he there?"

"No. He's in the bathroom. What do you want?"

"I want us to have Thanksgiving together," I started.

"Cool! You guys finally coming home?" Matty interrupted.

"No. Mom says she's not ready. I mean, I know she would really love to see you," I added quickly, "but I think it's still hard for her to think about being back in New York."

"Huh." Matty took a sip of something and continued munching.

"Has Dad said anything about Thanksgiving?"

"No."

"Well, listen. I want you to start dropping some hints to Dad about it, okay? And I want you to call Mom in the next day or two and, you know, talk about how much you miss her and want to see her and stuff."

"Why?"

"So we can get you guys out here for a visit." I bit back a second *idiot*. My brother's density might be irritating, but I needed his help.

"Okay, fine. Do you want me to cry and stuff?"

"Do whatever you think will get Mom to feel guilty. But don't overdo it. She's not stupid." Matty responded by snorting and hanging up on me. I put my phone away, a little uneasy about asking my brother to manipulate our mother, but as the saying went, desperate times called for desperate measures. We needed a reminder of why being apart was all wrong, before any of us got too comfortable with the way things were. *Assuming that hasn't already happened.*

All thoughts about my family were shoved to the side when I got my chemistry test back with another big red *D* at the top. Derek must have seen something in my expression when we met at his truck for our next lesson.

"What's wrong?"

"I tanked my chemistry test."

"That sucks."

I climbed into the truck and buckled my seat belt. "Yeah, it does. I don't suppose you know anything about chemistry?"

Derek made a face as he switched on the ignition. "'fraid not. I was pretty awful at it myself. Biology was more my thing."

"Same here." I slumped down in my seat with a sigh.

"Is there anyone in your class who can help?"

"Maybe. Only I'd have to actually talk to them."

"Yeah, there is that. Not terribly social, are you?"

I shrugged and began chewing a nail that was bothering me. "Not really. I was a little more outgoing at my old school, but I wasn't ever going to be voted Homecoming Queen."

Derek laughed. "No, I can't picture that."

"You don't need to sound so sure about my lack of popularity," I protested. Derek shot me a look.

"Would you ever want to be Homecoming Queen?"

"No," I admitted. "It's really annoying when you're right, you know."

"Don't worry. You'll have lots of opportunity to get used to that."

I rolled my eyes. "I probably should make a couple friends. It's just that I don't know how long we're going to be here, so it's kind of like what's the point?"

Derek pulled into our usual lot and parked before turning to face me. "So you guys might move again?"

"Maybe. I hope so." A strange expression flashed across his face and was gone. "I want my family to be back together in New York. I want to go back to my old school."

"That makes sense. Do you think that will happen anytime soon?"

"I don't know. Right now I'm just hoping we can have Thanksgiving together. I feel like if we're all together again, then maybe something will happen. My parents will remember how great it is. They're being really difficult about things right now."

"Ah, yes, difficult parents," Derek said. "They're always complaining about how much trouble we teenagers are when really *they're* the problem."

"Exactly," I said, matching his lighter tone. "Someone needs to write a help book for teens on how to deal with their troubled parents."

"Instant bestseller."

"For sure."

"Well, ready to do some driving?" We swapped seats and I went through my usual modifications of the mirrors and seat. I turned to him expectantly, my hand on the keys.

"Let's do a little warm-up in the parking lot first, and then we'll head out to a few neighborhood streets."

"Sounds good to me." I fired up the ignition and we were off. The next hour flew by, and I found myself laughing so hard at Derek's comments and his exaggerated horror at some of my less skillful moves that I had to stop or pull over multiple times to wipe tears out of my eyes.

"That was fun," I said, climbing out of the truck to trade places again.

"Right. Having your life flash before your eyes is *super* fun."

"Oh, shut up. It wasn't that bad. There weren't even any other cars around."

"Thank God for that, considering you seem to love driving down the middle of the road."

"I think I did pretty well."

Derek sighed and shook his head at me as we pulled onto the main highway. "Hardly."

As we turned onto my street, it was like someone flipped a switch in my brain, and I was suddenly overcome with a flood of worried thoughts. *I wonder if Matty called Mom? Maybe I should have told him to wait longer. Will she know I put him up to it?*

"...And you haven't heard a word I've been saying, have you?" Derek pulled up to the curb and gave me a wry smile.

"I'm sorry. I was thinking about my mom and my brother."

"That's okay." He was quiet for a moment, studying me. "You know, it probably wouldn't hurt for you to make another friend or two while you're here. Even if it's not for long."

"I guess." I looked down at my fingers wrapped around the strap to my bag. *I do have a friend,* I thought. *I just can't tell anyone about him.*

"I mean, I know I'm really all the friend anyone could ever need, but I can't be available to you all the time. You should probably get a number two, at least as a backup."

"Yeah, I'll get right on that." I unbuckled myself and opened the door. "Thanks, Derek."

"You're welcome. Same time next Tuesday?"

"Sure." I started to climb out, then leaned back to say, "Giant ego aside, you are a good friend, you know."

Derek leaned forward and opened his mouth, but then closed it again. "Thanks," he said a moment later. It felt like I had done something wrong. But what?

"Okay, well, see you later," I said.

"Yup. See you." He gave a small wave before backing away, his brake lights flashing briefly as he rounded the curve out of sight. I shivered in the darkening air.

⊶⥱◉ ◉⥲⊷

Though I watched her closely at dinner, my mother gave no indication that Matty had called. I didn't know whether to be relieved or disappointed, but it didn't really matter once Saturday morning rolled around. Elias appeared shortly after I got to the cellar.

"I was thinking yesterday that I really don't know very much about you," Elias said as he sat down. "That is, we've spoken of our families and the griefs we've endured. But I'd like to know more about *you*."

"Like what?"

"Well, what do you enjoy doing in your free time? What sorts of things interest you?"

I thought for a minute. "I like listening to music. Going to movies, hanging out with my friends—when I was back home and actually had friends to hang out with, that is."

"I see. I enjoy music myself, although I'm afraid I don't get to hear it very often. Do you have many musical performances in your area that you attend? Or perhaps you play an instrument yourself?"

"What? Oh, no. I'm not listening to live music. It's…" How could I explain this to him? "In my time, there's a way to save musical performances and replay them. My favorite way to listen is when I'm just lying on my bed, actually."

"Incredible," said Elias, his eyes wide.

"Yeah, I guess it is. And movies are like plays that have also been saved and you can watch them like they're happening live again." I saw him struggling and added, "I also like to read."

Elias's tense expression relaxed into a smile. "That's a favorite pastime of mine as well. What authors do you enjoy?"

I tried to think of some I'd read that he would also know. "I like Shakespeare's plays, or at least the ones I've read. And Jane Austen's novels." That pretty much exhausted my list of anything prior to 1850. I tended to prefer contemporary novels. "How about you?"

"I admire Shakespeare greatly as well. I have only read one of Miss Austen's novels, but I enjoyed it. Very witty. My father recently acquired a copy of Dante's *Divine Comedy*, which I am also enjoying."

"That's the one where the guy goes on a tour of hell, right?"

My description seemed to amuse Elias. "Yes, that's part of it."

"So what do you like to do besides read?" I asked.

"There's not much leisure time these days, but I do enjoy visiting with neighbors and helping my father with his practice. And when the weather's right, there's nothing like a lazy day of fishing at the creek."

"That sounds nice."

"It is. It's peaceful. I'd take you some time if I could."

"I wish I could go." It was an automatic response, but as soon as I said it, I realized it was true. I had a vision of sitting in the sunshine next to Elias, our feet dangling into the cool water of the creek while the leaves rustled in the breeze. *No point in thinking things like that.* I shook my head to clear it. "So have you always been interested in medicine?"

"It's hard to say, really. It's just been something I've grown accustomed to with my father. And now there is such a need." Elias's face darkened, and I searched for something to lighten the mood again.

"What's one of your favorite memories?" I could see that my question surprised him.

"A favorite memory? I'll have to think on that." He frowned with concentration for a minute, then began to chuckle.

"All right," he said, leaning in. "Back when I was ten or so, a farmer in the area gave my father an old mule for services rendered. My father didn't even want him, but this farmer was a proud man, so my father took it. And I don't know what it was, but that mule took quite a shine to Thomson. He wouldn't let me or Samuel get near him, though we tried more than a few times to jump on his back. But he'd follow Thomson around like he was lovesick. He'd walk behind him to the barn and out to the fields, and if we forgot to tie him, that mule would try to follow him to town. And Thomson, well, it just made him so mad." Elias grinned and shook his head. "Now there was quite a pretty girl who lived up the road—Louisa—and Thomson liked to stroll over her way and visit with her while she was hanging the wash or shelling peas and the like. So one afternoon when Samuel and I saw him heading up the road, we got one of my mother's bonnets and shawls and tied them on Jack."

"I thought he wouldn't let you get near him."

"Not usually, but he would for a carrot. So I fed him carrots and Samuel got to work with the bonnet and shawl. Once we had Jack gussied up, we untied him and set him after Thomson, then crept after him and hid behind some trees. Louisa was sitting on her porch, and there was Thomson, standing with his foot propped on the step and holding his hat like he thought he was some grown man, talking away. And up comes Jack, nuzzlin' in right next to him. As soon as he does, Samuel yells, 'Sorry, Louisa, but Thomson's already got himself a girl!' You should have seen his face."

"What'd he do?" I asked, laughing. Elias wiped his eyes.

"Oh, he tried to catch us and whip us, but we had too much of a head start on him. We made sure to stay away until supper, because we knew he couldn't do much in front of my mother. We still got a good cuff on the head from him, and my father made us do extra chores for my mother for a month for the loss of her bonnet and shawl. But it was worth it."

When he laughed, Elias looked like any other teenage boy. His usual grave manner always made him seem older to me, but now I was reminded that we were the same age.

"I like seeing you laugh," I said.

"I like getting the chance to laugh. It's been a long time." His eyes, blue and vulnerable, caught and held my own for several seconds. "Thank you, Julia."

"You're welcome." I wished, more than anything in that moment, that I could hug him. But I just gripped the sides of my chair instead.

Chapter 11

Monday morning, I woke up to the sound of my alarm and the gut-twisting pain of cramps. I groaned as I turned the alarm off and debated whether or not to ask my mother to call the school and say I was sick. Then I realized it would mean being at home all day with her, waiting for Matty to call. I didn't think I could handle that.

I forced myself to get ready and, with the help of some ibuprofen I swiped from my mother's purse, managed to get through most of my classes. But by the time I got to P.E. at the end of the day, all I wanted to do was lie down and curl up in a ball. When Ms. Jeffries blew her whistle at us and ordered us to divide into teams for basketball, I asked if I could sit it out. Her eyes narrowed.

"All right. Just for today, McKinley. But you better not be pulling something. I never forget the times of the month girls use this excuse, and you can bet that if you try it again at a different time, you'll be running laps around the gym."

"Okay," I answered meekly. The thought of Ms. Jeffries tracking my menstrual cycles was more than a little creepy, but I was too relieved to care.

"Go sit over there," she said, pointing to a raised slab against the wall where another girl was already sitting. When I got closer, I realized it was Samira from homeroom. She was reading a book, as usual, but looked up when I sat next to her.

"Hi," I said.

"Hello."

"I didn't realize you had P.E. too."

"I'm in Coach Connor's class."

"Oh." I drew my knees up to my chest. Samira was still holding her book open, but she sat looking at me as if waiting for me to say something else. "So do you have cramps too?" I asked. Her eyebrows went up and her mouth twitched.

"No. I'm fasting for Ramadan."

"Oh," I said again. What little skill at conversation I possessed seemed to desert me. Samira grinned at my discomfort, and the friendliness of her sudden smile made me relax. "How come you're in P.E.? You're a senior, right?" I asked.

"Yes. But my family went back to Pakistan for most of my sophomore year to take care of my grandparents, so now I have to make it up."

"Same with me. I used to go to a private school where they only made you do one year."

"This was in New York?"

"Yes," I said, surprised that she remembered.

"It must be very different here for you."

"It is. I'm still getting used to it." I studied her, trying not to be too obvious about it. She had large, black eyes fringed in dark lashes. Framed by the navy scarf she was wearing, her face had a kind of striking beauty. She put her book away, and we watched the clumsy game going on in front of us for a few minutes in silence. But my curiosity got the better of me.

"Do you mind my asking about your scarf? I don't mean any disrespect," I added quickly when she turned to face me. "I've seen them before, but never thought to ask why they're worn."

"It's called the *hijab*," she said, touching it. "I wear it out of respect for God and for my body."

"Huh." Her answer sounded nice enough, but I couldn't help thinking of it as some kind of oppression. "Do you have to wear it or do you get a choice?"

"Well, my parents definitely prefer that I wear it, but I don't think they would force me if I didn't want to. My cousins don't, and it's not a big deal."

"Do you ever think about not wearing it? I mean, it's got to be hard to have people judging you and making dumb comments." I stopped, thinking of some of the stores owned by Muslims and even one Punjabi Indian I'd seen vandalized in my neighborhood after 9/11. "I've heard what those guys in homeroom have said to you."

Samira shook her head. "I'm used to it. People see my *hijab* and assume I don't speak English or that I'm some kind of radical or I'm oppressed or something." I squirmed a little at that last bit, but she didn't seem to notice. "But I'm not going to stop doing something that's important to me just because other people are ignorant." She shrugged. "And really, it doesn't happen much. I find if I ignore it, people like those boys get bored and move on to other things."

"Do you mind that I asked you that?"

"No, I'm glad you did. Not many people do."

"Probably because they don't think it's polite. I, on the other hand, am not exactly known for my politeness, which I know is hard to believe given how popular I've become at this school," I said. Samira laughed. "Really, though," I said, "I'm making progress. I mean, assuming you'll keep talking to me after today, I can at least tell Derek I've made one other friend. He was just telling me I need to make some."

Samira cocked an eyebrow. "Derek is a friend?"

"Yeah. Why?"

"I just don't usually see friends watching each other the way Derek watches you." She smiled as my mouth dropped open. Just then, Ms. Jeffries blew her whistle, signaling the end of P.E.

"What would you know?" I said to Samira as we joined the stream of girls heading toward the locker room. "You've always got your head in a book during homeroom."

"That doesn't mean I can't see what's obvious."

"Well, I'd agree with you, except that you're totally wrong."

Samira laughed. "Right. You keep telling yourself that."

--->===◉ ◉===<---

When I got home, my mother's car was gone and I found a note taped to the refrigerator. *Going out for awhile. There's soup in the fridge.* I held the note for a moment, wondering what this meant. Had Matty called? I took out my cell phone and dialed our Brooklyn number, but no one answered. I grabbed my backpack so I could start on some homework while I waited for Elias and headed out the back door.

To my surprise, Elias was already in the cellar when I went down. He stood up, ducking his head under the low ceiling as I came down the final steps.

"Good afternoon, Julia."

"Hi." As I sat down, I saw that he was holding something. "What's that?" He glanced down and raised a handful of green stems with white flowers clustered at the top.

"Just some yarrow I found blooming out by the shed. There's not much left this late in the season."

"You brought me flowers?" I reached for them without thinking, and then let my hand fall.

Elias smiled and rubbed the back of his head with his free hand. "I did, although I'm not sure why seeing as I can't actually give them to you," he said. "I guess I'll just lay them here for now." He put them on the floor by his feet, and I found myself blinking away a sudden sting of tears. The last person to give me flowers was Uncle Denny on my sixteenth birthday. "Foolish of me," Elias said when I remained silent.

"No, it's not. It's very sweet. Thank you," I said. "You just improved my day by about a thousand percent." His shoulders relaxed.

"I must confess that I forget the…limitations at times. This is all so very strange to me still. If you don't mind my saying so."

"It's the same for me too. I mean, it's amazing, but there are times I think I must have dreamed it all up or that I'm going crazy."

"I've wondered that at times myself. Do you think anyone else has ever experienced such things?"

"I have no idea. Even if other people have, I'm not sure they'd talk about it. I haven't told anyone about this. Have you?"

Elias shook his head. "No, no one. I wouldn't even know where to start."

"Me neither. Plus, we'd probably get locked up."

Elias grinned. "That is a distinct possibility. But," he said, his face growing serious again, "it's more than that. This feels…"

"Private," I said. Elias nodded.

"Yes, but more than that. Special. Like something I need to protect, though I have no understanding of it." We were both silent for a moment, and then I remembered something.

"You know, I was thinking about it the other day and there was something I read when I thought you were, you know, a ghost."

"What?"

"Well, it was about this city in England—York—which was a Roman city centuries ago. And there's this story I read about a man working in the basement of some building in the 1950s, installing a boiler or something. He heard a noise behind him, and turned to see what looked like a group of Roman soldiers marching behind him."

Elias's eyebrows went up. "Interesting."

"It gets even better. The man could only see them from the top of their legs up, as though they were marching through the floor. When he ran upstairs and told people, no one believed him. But then later, when they did more excavation and research, they discovered that an old Roman highway ran right under that building and his description of them matched some of the artifacts they found."

Elias was frowning. "I'm afraid I'm not quite following how this relates to us. I mean, since neither of us is a ghost."

"That's just it, though. What if those Roman soldiers weren't ghosts either? If you factor in the road sinking over time and the foundation's thickness, wouldn't that account for why the man couldn't see the rest of their legs? What if they were marching on their own road in their own time, and he was standing on the floor in his time a few feet up."

Elias's expression shifted from skeptical to incredulous. "That's just like…"

"How you thought you saw me floating and I saw you disappear a few inches into the wall," I finished for him, unable to help myself. "That's what helped me figure out what was going on. Or sort of figure it out." Elias was quiet for a moment.

"What do you think this means?"

"Well, both of these things have happened underground, so maybe there's something about the earth or minerals or something like that that facilitates some sort of disruption in the time-space continuum."

"The what?" Elias was frowning again, and I realized that having sci-fi junkies for a dad and brother, not to mention the age I was living in, had exposed me to concepts Elias couldn't possibly know. I wracked my brain for a way to explain it in a way he could understand.

"Okay, imagine a string, and that string is our timeline. Our lives moving forward."

"All right."

"Now imagine if that string somehow looped around and crossed other parts of itself that came before. You're still moving forward on the string, but you're also intersecting with another time. Maybe that's what's happening with us." *Not bad,* I thought, feeling triumphant. *Matty and Dad would be proud.*

"Hm." I could see that Elias was still struggling. After a moment, he said, "So you're trying to find an explanation in natural philosophy?"

"Uh, is that the same thing as science?"

"I believe so, although that is a newer term. I saw it in something my father had me read."

"Then yes. I'm curious to know how this is physically possible. Aren't you?"

"I suppose, although I haven't really been considering it from that perspective."

"What do you mean?" It was my turn to be confused.

"I've been thinking about it more in terms of meaning. It seems significant that we're both living through such similar situations, doesn't it?"

"I guess. But how does that explain anything?"

"I don't quite know. I am still working it out, if such things can be understood at all. I think I understand what you're saying about the physical properties and your string metaphor, but it still doesn't quite answer the question of why—why should we two be able to see and talk to each other?"

I pressed a fist against my lower abdomen, which was beginning to ache again. "But that's just what I've been trying to explain. There are scientific theories out there that can probably explain the why—how this is physically possible."

"But is that really enough, to just know the mechanics? All of this seems like so much more than that. Really, it's almost..." Elias paused and started again. "It seems rather miraculous. That you and I should find each other at a time in both of our lives when our need is so great, that we should be able to have so much in common despite our living in such different times—doesn't that seem beyond the realm of minerals and science?"

It sounded so poetic and grand when he put it like that, but I still couldn't figure out what he was getting at. "What do you think this is, then?"

"A precious gift. Something given to us."

"Are you talking about God?"

"I suppose I am."

I shifted uneasily in my chair. It occurred to me that Elias lived in a time where most people were probably a lot more religious than they were now. I hadn't quite decided about God one way or the other, and stories I'd heard from the Bible seemed no more real than the fairy tales my parents had read me as a child. But how could I say this to Elias without offending him? "Look, I don't really, um…I not sure I believe in God. I mean, I believe that God or some kind of greater force in the universe is possible, but mostly I believe in what I can see around me. What can be proven. People make up all kinds of things and believe in them, but that doesn't make them real." Elias's face was pensive. I wished for the hundredth time that I knew how to say things better. "I'm sorry if I've upset you, Elias."

He looked surprised. "Why do you think I would be upset?"

"Because I just said that God might be something people make up. And I figure you and everyone else in your time is more religious than I am."

"You are right that I believe in God, but I am not offended by what you said. Things are not so uniform in my time as you might think. There are all kinds of people who either have no faith or have lost it in this bloody war, and there is evidence of that all around me." His mouth twisted into a grimace. "You can't see the cellar I'm in, but if you could, you would see that it is quickly growing bare. The two armies cross back and forth across this area in one battle after another, and each time they do, they strip it even more. I've seen men behave like animals, taking food and livestock from widows and orphans to feed and supply themselves so they can go and kill more men. Such things have made many question the existence of God, including my own father."

His voice was gentle, but I still felt a small twinge of guilt. Though there might be some similarities to our family situations, the chaos and suffering Elias was going through was far greater than anything I had ever experienced.

"I'm sorry. I guess sometimes it's easy for me to feel like, I don't know, more advanced or something and make assumptions."

"Oh, I'm sure you are more advanced in things like medicine, inventions—knowledge itself, I suppose. You mention things from time to time that I can't begin to understand or conceive of, and yet they are as natural to you as the air you breathe. And yet, for all of that, you still have suffering and death. I would imagine war as well."

I flinched. "Yes, we still have all of that."

"Now I am sorry, Julia. I didn't mean to upset you."

"No, you're right. I guess in some ways we haven't made any progress at all." We sat in silence for a moment, then Elias reached for his lantern.

"Before I go, has there been any change with your mother?"

"No. How about with your father?"

"None." We both stood up. "I hope your mother has a change of heart, Julia."

"I hope your father does too." Elias's serious expression suddenly brightened. "What?" I asked.

"Just that we've lost our ability to hope for ourselves, and yet here we are hoping things for each other." He paused, then added, "It's good not to have to be carrying this alone anymore."

I had a sudden memory of my first time in a swimming pool. The water had terrified me, but Uncle Denny had carried me in and ducked under the water with me after a quick count to three. I'd hated the way the water engulfed me, had poured into my ears and muffled everything into strangeness. But I also remembered the feel of Uncle Denny's arms around me and my own twined around his neck. I had never felt so lost and so safe at the same time. Until now.

"Yes, it is good," I said.

Elias's smile widened and his dark hair fell forward as he ducked under the low ceiling toward the stairs.

⤞⥿ ⥀⤝

I was eating soup and watching *Jeopardy* on the small TV in the living room when my mother finally came home. I turned down the volume and took my feet off the couch.

"Want to sit down?"

She stood in the doorway with her coat on, holding a plastic bag stretched with the weight of its contents. "No, I need to put this stuff away."

"You could come watch with me after."

My mother seemed not to hear me. "Matty called this afternoon."

I tensed and looked down at my bowl. "How is he?"

"He said he wants to visit with your dad. For Thanksgiving." I braved a look up at my mother and immediately wished I hadn't. "I don't know if you put him up to this or not, but I'm too tired to care anymore. I doubt your father will even want to come, but if you want to try, I'm not going to stop you."

I wanted to jump up from the couch and dance around, but she looked so tense and unhappy, I resisted the urge. "Thanks, Mom. It's gonna be great."

Her mouth twisted. "We'll see."

As she headed for the kitchen, I turned the volume back up, but found I couldn't concentrate on the show anymore. My mother might not think so, but I knew being together would be good for us all. Then why did I feel so guilty? She needed to be reminded of what it was like for us to be a family, and I had a feeling my father did too. I'd been so focused on getting my mother to agree that I hadn't really thought about whether he would even want to come. *I can't wait to tell Elias.* At least he would be happy about this.

Chapter 12

For once, Samira looked up from her book when I came into home-room the next morning and smiled. I smiled and nodded hello back and took my seat as the bell rang. Apparently, this didn't go unno-ticed. The shorter member of the Dummy Duo that sat between us muttered, "Looks like the terrorist has a girlfriend," and they both laughed. I found myself leaning forward in my seat. Samira might find it better to ignore them, but I didn't.

"Let me guess—still trying to meet your quota for dipshit com-ments?" They turned, and I saw Samira stiffen out of the corner of my eye.

"Excuse me?" the larger boy, Phil, asked. The bell rang, and we stood for the pledge. "Bitch," Phil mouthed at me as we sat back down. I flashed him my brightest smile and rubbed the side of my nose with my middle finger. His face darkened, and I saw that Derek had turned in his seat and was giving me an incredulous look, but Mrs. Davenport cut off any further exchange by passing out some forms from the counseling office and going over them in excruciating detail.

Derek was waiting for me outside the door after the bell rang. "What was that about?"

I shrugged. "Nothing."

"It didn't look like nothing to me."

"Really, it's no big deal. I have to get to class." Derek frowned, so I added, "I'll tell you more later. I promise."

"Fine. Driving lesson tomorrow?"

"Great." Elias was going to be busy helping his father for the next couple days. I headed off to class and spent the rest of the day trying to figure out the best way to approach my father about Thanksgiving. I decided to call him on my way home from school. He'd be at work, which meant that if he said no, I could still work out a Plan B with Matty before he got home. He sounded glad to hear from me, which was a good start.

"How are you?"

"Good. School's going well and I'm making progress on my college applications." I hoped he wouldn't ask me any specifics. It would be a lot harder to lie outright about chemistry. And I was going to fix that soon anyway.

"Glad to hear it. Let me know if you need any help."

"Well, actually, Dad, I could use your feedback on a couple of my essays."

"Of course. Just e-mail or fax them."

"It would be better if you could help me in person. Like at Thanksgiving."

"Are you planning to come home for that?" I could tell from the careful way he asked that the 'you' meant me *and* my mother. And maybe I was imagining it, but I heard a slight lift in his voice.

"Actually, we want you to come here. Just listen and think about it before you say anything," I added when I heard him take a breath. "I've been missing you and Matty like crazy, and I know Matty has been missing Mom, and we really want to have Thanksgiving all together here in Virginia. It's really pretty here, Dad. Matty would love it and it'd just be for a few days." My father was silent for several seconds.

"What does your mom think about this?"

"She really wants you guys to come." She might not admit it, but that didn't mean it wasn't true. At least deep down.

"Huh."

"Dad, it's Thanksgiving. We've never been apart for Thanksgiving. We've never been apart like this at all before." I could picture him thinking, squeezing the top of his nose like he always did, and I was filled with longing to see him. To feel him hug me and lift me off the ground. To feel his stiff shirt collar poking my cheek. "Please, Dad."

He let out a deep sigh. "All right, Julia."

"Really?" My voice came out in a squeak.

"Yes. I've got to go, but I'll book our flights and get back to you with the details. You're sure your mother's okay with this?"

"I'm sure, Dad. We just talked about it last night."

"All right, then. Talk to you soon."

I let out a whoop, jumping up and down until my bag slid off my shoulder and hit my leg, almost making me fall. I looked around, but luckily no one was around to see this. I dusted off my bag and walked as fast as I could to the house, anxious to tell my mother. But the car was gone. I had to tell someone. I got my phone back out and called the apartment.

"What?" Typical Matty.

"I talked to Dad. He said yes. You guys are coming out for Thanksgiving."

"Cool." He was trying to pretend otherwise, but I could tell he was excited too.

"I know, right? We're finally going to be together. At least for a little while."

"Yeah."

"Matty, does it seem like Dad misses Mom?"

"I don't know. We eat a lot of takeout."

"That's not what I mean. Does he seem sad? Does he talk about her or say anything about wishing she'd come back?" I realized how dumb my questions were as soon as I asked them. My father wasn't the type to talk about his feelings to anyone, much less my thirteen-year-old brother.

"No." I could tell from my brother's tone that he also thought my questions were dumb.

"Fine. Sorry I asked."

"Me too."

I hung up on him and went into the kitchen, opening cupboards and studying the contents of the fridge until I could figure out something to make for dinner. When my mother came home, I had a pot of chili going and a salad already on the table.

"What's all this?"

"We're celebrating," I said, turning off the stove.

"What are we celebrating?" My mother took the steaming bowl I handed to her and followed me into the dining room.

"Dad and Matty are coming here for Thanksgiving."

"Oh." My mother let out a small breath, her expression caught somewhere between gladness and terror. She poured herself a glass of wine. "Well," she said after she had taken a swallow, "that will be nice."

"It's going to be way more than nice," I said. "Only Matty's going to freak that there's no cable here." I reached for her hand and squeezed it. "Thanks for saying yes, Mom. You won't regret it. I promise."

My mother smiled, but her grip on my hand hurt. "If you say so."

→▰ ▰◀

"So what's the deal between you and Phil and Donny?" Derek asked as we climbed into his truck for our next lesson.

"They're just asses."

Derek threw me a look. Clearly, that wasn't going to cut it. "Yeah, I know that. Unlike you, I've known them since elementary school. But what I can't understand is why, after ignoring just about everyone else at school, you're suddenly being so…interactive with them."

"They started it." Realizing I sounded like a six-year-old, I added, "And actually, it's kind of your fault."

"My fault?"

"You told me to make friends, so I did. Samira. We talked the other day in P.E., and when I said hi to her in homeroom, Donny and Phil said something stupid and I said something back. That's it. Nothing to worry about."

Derek frowned and pulled over. "I don't like it."

"Well, it's already happened, so I can't really do much about it at this point."

"You might think it's over, but I doubt it is for them. They're the type to hold grudges and get back at you sometime later." Derek was making them sound like the Mafia.

"Relax. They were both so stoned this morning that they didn't even look my way. Besides, I can take care of myself."

"You might think you can," Derek said, eyeing me doubtfully, "but maybe I should have a talk with them anyway."

"Uh, no. Don't do that. It would just make a bigger deal out of this than it already is. Really," I said when Derek's mouth tightened, "I'll be fine. Now can I please do some driving?" Derek looked as though he were going to argue, but to my relief he just sighed and opened his door.

"Fine. Let's switch."

After driving up and down small side roads, Derek had me try some three-point turns. Since there were no curbs to bump into, I ended up driving onto the edges of more than a few lawns. Apparently, my depth perception still needed a little work. Derek's distress about this struck me as funny, and every time he yelled at me to stop, I started laughing. His obvious irritation with me just made me laugh even harder.

"You're awfully happy today," he said as he drove me home. "Any particular reason why you find ruining private property so funny?"

I coughed to cover the laugh bubbling up. "It's not that. It's how mad you were getting about it."

"And that's funny?"

"Yes. Very."

"You are one strange girl."

"And you're just noticing that now?" I was grinning again. "I'll admit, I am a little more loopy than usual today. I just found out my dad and brother are coming to visit for Thanksgiving."

"Really? That's great."

"Yeah. It'll be the first time we've all been together since my mom and I came out here."

"I hope it's a good visit." Derek's tone seemed harmless enough, but something about his comment put me on edge.

"Why wouldn't it be?"

Derek seemed taken aback by my question. "I don't know. I didn't mean that it wouldn't. I just meant what I said—that I hope you have a good time together. What's wrong with that?"

He was right. I took a deep breath. "Sorry. I'm excited about it, but I guess I'm a little nervous about it too." We'd pulled up in front of the house.

"Because?"

I stared down at my bag, sliding the zipper back and forth for a minute. How could I explain? Derek was my driving buddy, one of the few people in my life these days that I could just laugh and joke with. Trying to explain everything would be too hard, and this hope about my family was so new and fragile, I didn't want anything to ruin it.

"It's hard to say. Thanks for the lesson," I said, opening the door. He opened his mouth to speak, but I slammed the door shut and waved like I hadn't seen.

⟶⟞▧◉ ◉▧⟝⟵

My eagerness to tell Elias about Thanksgiving was so great that it woke me up early on Saturday morning. I looked at the clock. 7:30. I groaned and rolled over. There was no use getting up yet. It would just mean hours of sitting around waiting. I tried to go back to sleep, but when another hour passed without success, I finally gave up and headed downstairs. My mother hadn't emerged yet, so I got some coffee going and opened the cupboard to grab a mug. I froze when I saw what was in my hand. Uncle Denny's mug. I started putting it back on the shelf, then changed my mind. Uncle Denny would want me to use his mug, not let it get all dusty and neglected on the shelf.

I sat at the dining room table with my hand cupped around its warmth and took small sips of its scalding contents. I could picture Uncle Denny as he usually was on the weekends—in a pair of battered jeans and a sweatshirt, making himself at home in our kitchen or sprawled on the couch watching sports with Matty and my dad. I pressed the mug against my forehead and closed my eyes.

"I miss you, Uncle Denny," I whispered. The familiar ache sprang up in my chest, but it had softened somehow. Imagining him sitting across the table from me felt more good than bad, something I wanted to last instead of trying to avoid. "You know, Mom hasn't been doing very well without you, but we're hanging in there. She said yes to Thanksgiving, so that's good. And I'm about to have a date, or something like that, with a boy from the 1860s, so that's kind of interesting. You'd probably like it that he can't touch me." Uncle Denny had once offered to chaperone all my dates, making my parents laugh, but not until they'd thrown a considering look my way. I thought about what else I wanted to tell him. "I'm learning to drive."

"Who are you talking to?" I jerked in surprise at my mother's voice, spilling hot coffee on my hand. My mother's eyes went to the mug in my hands and widened before glancing away.

"No one," I said, grabbing a napkin to wipe my hand. I watched her carry in her own mug, stirring in the cream she'd added. "Actually," I said, my heart beginning to beat faster, "I was talking to Uncle Denny." Her spoon clattered against the mug and she raised a hand to grip the door frame.

"Is that so?"

"Yes." I caught her gaze and held it. "I miss talking to him, so I thought I'd just go ahead and do it. Maybe you should too."

"I'm going back upstairs."

"Mom!" I called after her. "Can't we ever just talk about him?" But I was speaking to the air. Maybe I was pushing too hard, but I missed Uncle Denny being in our lives. And even though we were living in the same house, I missed my mother. *It will get better when Dad and Matty are here.* Remembering their visit turned my longing into excitement.

I managed to kill an hour reading the paper, and another eating cereal and watching cartoons on the one channel that came in clearly. I went down to the cellar almost a half hour early, hoping Elias might show up early as well. About ten minutes later, I saw the dim, bobbing glow of his lantern and his own form emerge soon after it. He looked surprised to see me already waiting there, then smiled.

"It seems we are both eager to see each other today."

"I have some good news, for once. My mother finally agreed to let my brother and dad come visit for Thanksgiving, and my dad agreed. They'll be here in just two weeks." Elias's reaction was just what I'd hoped it would be.

"That's wonderful news, Julia. I'm so very glad for you. It's just what you wanted."

"I know. It's still hard for me to believe. How about you? Any progress with your father and Samuel?"

"Nothing as wonderful as your news, but yes, there's been some progress. I finally worked up the courage to tell my father that I was going to get Samuel and bring him home."

"Oh, wow. That's huge. How'd he take it?"

"I could tell he was angry, but he didn't say no. He just said that if I could manage to figure out a way to do it, he wouldn't stop me."

"You know what's weird? My mom said something similar. It's like they both want what we want deep down but they're not willing to admit it. So then it's up to us to make it happen. Is bringing your brother home going to be hard?"

Elias sighed. "I'm afraid so. Virginia—especially this part of the state—is like the rope in a tug-of-war. It goes back and forth, and it's never quite clear when you're traveling if you're going to run into Federal troops or be stopped by Mosby's Rangers. They're a Confederate militia group," he clarified when he saw my puzzled expression. "And both sides are more than happy to relieve you of any able-bodied horse that you might have."

"So what are you going to do?"

"I'm still figuring that out. Union troops took our two horses last spring, but a neighbor of ours—Zachariah—still has a mare. She and Zachariah are both so old, I guess both armies decided to leave them alone. Zachariah knows our family well and would probably loan her to me, but there are still a lot of other problems that have to be worked out."

"Do you think you'll be able to?"

"I have to. Samuel needs to be home." The quiet conviction in his voice seemed to pierce all the way through me.

"I guess you'd better go get him then."

Elias smiled. "I will." We sat quietly for a moment, and as Elias's gaze drifted to the side and he became lost in thought, I took the opportunity to study him. In all the excitement of sharing our news, I hadn't noticed it, but now it occurred to me that something wasn't quite right. Even though I was straining, I couldn't seem to see Elias as clearly as I had before. His features seemed fainter and he had taken on more of the translucence of our earlier visits.

"Elias," I said, interrupting his musings. "Do I look as clear to you now as I did the last time we met?"

He stared at me for a moment. "Now that you mention it, no," he said slowly. "You seem a little more...faded, I suppose." I felt a faint chill that had nothing to do with the temperature of the cellar.

"Why do you think that is?"

"I don't know." His face was troubled.

"It's probably nothing. Maybe the colder weather affects things or the phase of the moon or something like that..." I trailed off, my words doing nothing to alleviate the dread that was beginning to creep in.

"Perhaps. But as much as we have come to count on our meetings, we don't know any more about how or why they might come to an end than we do about how or why they began."

My throat closed as he spoke aloud what I had been too afraid to even think. "Can we please not talk about this? I don't want to think about this, about us, ending. At least not right now. This is a good day for us. We're making progress with our families, right?"

"Right." Elias seemed glad to change the subject as well. "I'm going to see Zachariah this week."

"If he says yes, will you be leaving soon?"

"Possibly. It's hard to say at this point."

"Should we try to meet again before Saturday? I mean, in case you have to leave."

"Yes, let's try. It's harder for me to get away during the week, and I may not be able to come," he warned me.

"That's okay. I can come for a while in the afternoon and you can just show up if you're able to."

Elias looked doubtful. "I don't really like the idea of your having to spend so much time waiting."

"It's okay. I don't mind—really. I'd rather do that than have you leave for weeks and not be able to see you or know what's going on."

"It would be hard for me to leave without saying goodbye as well. It is selfish of me, but yes, let's try it."

"I don't know if I'll be able to make it every day, but I'll try. Between 3:30 and 4:30, let's say. I don't think I can stay longer than that. My mother usually comes out closer to dinner time, and she would definitely find it weird if I'm down here now that it's so cold."

"Yes, of course. Whatever you can manage is more than enough, and I will do my best to come as well. But please understand that if I don't, it's because it is impossible for me—not that I don't want to or haven't made every effort to. Because I would, to see you," he added in a low voice. He cleared his throat and shifted stiffly in his seat, but his gaze held mine steadily and I felt my face flush with a warmth that went all the way to my stomach. He stood up abruptly. "I think I hear my mother. I must go." He picked up his lantern and said, "I am very glad for your good news, Julia. I will continue to hope for you."

"And I for you," I said, and then he was gone.

Chapter 13

ON MONDAY, I was full of restless energy, bouncing between excitement about my father's and Matty's upcoming visit and anxiety about whether I'd be able to see Elias again. I raced home at the end of the day and sat staring at the cellar steps for about ten minutes before I realized that intense staring wasn't really helping anything. I got out some homework to distract myself, but couldn't help looking up every five minutes. When 4:30 came and went, I put my books back in my bag and leaned back in my chair. He hadn't come. Even knowing it would be hard for him to get away and knowing there were probably dozens of reasons why he hadn't shown up, I couldn't rid myself of the small pocket of dread forming in my chest. I waited another fifteen minutes, then finally gave up and went back upstairs. I was beginning to shiver, and I knew my mother would be coming out for dinner soon.

The next morning, Derek was waiting by the door of homeroom when I arrived. "So are we on again this afternoon?"

"Oh, no, sorry. I can't. And I probably won't be able to all this week," I said, scrambling to come up with a reason. "I need to help my mom get ready for Thanksgiving, and I want to get my college applications finished so my dad can look them over." Derek's smile faltered and he shrugged.

"Sure, no problem. We can start up again after Thanksgiving."

"That would be great." The bell rang, and as we made our way to our seats, Samira caught my eye and raised her eyebrows knowingly. I rolled my eyes and shook my head at her. *You don't know what you're talking about.*

That afternoon in the cellar, I was in the middle of reviewing Spanish verbs when I heard the faint but distinct sound of steps. I slammed my book shut and stood up, straining to see. Elias appeared a second later.

"Elias." I wanted to fling my arms around him, but settled for moving a step closer.

"Julia." He held his lantern aloft and stood studying me intently for several seconds. I could see his eyes, faintly blue, and make out his features, but just like last time, he still looked somewhat transparent.

"I'm sorry I couldn't come yesterday," he said, sitting down. "Were you waiting?"

"Yes, but it was fine. I did some homework," I added when I saw him frown. "And now you're here. Did you have any luck with the horse?"

"I did. I went to see Zachariah, and he said I could take Constance, but in exchange for borrowing her, I must help him with some work around his place. I was chopping some firewood for him yesterday. Tomorrow he needs help repairing his outhouse." The expression on Elias's face made me laugh.

"Well, sorry about that part of it, but that's great he's loaning you his horse."

"Yes, it is. I'm more pleased than I can say."

"When will you leave?"

"I hope to leave early Friday morning."

"How long will it take you to get to Samuel? And will it be dangerous?" I had a sudden, irrational urge to offer him a ride. *My mom and I can drive you.*

"It's hard to say. Maybe two or three days. Constance isn't exactly fast-moving these days, and I'll need to keep away from the turnpikes, so we'll be zigzagging around the countryside."

"And the part about the danger?"

"Well," he said wryly, "there is a war going on. But I should be able to keep out of the way of any troops. And I'm hoping that even if I do run into any, they won't have any use for a ragged country boy on a rickety old horse."

"You're not ragged."

Elias grinned. "I will be. I intend to look so poorly it would seem a waste of time to bother with me. It shouldn't be hard with Constance already on the verge of collapse."

"That's clever."

Elias shrugged. "We'll see. The hard part will be getting Samuel back home. With his injuries, we're going to need to get a wagon and take the main roads. And you need permits and such for that sort of thing. But," he said, his voice taking on a kind of quiet determination, "I'll figure that all out when I get there. One way or another, I'm bringing my brother home." His words filled me with admiration.

"I believe you. I believe *in* you. You're pretty incredible, you know."

Elias shook his head. "I'm just doing what I need to. I love Samuel, I love my father, and this needs to be made right. You'd do the same. You *are* doing the same," he amended. It was my turn to shake my head.

"I just talk to people. That's not exactly sneaking through the woods in the middle of a war."

"Perhaps not, but I'm certain you would if that were required of you." I couldn't imagine myself doing any such thing, but it was nice that Elias could. We sat quietly for a moment, and then I finally spoke aloud the doubt that had been weighing on me since Saturday. "Do you think we'll still be able to see each other when you come back?"

Elias sighed and leaned forward. "I don't know. I certainly hope so. I don't know why we wouldn't be able to."

"What about the fact that we're growing fainter to each other?" The words seemed to force their way out.

"Yes, there is that." Elias stared at the floor between our feet, his face troubled.

"Maybe whatever weird physical time/space disruption that allows this is changing. Maybe…" I had to stop and swallow hard before continuing. "Maybe our window or whatever you'd call this is closing."

"That's possible. But again, perhaps this has more to do with us and what is occurring in our lives than with physical or elemental factors." He looked up and my confusion must have shown because he said, "Think about when we were the most clear and solid looking to each other. What had just happened to both of us?"

"We'd both just had big fights with our parents," I said slowly. What he was suggesting was starting to become clear. "And now we're both getting what we want. Or at least getting closer." He nodded, but I wasn't convinced. "So you're saying that our ability to see each other is proportional to how miserable our lives are?"

"It sounds rather unpleasant when you put it like that, but yes, I suppose that is what I'm suggesting."

"But if you take that all the way, it means that our families being reunited and happy equals us losing each other."

Elias frowned. "Look," he said, reaching a hand toward me and then dropping it again. "I could be completely wrong about this. There's just as much possibility that we'll meet again and that we'll be as clear as we ever were."

"Sure." But I didn't feel sure at all. I wanted to believe what he'd just said, but there was something about his theory that I couldn't shake. I didn't want to send him on his journey full of gloom and doubts, so I forced myself to smile. "I'm sure we will meet again, and many times after that. There's no way you're leaving me hanging about what happens."

"I'll be wanting a full account of how your family gathering goes as well." He paused, his expression becoming almost tentative. "Is that a very important holiday in your time, Thanksgiving?"

"Yeah, it's a big one. Don't you guys have Thanksgiving? Turkey? Stuffing and mashed potatoes? Pumpkin pie?"

"We do have Thanksgiving of a sort, but it's neither major nor official. Especially with the war. People are finding things a bit lean this year."

I felt like a jerk. "I'm sorry. That was pretty stupid of me, going on about food like that."

Elias laughed. "No, not at all. It's good to hear you talk about those things, to hear that our country values Thanksgiving and there's that kind of solidarity." He broke off and cleared his throat, shying away as usual from anything too specific about the future. Seeing his discomfort, I changed the subject.

"How long do you think you'll be gone?"

"It's hard to say. A lot depends on Samuel's condition and how easily we can arrange to travel back home. I would imagine at least a week—possibly two. Hopefully not more than that."

"So you probably won't be back until after Thanksgiving." It was just a week away. "I guess that works out since I won't really be able to come down here while my dad and brother are visiting." I caught my breath. "It's crazy they'll be here so soon. I can't wait to see them. How do you think it will be to see Samuel again?"

"We haven't been together in over a year now, and while we may not have always gotten along, so much has happened, I think we appreciate each other a great deal more now. Or at least that's what it seems like in our letters. To see one of my brothers again would be a very great joy." Elias turned away for a moment, struggling to control his emotions, and I wished for the hundredth time that I could hug him.

"Elias, we *have* to be able to see each other again. I don't think I could stand it if I didn't know what happened with you and Samuel."

"It does seem only right that we should be able to finish our stories with each other. I don't know why, exactly, but I believe we will, Julia. I'm almost certain of it." He sounded so sure that it made me feel almost certain myself even though I didn't know what he was basing his conclusion on. I didn't care anymore if it was logical or not. I just wanted it to be true. Elias stood up slowly.

"I must go. There are a great many preparations to be made, so I'm afraid I won't be able to come down here again before I leave."

I stood up as well. "As soon as my dad and brother are gone again, I'll be down here as many afternoons as I can during this hour. And during our usual time on Saturday. And I'll keep being here until you show up again. Don't keep me waiting too long, okay?"

Elias smiled. "I'll do my best. A gentleman should never keep a lady waiting, after all." His expression grew serious again as he said, "I will hold you and your family in my heart as I travel, Julia. May your family experience great joy in your time together."

There were so many things I wanted to say, but all I could manage was, "Be careful."

Elias held up his lantern and we studied each other's faces in the dim light for several seconds. And then, without another word, he turned swiftly and was gone.

⇥⊙ ⊙⇤

In the days following my meeting with Elias, I threw myself into working on my college application essays, studying for my classes, and nudging my mother into preparing for Thanksgiving. She came into the kitchen one evening and found me standing at the counter, flipping through a cookbook.

"What are you doing?" she asked, coming to peer over my shoulder.

"I'm trying to come up with a menu for Thanksgiving. What do you think? Should we do the traditional or try something new?"

"Oh, I don't know." She moved away to pour herself a glass of wine.

"I'm thinking we can order the turkey, mashed potatoes, and stuffing from the grocery store," I said. "I saw some ads in the paper the other day. But there are some interesting vegetable dishes in here, and I think we should try making a pie."

"That's ambitious of you," she said, taking a sip from her glass.

"Well, I'm expecting help from you. C'mon, doesn't homemade pie sound good?"

My mother leaned against the counter, frowning. "I suppose we could give it a try. We're going to need to buy a few things, though. I don't think this kitchen has everything we need." She set her glass down on the counter.

"I know. I'm making a list. I noticed we're short a set of towels."

"You can add a blanket and pillow for your brother. He's going to need those for the couch." I started to ask why he'd be on the couch instead of the other bedroom, and then it sank in. My father would be in the third bedroom.

"Okay," I said, writing it down. "I'll leave this out in case we think of anything else. You want to go shopping this weekend?"

"All right. How about Saturday afternoon?"

"Works for me." I felt an automatic spurt of anxiety at the thought of missing Elias until I remembered he would be gone. I helped my mother make dinner, and as we carried our plates into the dining room, she paused to jot something on the list. I felt a small frisson of excitement. *She's thinking about the visit.* It was such a small thing, writing something down on a paper, but I was more than ready to find hope in small things.

The days passed quickly after that, full of activity and antici-pation, while the nights were full of vivid and jumbled dreams. I hadn't dreamed about Uncle Denny in awhile, but now he was mak-ing frequent appearances. I couldn't remember much once I woke up, but there was one that stood out from all the rest. I was in the kitchen preparing food with my mother, and when I turned around to bring it into the dining room, my father, Matty, Uncle Denny, and Elias were all sitting at the table smiling at me. I was flooded with happiness at the sight and started to call out to them, until some insidious voice from outside the dream whispered that this wasn't possible, that none of it was real. I woke in the cool, dark silence of the early morning, feeling as though I had been torn out of that other world, leaving pieces of myself behind.

Between the dreams, Elias's absence, and the upcoming visit, I was full of restless energy, alternating between bursts of anxiety and bursts of excitement. Most of the other students at school seemed to share my fidgets, and by the Tuesday before Thanksgiving, most of our teachers had given up on us. Mrs. Davenport didn't even bother getting up from her desk after announcements finished in homeroom, so everyone drifted over to their friends and the room was soon loud with conversation. Derek came back and perched on the edge of my desk.

"So when are your dad and brother coming?"

"Tomorrow. My mom and I are driving to Dulles to pick them up. Traffic's probably going to be awful."

"Yeah. But hey, it'll give you more time to catch up, right?"

"I guess."

"You don't sound very excited about that."

"My mom's not much of a talker these days. It can get awkward." I didn't want to think about it. "What's your family doing?"

"We're having a big shindig at our house like we do every year. Aunts, uncles, cousins. It's kind of crazy, but it's fun. Everyone brings a ton of food, which is awesome, and we always play a kids vs. adults game of touch football."

"That sounds great."

"It is. I'm lucky to have so much family around." Derek stopped and cleared his throat, probably remembering what I'd told him about Uncle Denny. I started to tense, but Derek started up again. "I was going to ask if you and your mom wanted to come over, but then you told me about your dad and brother visiting, so I figured you'd probably want the time to yourselves."

"Thanks," I said, surprised. "That was nice of you to think of us."

"Sure." Derek shrugged and then grinned. "It's not like a couple extra people would have made much difference with that crowd."

"Derek!" Natalie was calling.

"You're being summoned."

Derek rolled his eyes. "Better see what she wants. Her boyfriend's coming for a visit too, so she's been more uptight than usual, lately." He stood up and paused for a second, his face growing serious. "Have a good Thanksgiving, Julia."

"You too."

Derek held my gaze for another second before rapping his knuckles on my desk in a short staccato and sauntering back up the aisle toward Natalie. I watched him tease Natalie about something and her pretend to punch him in the shoulder. I didn't know what to make of him sometimes. He could go from cocky jokester to sensitive and serious, then back again in a matter of seconds. It was unnerving.

"I can't wait for this day to be over." Samira moved into the empty seat next to me.

"I know, me too. What are you doing for Thanksgiving?" I asked her.

"My aunts, uncles, and cousins will probably be coming over. We're still in Ramadan, so no big feast during the day for us. But we make up for it in the evening. After we eat, my uncles all go into the living room to argue, and my aunts go into the kitchen to gossip."

"And what do you do?"

"I go up to my room and read."

"Of course you do," I said laughing.

"Think they'll make us dress out for P.E. today?"

"Ugh, I hope not. But they probably will. And make us run laps or something."

But as it turned out, even the P.E. teachers seemed ready for the holiday. They showed us a video about nutrition from the early '80s, and we spent the period making fun of everyone's poufy hair and shoulder pads.

When I got home, I found my mother pacing up and down the front hallway. She didn't even seem to notice me and jumped when I shut the front door.

"What time is it?" she asked, looking down at her bare wrist.

"Ten after three," I said. She groaned and clutched her head.

"Where has the day gone?"

"What's the matter? Why are you so stressed?"

My mother looked at me in amazement. "What do you mean why am I so stressed? Your father and brother are arriving tomorrow, and according to your plans, we are having Thanksgiving dinner with all the trimmings, including homemade pie!" I almost laughed, but then I saw how genuinely agitated she was. This wasn't about the pie.

"Mom, everything's going to be fine." I gripped her shoulders and tried to give her a steadying look. "I'll go clean the bathroom and you can make sure the other bedroom is ready. We'll pick up the turkey and the sides from the grocery store in the morning, and then we'll still have a couple hours to make the pies before we have to leave for the airport, okay? It's going to be fine," I repeated. My mother nodded slowly, her expression dazed.

"Okay, yes."

I gave her a gentle push toward the stairs. "Now go work on the guestroom, and I'll be up in a minute." I watched her head up the stairs before going into the kitchen to make myself some tea. I stood at the sink as I waited for the water to boil, and as I stared out the window at the darkening sky, my thoughts drifted to Elias. Where was he? Had he reached his brother yet? Some part of my brain reminded me that Elias and Samuel were long gone, that their story had already played out more than a century ago. And yet, it was still happening. His reality was still occurring at the same time as mine, and surely whatever made that possible could also let me wish a good outcome for him as though it were still an unknown.

"Julia!" My mother's call interrupted my thoughts. "Can you bring up a broom and a dustpan?"

"Coming!" I hollered back. I poured hot water into my mug and headed for the hallway closet. It was time to get ready for my own upcoming reality.

Chapter 14

My mother was already in the kitchen when I came downstairs the next morning, holding her mug against her chest as she stared out the window.

"Good morning," I said from the doorway. She jerked in surprise, but quickly recovered, giving me a small, tense smile.

"Good morning. I thought we could get started with the pies first and then go to the grocery store while they're cooling. Unless you think it would be better to go to the grocery store first. I'm sure it's going to be a madhouse today."

"No, pies first is fine," I said, pouring myself a cup. My mother was so jittery, I wondered how many cups she'd already drunk. I glanced at the clock. "We have plenty of time, Mom. We don't have to leave for the airport for another four hours."

"Right. Okay." She drew in a breath and looked around before putting her mug in the sink. "I'm going back upstairs. Holler when you're ready to get started."

I hoped she would be able to calm down a little. If she was going to be wound up that tightly all morning, we'd both be exhausted before Dad and Matty even got here. I looked at the clock again. It was hard to believe they would be here with us in just a matter of hours. I could picture them crowding the kitchen and the sound of their voices echoing around the house instead of its usual silence, and it made me do a little jig of happiness as I opened the cupboard to get some cereal. It had taken longer than I'd thought it would, but our family was finally going to be together. And once they were actually here, once she remembered what it was like, I knew my mother's nerves would go away and she'd be happy too.

By the time we had finished the pies—one apple, one pumpkin—my mother seemed a little calmer. "Not perfect, but I think we did a pretty good job," I said as we slid them into the oven.

"I'm going for a little walk," my mother said, rolling her sleeves back down.

"Just don't be gone too long. We still need to go to the grocery store once these are out of the oven."

"I know. I'll be back in a bit."

I busied myself over the next half hour with cleaning up the pie mess and peeking into all the other rooms to make sure everything was ready. In the library, my mother's art supplies were arranged neatly on the desk and her canvases were all stacked against the far wall and covered with an old sheet. She returned when the pies were cooling on the kitchen counter, and we made our run to the grocery store.

Before I knew it, it was time to go to the airport. My mother disappeared upstairs for several minutes, and I waited in the living room, flipping through a magazine.

"Julia?"

"In here," I called. Anyone looking closely could see that she had lost even more weight and that her face was drawn, but it was obvious that she had taken care in dressing and some of her old elegance was back. She wore beige slacks and a cream cashmere sweater, her hair was swept up in a French twist, and when I walked out to the car with her, I caught a whiff of Chanel No. 5. "You look nice, Mom," I said.

"Thanks." She gripped the steering wheel tightly and took a deep breath. "Ready?"

"I can't wait to see them!" As bad as I felt about my mother's nervousness, I couldn't contain my own excitement.

Dulles Airport was packed, which wasn't exactly surprising on the day before Thanksgiving. "The plane landed ten minutes ago," I said, checking the arrivals monitor. I hugged my mother's arm and did a little bounce of excitement. Her eyes were flitting back and forth, searching the crowds of people coming out of the terminal. And then there they were, Matty in his blue jacket and my father with a black carry-on bag slung over his shoulder, riding down the escalator.

"Dad!" I shouted. I felt my mother stiffen beside me as he smiled and waved. Matty almost pushed the elderly woman in front of him over so he could run down the rest of the way.

"Mom!" He sprinted toward us and flung himself at my mother, who rocked back under the force of his weight. They hugged each other tightly for several seconds, and when they finally pulled apart, my mother was wiping away tears.

"Hey, butt-face," Matty greeted me.

"Hey, garbage-breath." And then we too were hugging. I was surprised to find my brother was now taller than I was. My father walked up, and I tore myself away from Matty to throw my arms around him instead. He lifted me off the ground, and the familiar roughness of his cheek and faint smell of his aftershave made my throat ache.

"Daddy, I'm so glad you're here," I whispered in his ear. He released me and straightened back up.

"Me too, Tink. Me too." He turned to my mother, and there was a slight pause before he leaned forward to clasp her shoulder and kiss her cheek. "Hello, Carolyn."

"John." Her hand touched his face before fluttering away. "Well," she said, her voice turning brisk. "Let's get your luggage and get out of here."

Matty and I filled the car ride back to the house with chatter about school, college applications, and the latest movie Matty had seen, whose special effects were apparently worthy of a twenty-minute description. Normally one of my parents or I would cut him off at some point when he went into these rhapsodies, but I think we were all a little bit glad not to have any awkward silences. I relished the feeling of all of us being in the car together, but I could not stop a small stab of sadness at the sight of my parents so stiff with each other, some vast distance between them though they sat inches apart in the front of the car.

"Nice house," my father commented when we pulled into the driveway. "What year does it date back to?"

"Eighteen-fifty," I said, remembering what Susan had told me.

"That's fantastic," my father said, climbing out of the car. "Looks like they kept most of the original structure, at least from the front."

"Given how small the rooms are, I'd say that was accurate," my mother said. "It has a cellar in the back," she added, turning to Matty. My heart stuttered and then resumed its normal pace. "Julia can show it to you. She's taken a real shine to it." There was an edge to her voice, and I felt a twinge of annoyance at her hypocrisy. It wasn't like I was making any nasty comments about her and the library. I took a deep breath and pushed my annoyance aside. This was going to be a no-fighting holiday.

"Sure, whenever," I said. It's not like we'd be running into Elias. We helped my father and brother carry in their bags, and my mother took my father upstairs while I showed Matty the living room. He flopped noisily on the couch.

"Awesome. I'm right by the TV."

"Yeah, but there's no cable."

"What?" His mouth dropped open in shock.

"And no internet," I added. My mother popped her head in just then.

"What?" she asked, seeing Matty's face.

"Matty's just been informed about the lack of cable and internet."

"I didn't know staying in an old house meant going back to the Dark Ages," Matty muttered. My mother laughed, the first real laugh I'd heard from her in a long time.

"You'll survive a few days without all that stuff, Matty."

"I don't know about that." He picked up the ancient remote and examined it glumly.

"Why don't I show you the cellar?" I said, taking pity on him now that I'd had my fun.

"All right." He hoisted himself up and clumped down the hallway after me. My mother followed.

"I'll get started on dinner." As we passed through the kitchen, Matty perked up.

"What smells so good?"

"We made a couple of pies this morning," I said.

"From scratch?"

"Yes."

"Awesome!" He walked over to inspect them more closely, but my mother swatted him away.

"We're not eating them until tomorrow," she said. My brother sighed and my mother gave him a nudge. "Go see the cellar and get out of my way." I couldn't help smiling as I opened the back door. It was almost like it used to be.

Matty stood next to me as I pulled out the key chain and unlocked the doors. He helped me prop them open and followed me down the steps. I pulled the cord for the light. "This is it," I said. He looked around at the bare concrete walls and at my chair with the scattering of books and magazines next to it.

"That's it?" He looked around again, as though he might have missed something. "So you, what, hang out here?"

"Kind of. It's a quiet place to study." My explanation sounded weak even to me. It was strange being down here with him, the open doors letting the afternoon sunshine flood in, illuminating just what a bare and lonely place it was without Elias. "Let's get out of here."

"Fine by me," Matty said, shrugging. Back in the house, Matty headed for the living room and I heard the TV go on. My mother was tossing a salad in the kitchen.

"I think we're about ready. Go tell your father."

"Okay."

As I climbed the stairs, I could hear Matty flipping back and forth between the two channels that got reception. Grinning to myself, I went to my father's room. His door was ajar, and as I pushed it further open, he shoved a paper he'd been reading into his bag, his expression startled.

"Dinner's ready," I said. His face cleared and he smiled.

"All right. I'll be down in a minute."

"Is everything okay?"

"Yes, everything's fine." He lifted his bag off the bed and put it on the floor. "I'm just going to wash my hands," he said, moving toward me so that I had to back out into the hallway. He closed the door behind him. "Tell your mother I'll be right down." I stood in the hallway for another minute, staring at his door. What had he been reading? I shook my head at my own question. It was probably just some work thing.

--->=⊙ ⊙=<---

On the surface of things, Thanksgiving went well. It was like we all made some secret agreement to be on our best behavior. It also helped that there was so much to do—setting the table, heating the turkey, mixing the stuffing, putting together the salad, and keeping Matty from sneaking an early taste of the pies. When we finally sat at the table to eat, my mother and father were at either end, while Matty and I sat across from each other on the sides. Perfect symmetry. The lack of an obvious gap was a relief, however small. At home, sitting at the kitchen table where we always ate our meals, Uncle Denny's absence would have been obvious. But even though no one spoke his name, he still shadowed everything. I could almost see all of our private memories flickering away like silent films in our minds whenever someone would lower their eyes or drift away for a moment.

When the dishes were cleared away and the leftovers stored in the refrigerator, Matty tugged at my father's arm. "Let's go watch the game." He started down the hall, then stopped and pivoted, an agonized expression on his face. "Will this TV get the game?"

"I don't know if it's the game you'll want, but you'll probably get something," I said. As he and my father headed for the living room, I turned to ask my mother if she was coming, but stopped. She looked as though a set of invisible strings that had been holding her upright all day had been snipped while my back was turned. She sagged against the counter and her face was grey. "Mom? Are you okay?" I moved toward her, but she pushed away from the counter.

"Yes, I'm fine. Just tired is all. We've had a busy few days."

"Maybe you should go take a nap."

"I think I will. Go enjoy the game."

"Okay." I glanced back when I was halfway down the hall and saw her draining a glass of wine in large, thirsty swallows. I could hear Matty say something in the living room and my father laugh. My mother poured a second glass, but I turned away before I could see her drink it.

⊷⊶ ⊷⊶

When I woke the next morning, I worried a little about what condition my mother would be in, but she must have had a decent night's sleep, because she emerged from her room looking almost cheerful. No hangover in sight. My father had taken charge of breakfast and was hard at work flipping pancakes and prodding sausages. My mother poured a mug of coffee and set it on the counter next to him.

"Thanks," he said.

"You're welcome."

Even the weather seemed like it was making an effort. The sun was shining and the thermometer read fifty-eight degrees. My mother came to stand next to me at the window.

"I thought we'd take the boys out for a drive around the countryside today," she said. She gave me a tentative smile and reached up to push a stray lock of hair behind my ear.

"Great." I smiled back, trying not to study her too closely. We sat at the table and let out a cheer as my father set down a plate piled high with pancakes. After we'd stuffed ourselves, we piled in the car and drove up and down the two-lane highways winding through the countryside, pulling over whenever we saw a pretty place to take a short walk or snap a photo. We had lunch in Middleburg and hot chocolate in Leesburg, browsing the shops that lined the center of town. At one point, my father put his arm around my mother, and she leaned into him as we walked down the sidewalk. When she bought some Christmas ornaments in one of the shops, I felt a small flutter of hope. They had to be for our tree at home.

The drive home was quiet in a drowsy, content kind of way as we were all lulled by the motion of the car and the rapidly fading light. At the house, we helped ourselves to leftovers in the kitchen, not even bothering to sit down as we reached across each other to fork up bites of cold turkey and stuffing. Before my mother went upstairs, she gave each of us a hug.

"This was a good day," I whispered in her ear when it was my turn.

"It was." Her face was lined with fatigue, but she looked more relaxed than she had yesterday.

My father and I cleaned up in the kitchen while Matty went, as usual, to go turn on the TV.

"I'm so glad you guys are here," I said as I rinsed off a plate. "Thanks for coming, Dad."

"You're welcome."

"Mom's the happiest she's been since we got here."

My father made a noncommittal sound and absorbed himself in drying the dish he was holding. I turned off the faucet.

"What's going on?"

"What?" My father looked up, startled.

"I'm talking about how much better Mom is doing with you guys here, and you're being kind of weird about it."

"Sorry. I didn't mean to be 'weird.' I'm glad you're glad and that your mom seems happier." When I continued to stare at him, he reached forward to ruffle my hair. "It was a nice day, Tink. Just enjoy that and don't overthink it, okay?"

"Okay."

But I couldn't shake the feeling that he was hiding something.

⇢⇢▬◉ ◉▬◂◂

The next morning, I woke to overcast skies and a misty rain. I lay in bed, watching it for several minutes and thinking about Elias. Was he out in the rain? Had he reached Samuel? Would he be able to get them both home again?

The house was quiet. Downstairs, I found Matty still asleep on the couch, breathing heavily through a slack mouth. My father was sitting at the dining room table, drinking coffee and reading the paper.

"No pancakes today?" I asked, sitting next to him.

"Nah. Don't want you guys getting spoiled."

"Right." I stole a sip of his coffee and studied him across the top of the paper. Dark circles shadowed his eyes and his hair was sticking up in the back. "You sleep okay?"

"Yes, fine. Or at least as fine as I can in a strange bed. You know how that is." He began folding the paper back into a neat rectangle. "So I was thinking that since it's supposed to rain all day, maybe we could go see a movie."

"Fine with me."

"Right, then. I'm off to shower."

My mother and Matty emerged an hour later, and we all got back into the car and drove to the nearest movie theater, which was about a half hour away. There wasn't much to choose from, so we let Matty talk us into the latest action thriller. It was either that or a romantic comedy, and none of us was in the mood for that. After an early dinner at a nearby restaurant, we headed back to the house. The fact that it was our last evening together seemed to be weighing on all of us. We all hovered in the front hallway for a minute, not quite sure what to do next. My father busied himself with collecting all of our jackets and hanging them on the coat rack standing in the corner. Then he cleared his throat.

"Kids, there's something I need to speak with your mother about privately. Do you mind just..." He gestured toward the living room. We all stared at him dumbly for a moment, surprised by this turn of events.

"Sure," I said finally. Matty followed me, both of us moving slowly, and my father touched my mother's arm.

"Upstairs?"

"All right." From the look on her face, she didn't seem to know what this was about either.

"What's going on?" Matty asked, flopping onto the couch and turning on the TV.

"I have no idea. Turn that off," I ordered, walking over to grab the remote from Matty's hand. He thrust it behind him.

"Why should I?"

"Because, idiot, I want to hear what's going on upstairs."

"Fine." Matty pulled the remote back out and the TV went quiet. He followed me as I crept over to the base of the stairs. I could hear the low murmur of my father's voice for a minute or two, and then there was a loud cry from my mother. Matty and I jumped. The sound of my mother's sobbing drifted down to us through the closed door, and my father's voice resumed its low murmur. We stood there, frozen and straining to hear, until there was only silence. When we heard the bedroom door start to open, we bolted back into the living room and turned the TV on again.

My father appeared in the doorway seconds later. His face sagged with grief and fatigue, and I saw him holding a paper in his hand. I thought of the one I'd seen him shove into his bag the other night and was filled with dread.

"What's going on?" My voice shook. My father slowly lowered himself into a chair across from us and smoothed the paper against his leg.

"This is a letter from the Office of the Chief Medical Examiner in New York." He paused and said, "They've identified some remains as Uncle Denny's."

It felt as though someone had taken a hammer to my chest. The pain that had settled into bearable dullness in the last few months suddenly turned sharp and raw again. I had forgotten all about it, but now I remembered my father taking Uncle Denny's hairbrush in so they could extract some hairs for DNA. It was real, then. Uncle Denny was really gone. Of course we had already known that. But without any physical proof, I think we had all harbored—however irrational and impossible—the fantasy that maybe he was still out there somewhere. Maybe there was still some remote chance that he would walk through our door one day with a great story about what had happened to him.

But now there was DNA. There were parts. A sob tore through me, and my father leaned forward and rubbed my back as I hunched over and cried. "I'm so sorry," he said. I sat back up, a flood of anger pushing through the grief.

"How long have you known?"

"What?"

"How long have you known? When did you get the letter?"

My father sighed and leaned back in his chair. "I got it the day before you called to invite us to Thanksgiving," he said.

"So you came here knowing what we were all expecting, what we were all hoping for—a nice holiday reunion—and you decided this was the time to tell her, to tell us, *that*?"

"Honey," my father began. He reached over to touch my arm, but I shook him off.

"No." I stood up and began to pace. I couldn't bear to sit still. "How could you do this?" I was conscious of my mother in the room upstairs and struggled to lower my voice. "You saw how much better she was doing," I hissed. "We were finally starting to be a little bit happy again. Why did you have to ruin that?"

My father ran a hand over his face. "What was I supposed to do, Julia? It's not like I wanted this to happen."

"But why now?"

"When should I have told you? This isn't the kind of thing you do over the phone. I knew I had to tell you in person, and when you called the next day, it just seemed like the best option."

"Well, it wasn't." I continued to pace, the tears still streaming down my face. Matty was hunched over on the couch, pale and mute with misery.

"And what would you have suggested, Julia?" My father was starting to sound angry himself. "That I never share this news? That I pretend I never got this letter? That I wait until your mother finally came back—which might not ever happen, by the way—and spring it on her then?"

"I don't know." I came to a stop in front of him. "I just wanted this weekend to be happy." His face softened and he stood up.

"I know, kiddo. I know." He pulled me against him. I wrapped my arms around him and buried my face in his chest, all my anger spent. "Come here, Matty," I heard him say, and then Matty was with us and we were all clinging to each other. After a few minutes, my father gently disentangled himself. "I need to make a few phone calls. I don't think your mother's going to be up to driving us back to the airport tomorrow, so I'm just going to call a shuttle." He started through the doorway and then paused. "You know, Julia, you can come back with us if you want to." I stiffened.

"And leave Mom behind? After what's just happened?"

"She knows she can come too. I asked her to." He looked away, his jaw tightening. "I even begged. But she won't," he said turning back to face me. "That's her decision, Julia, and I want you to know that you can make your own. You need to do what's best for you now."

What was the best for me? I didn't even know anymore. "I'm going to stay, at least for now."

My father nodded. "I figured you'd say that. You're a good kid, you know that?" He touched my cheek and headed down the hallway. *Yeah*, I thought. *If only that were enough.*

Chapter 15

I STOOD ON the front porch with a blanket around me, watching my father load his and Matty's bags into the back of the shuttle. He slammed the door shut and walked up the steps toward me.

"You know you're welcome to come home any time," he said, pausing on the step below me.

"I know."

"I love you."

"I love you too." My words got muffled against his shoulder as we hugged. He released me and went back to the car. Matty had been waiting next to me, leaning against the porch rail. He straightened and glanced back at the front door.

"She wants to say goodbye, Matty. She just can't. You know that, right?"

"Not really." He kicked his foot against the base of the rail, dislodging a flake of white paint.

"Come on, Matty," my father called. Matty turned and gave me a quick, hard hug.

"See ya."

"Bye, Matty." And seconds later, with a fluttering of dead leaves at the end of the driveway, they were gone. I stood staring at that empty space until my nose and feet were numb. Back inside, the silence was oppressive. I made coffee and took a mug upstairs. I knocked gently.

"Mom?" There was no answer. "Mom?" I repeated, a little louder. "Can I come in?" When the silence continued, I opened her door. "I brought you some…" My voice trailed off as I took in the bottle of sleeping pills on her nightstand. I picked it up and shook it—it was still about half full. Her head was barely visible from beneath the covers, and I leaned in close to hear her breathing. I put the bottle back and crept back out of the room.

I busied myself with washing the sheets and towels Matty and my father had used and giving the bathroom a once-over. When I ran out of things to clean, I sat at my desk and tried to work on some homework, but mostly I found myself just staring out the window, replaying the weekend's events and trying to think of some way things could have played out differently. Which, of course, was impossible. With my mother wrapped back up in her cocoon of misery just across the hall, even thinking about the good parts of our time together hurt. It had simply been a glass illusion waiting to shatter the moment my father shared his news.

I pulled out my phone and thought about calling Sarah, but I doubted she'd want to listen to my problems right now, especially since she'd be busy with her own family. I didn't think I could bear hearing them all in the background. Derek? No. We were just driving buddies. Samira? It was too much to lay on someone I was just getting to know. I didn't want to lay it on anyone, really—not when they were all with their own families and probably having a really nice weekend. Elias was the only person I wanted to talk to, the only one who would really understand, and who knew when I would see him again? *But I will see him again,* I thought as I stared at the bare branches of the oak tree stretching out to the sky in the fading light. It was the one small thread of hope still keeping me stitched together.

⊶⊷

While all the other students were probably being dragged by their parents out of bed the next morning, I left the house early, eager to be around anyone and anything that could distract me from the pit of awfulness my life seemed to have fallen into. Once I was at school, though, I realized that as glad I was to be around people in general, I wasn't really ready to talk to anyone in particular. I flashed a quick smile at Samira and Derek before sliding into my desk, digging through my bag to avoid their curious glances, but Derek caught me on the way out.

"Hey, Speedy. Hold on a sec. How was your Thanksgiving?"

"Fine. How was yours?"

Derek ignored my question. "Fine? You look like your cat just died." To the surprise of both of us, my eyes suddenly filled with tears. "Aw, man, I'm sorry," Derek said, pulling at his hair. "I didn't mean to upset you."

"No, no," I said, swiping at my face with my jacket sleeve, mortified. This was exactly what I'd been trying to avoid. "It's okay. It just…didn't turn out that great."

"Listen," he said, moving closer to me to make way for the students pushing past us. "Why don't we meet after school? You can practice your driving and tell me what happened without five hundred people around."

"Okay." That sounded better than going home right away to sit around by myself.

"See you later, then. And hang in there." He squeezed my arm as he moved past me, and I went to my next class feeling slightly less awful.

When we were in his truck driving down one of the quiet neighborhood roads that had become our usual practice area, Derek pulled over and turned off the ignition.

"You want to talk or drive first?"

"Drive." I still didn't feel quite ready to share.

"Okay," he said, shrugging, and we went through our usual routine of trading places and adjusting the mirrors and seat to accommodate my lack of inches. When I looked over and saw Derek's knees scrunched up against the glove compartment, I couldn't help smiling, probably for the first time in the last two days. "What?" he asked.

"Nothing." I turned on the ignition and we spent the next hour cruising up and down side roads. At one point, he even had me try the highway. Unused to accelerating more than 25 miles an hour, I got a little spooked by all the cars flying by and pressed the gas pedal too hard, sending the truck leaping forward in a jerk that made it shudder in protest.

"Easy there, Tiger," Derek said. "You've got to be smooth. Like my moves with the ladies."

I laughed. "That's hardly an example of smoothness."

"Then you haven't been paying enough attention."

He directed me to a local drive-thru, where we ordered some fries and chocolate shakes. I rubbed the tires against the curb a couple times going around the bend, but handled it pretty decently overall. Even Derek seemed a tiny bit impressed.

"Not bad, for a rookie. I mean, it would have been nice if you hadn't left half my tire tread behind just now, but not bad."

"I'm doing great and you know it," I said, climbing out to switch places again. Derek snorted as he readjusted the seat and mirrors. "Don't get cocky. You drive about as well as a partially blind eighty-year-old. It's going to take a lot more practice for you to work your way down the decades."

"Whatever. You're just trying to get me back in your truck," I teased without thinking. Derek laughed, but his face reddened. I looked away and changed the subject to college applications, and we took turns complaining about how hard it was to write application essays until we reached my street. Derek pulled up in front of the house and turned off the ignition.

"So what happened?"

I fidgeted with the edge of my scarf for a minute, unsure of how to begin. Derek leaned back into his seat and waited, his left arm draped over the wheel. I took a deep breath and forced myself to speak before the silence could get any more uncomfortable. "Everything was going really well. I mean, it was a little tense at first, but I was expecting that. But the more time we spent together, the easier it got. It's like we had to warm up or something, and once we got the hang of being a family again, everything was great. My mom's been so closed off from everyone—she and I have hardly talked at all in the last month. But she was starting to open up again. She was even smiling, and I started to actually think…" I broke off, choked by the lump forming in my throat. I swallowed hard and started again, my hands still working the fringe of my scarf, twisting and smoothing it over and over again. "And then on Saturday, my dad dropped a bomb on us. He had a letter confirming that they've identified some remains as my uncle's." My voice came out flat, almost robotic as I tried to suppress my emotion. Just saying it aloud hurt.

Derek drew in a sharp breath, but he didn't say anything, so I continued. "Of course my mom completely freaked out. She stayed in her room for the rest of the weekend. She didn't even come out to say goodbye to my little brother. And now I don't know what's going to happen. I thought things were finally getting better, but now everything's just worse." My voice cracked, and to my mortification, I began to cry. "I'm sorry," I said, wiping the tears away with my scarf.

"Why are you sorry?"

"For getting all emotional on you."

"Why would you need to apologize for that? It would be weird if you *didn't* get emotional. Your uncle is gone, your mother's a mess, and your family's falling apart. Of course you're going to cry."

"You sound mad."

"I'm not mad." He leaned toward me, his expression intent. "I just don't get why you shut yourself down like that. Go ahead and cry. You can howl if you want to—I don't care." I let out a small laugh that somehow ended in a sob, and then I was really crying—ugly, jagged sobs—my face pressed against my arm. At some point, Derek began stroking my back in a soft, steady rhythm that continued until my tears stopped. "Come here," he said, when I finally lowered my arm. I let him pull me toward him and put his arms around me. I lay with my head against his chest, the wool of his sweater scratchy against my cheek, and felt myself relax for the first time in days. Though the heater had stopped running when he'd turned off the engine, the cab of the truck was still warm. He continued to stroke my back until my mind emptied of everything and I began to feel sleepy. He seemed to sense my lethargic state. "Don't go to sleep on me."

"I'm not." I pushed myself up and brushed my hair out of my face. "Thank you, Derek. It felt good to be able to talk about it." I felt a faint twinge of guilt as I said this, my mind flashing to the empty cellar and Elias.

"Any time. I'm glad you told me. You're going through a lot, you know."

"I know. I just don't usually like to dump all my problems on people."

"There's a difference between dumping and sharing."

"Is there?"

"Of course. Do you get bothered by people sharing their problems with you?"

"No."

"Then why do you assume others would?"

"I don't know." And I really didn't. I'd always been a good listener, someone others would confide in, but I found it hard to share in return. I glanced toward the house, a sense of cold dread blooming in the pit of my stomach. Was my mother still in her room or had she finally come out? "I should probably go in."

Derek reached over and turned me to face him, his hand spanning the side of my face. "Call me any time, and I'll pick you up and we can go driving or get something to eat or whatever. Okay?"

"Okay." I tried to smile and felt it wobble. He sighed, his eyes darkening, and then he leaned forward, pulling my face toward his own. It was a soft kiss at first, tentative and sweet, and I let myself savor that sweetness and the warmth spreading through me. But soon it began to deepen into something else, something more urgent, and just as I was on the brink of falling into it, the image of Elias's face, his eyes blue and clear and staring into my heart, flashed with vivid clarity in my mind. *What are you doing?*

I gasped and pulled away from Derek, shaking with the surge of conflicting emotions flooding me—longing, guilt, confusion. Derek also drew a shaky breath, his eyes dazed and unfocused for a moment before widening in bewilderment.

"What's wrong?"

"Nothing. It's just…" I looked away, struggling to compose myself. "I don't think I can do this."

"Okay." Derek blew out a gust of air and pushed a hand through his hair. "Sorry if I moved too fast. I just thought… Well, I guess I didn't really think. It just felt right. God, that sounds cliché."

"No, it doesn't. But things are really complicated right now and I can't do this," I repeated. I could almost feel the waves of confusion and hurt radiating from him, and combined with my own riot of emotions, the truck felt unbearably close. I wanted nothing more in that moment than to get out of there. "Look, I'm sorry. You've been really great about everything, but I need some space to figure stuff out." I unlocked my door and hoisted my bag off the floor.

"What does that mean? Does that just mean I'm not supposed to kiss you again, or does that mean I can't even talk to you?"

I was too tired to handle any more. "I don't know. I'm sorry, okay? I just don't know, and that's the best I can do right now." I slid out of the truck and slammed the door shut behind me.

"Julia!" I heard him shout through the window, but I walked across the yard and up the front steps as fast as I could. As I fumbled with the key to the front door, I heard the engine start up and his truck peel away with an angry squeal. The keys fell in a clatter at my feet.

"Shit!" I leaned my forehead against the front door and took a deep, shuddering breath. Just like every other possibility of happiness in my life lately, this one had crumbled into bitter ashes. And this time, it was my own fault.

⇥⊙ ⊙⊷

That night, after making myself a peanut butter sandwich, I went into the living room to watch some TV. Despite the limited channels, I was able to find a crime drama, which was perfect—something to distract me from my own drama. Partway through, my mother came downstairs and paused in the doorway. Her hair was a nest of tangles and her clothes hung on her lopsided and rumpled.

"Hi," I said, turning down the volume.

"Hi." She fiddled with a button on her shirt for a minute. "Did your dad and Matty get home okay?"

"They're fine." *Except Matty was devastated that you didn't say good-bye*, I thought to myself. Not exactly the kind of thing to say to an emotionally unstable mother.

"Good. That's good." She gestured toward the kitchen. "I'm going to get something to eat and go back upstairs. You okay?" *Of course not.*

"Yeah. Are you?" But she was already turning away.

"I'll let you finish your show. Sorry to interrupt."

"You're not..." My voice trailed away as she disappeared from sight and another voice popped into my head. *Why are you sorry?* But I didn't want to think about Derek right now. I didn't want to think about anything.

The next morning, I got to homeroom before Derek and opened my notebook as soon as I sat down, trying to look occupied. I didn't look up until Mrs. Davenport asked for our attention to review the school's zero-tolerance policy about drugs on campus. She was standing directly in front of Derek's row, and he turned to look back at me. He wore an expression somewhere between hurt and angry, and when he raised his eyebrows at me in a mute question, I kept my expression blank and flashed him a quick, fake smile before fixing my gaze on Mrs. Davenport. I had never stared so hard at someone with such little attention in my life.

When the bell rang, I lingered over putting my things back in my bag, but I needn't have bothered. Derek shot up from his desk and slammed out the door before the bell had even finished ringing.

"What's going on?" Samira asked, following me up the aisle.

"What do you mean?"

"I mean, why does Derek keep staring at you like a lost puppy and you won't look at him at all?"

"Things are just a little tense between us right now."

"Why?" Clearly, Samira wasn't going to be so easily put off.

"Because I'm kind of confused these days and I think I might have given him some mixed signals."

"Oh." Her eyes were solemn, and I appreciated that she didn't immediately start prying or telling me what I should do.

"See you in P.E.?" I said.

"Yeah, see you."

To my relief, Samira and I got put on different teams for volleyball and there wasn't a chance to talk. I needed time to figure out what I was feeling before I could talk to anyone about it, however nice and understanding they were. I walked quickly on my way home, anxious to get out of the cold air and down into the cellar. It was highly unlikely that Elias would be back already, but as long as there was even a small chance he'd show up, I wanted to be there.

When I got home, I saw my mother had taped a note to the refrigerator saying she'd gone out and wouldn't be back until late. *So we've started that again,* I thought. At least I didn't have to worry about sneaking out to the cellar. I made myself a mug of hot chocolate, grabbed my schoolbag, and headed out the back door. It wasn't even three-thirty yet, but the afternoon sunshine had already lost its brightness, and before long it would be dark. Winter wasn't far off, and the days were getting shorter. It was hard to believe we'd been here over three months.

I settled into my chair and pulled out my English book, but I didn't open it. Instead, I closed my eyes and let all the thoughts and emotions I'd locked up in the past twenty-four hours come tumbling out. The truth was, I had liked kissing Derek. I'd liked being held and having someone pay attention and be concerned about me. But I was also full of guilt. Elias had given me *his* full attention, caring, and concern. I'd opened up more to him than I had to anyone since Uncle Denny died, and after barely a week of him being gone, struggling to get his injured brother home, I was making out with someone else.

But why should I feel guilty about that? Elias and I had never made any promises to each other. We were living in different centuries. We couldn't even touch. So why did it feel like I was cheating on him? *Because I love him.* The thought came out of nowhere, and as shocking as it was to me, I knew it was true. I loved Elias. I loved his gentleness and thoughtfulness. I loved the glimpses of humor he showed beneath his seriousness, and his kindness in listening to me and supporting me. But then why was I so attracted to Derek?

I groaned and leaned back against the wall. I had somehow managed to get through all of junior high and most of high school without ever having a boyfriend, without any guy—to my knowledge, at least—seeming to have any interest in me, and here I was torn in two directions like some heroine in a teen movie, minus the cheesy resolution at prom. And how was I supposed to explain any of this to Derek? I hated hurting him, especially after he'd gone out of his way to help me. Maybe I couldn't avoid hurting him, but at least I could stay away from him and avoid lying to him outright, which seemed like the worst insult of all.

I waited awhile longer, and when it became clear that Elias wasn't going to show, I gathered my things and started back up the stairs. My book slipped out of my bag toward the top, and as I bent to pick it up, I saw something where the paint had chipped away that I'd never noticed before—the letters *E* and *J* carved into the edge of the door. I wondered when he had carved them. *Elias and Julia.* The letters blurred in front of me. *Please, Elias, come back soon.*

Chapter 16

FOR THE REMAINDER of the week, I found myself entering a weird cycle of waiting, watching, and avoiding with Derek and my mother. I could feel Derek watching me while I did my best to avoid him, just like I watched my mother as she avoided me. As the days moved toward December and Christmas music and decorations began invading every public space in town, my mother had once again retreated behind closed doors, frequent absences, bottomless glasses of wine, and a kind of absentminded politeness whenever we did see each other. As I sat in the cellar in another vigil of waiting for Elias one afternoon, it occurred to me that in some ways I was living with *two* ghosts who weren't really ghosts, and the future of my relationship with both of them was equally unclear.

The one bright spot was now that I had so much time on my own, I started improving in school. Samira and I had started working together on whatever common assignments we had during homeroom—another good way to avoid talking to Derek—and I found it helped the hours in the cellar go by faster if I studied. It also helped keep me from worrying about Elias and what decisions

I might have to face once the winter holidays rolled around. Given how things were lately, I was pretty sure my mother wouldn't want to go home for Christmas. The question was whether I would want to go home without her.

When almost three weeks had passed since I had last seen Elias, I began to feel the dark pull of doubt and despair. What if he couldn't get back? What if I never saw him again? Since it was Saturday, I left my schoolbag upstairs and settled into my chair with a magazine. I was looking through a photospread of gift ideas when I heard it—the faint scrape and shuffle of someone on the stairs. I wanted to yell and cry and laugh all at the same time. I settled for throwing the magazine on the floor and jumping out of my chair instead.

"Elias!" I exclaimed as he appeared on the last step and moved toward me.

"Julia!" His voice wasn't as wild as my own, but I could tell he was glad to see me.

"I'm so glad you're finally here. I've been waiting every day for over a week, imagining all kinds of terrible things. How did it go? Were you able to get Samuel? Is he okay?" My questions tumbled out until I ran out of breath. Elias and I sat down in our usual spots, and I leaned in, anxious to hear his story. Maybe it was my imagination, but he looked thinner to me and the bones of his jaw and cheeks stood out sharply.

"Yes, Samuel is home. We returned Wednesday night, but it was impossible for me to get away. The journey was about what I had expected. Getting to my brother wasn't so difficult, but figuring out a way back was. It took me several days to get the right permits and to find someone who could sell me a wagon. There weren't many to be had, and those that had them weren't ready to let them go easily. The one I finally purchased cost me not only all the money I'd brought, but everything else I had, including the pocket watch my father had given me and all the food I'd brought for our journey back."

"How did you manage?"

"One of the workers at the makeshift hospital where my brother was gave me half a loaf of bread. I'm pretty certain he stole it, but I couldn't let Samuel get any weaker than he already was. I loaded him into the wagon and we made our way home on the main roads." He stopped and swallowed hard. "It took a long time. Every jolt of the wagon hurt Samuel terribly. By the time we reached home, he had a high fever. We've been taking turns—my mother, my father, and I—sitting with him and doing everything we can to keep it down. That's why I couldn't come to you. I wanted to, Julia—I thought of you constantly on the ride back—but I couldn't come." His voice cracked, and he wiped a hand across his face, though his eyes remained dry. It was like he was too tired to even cry.

"It's all right, Elias. I understand. Of course you had to be with your brother. I'm glad you could come at all. I'm so sorry. This must be so hard for you all."

"It has been difficult. But I am very glad to see you again." The grimness in his face softened as he smiled at me. "You are the one bright spot in the midst of a very dark time, and I am anxious to hear your own news and how the visit went."

"Not well. I mean, it did at first, and there was one afternoon where I thought things were going really getting better. My mom was relaxing and opening up. It was great." I paused, the memory of that hope still painful.

"And then?" Elias prompted gently.

"And then my father dropped the news on us that they've identified some of my uncle's remains. My mother completely fell apart. She didn't even come out to say goodbye to my brother. It's like we took a tiny step forward and then got shoved back about twenty. Now my father and brother are back in New York, and I'm starting to wonder if my mother will ever get better or be ready to go back home. Christmas is coming and I have no idea what I'm going to do. Do I go home and leave her here by herself? Do I stay and just sit around watching her be miserable? And what about after that? I never thought we'd be here more than a month or two. Do I stay and finish school here or go back so I can graduate with my friends?" Everything that had been stewing inside me the last several days came pouring out. "It's all gotten so complicated."

Elias nodded. "It sounds that way. How do you choose between two such flawed alternatives, especially when the outcome is so unclear?"

"Exactly." I let out another sigh and leaned back in my chair, stretching my legs out in front of me. There was something so comforting about someone understanding immediately, especially when lately everything I said to everyone else in my life seemed to come out the wrong way. My chest tightened as something I'd avoided thinking about rose to the surface, and I forced myself to speak it out loud. "You're part of it, you know." Elias looked at me in surprise. "Getting to know you, being able to talk to you—I don't think I could have made it through these months without you. So it's not just that I'm having a hard time with the thought of leaving my mother behind," I admitted slowly. "I don't want to leave you either."

Elias bowed his head for a moment and looked up again, his face grave. "Selfish as it is, I would not want to be left behind. In fact, I think it would be rather pleasant seeing you and continuing these conversations for, oh, say, the rest of our lives." His mouth tilted up and I laughed, a jolt of happiness running through me.

"Yes, that would be nice."

Elias's face grew thoughtful again. "But even if that were possible, would it really be enough, Julia? Would that be the life we are meant to have, sneaking away from our families to meet in a cellar for a few minutes here and there? Fixed to this house until we are old?" I'd never thought it out like that. He made it sound so...sad. Some of my feelings must have shown on my face because he added, "I don't mean to cause you distress or diminish what this has all meant to me—what *you* mean to me. But while there is that selfish part of me that would like this to go on forever, there is a part of me that wants you and your mother to go back to New York and reunite with your father and brother. I want you to be free to live with people you can go places with and build a life with." His voice dropped almost to a whisper. "More than anything, I want you to be happy."

It took several seconds for me to be able to speak. "I want you to be happy too. I'm just tired of losing people. I don't want to have to keep saying goodbye."

"I know." We were both quiet for a moment. "We are here now, though, face to face. And that's a wonderful thing." Elias smiled and I forced myself to smile back. As I did, I noticed something.

"You know, you're really clear to me again. More solid looking."

"You are to me as well," Elias said, holding up his lantern for a better look.

"And things are pretty awful for both of us right now, aren't they?"

"I suppose they are. Do you really think there's a connection?"

"Maybe."

Elias cocked his head. "I think I hear my mother. I'd better go up."

"I hope your brother gets better soon."

"So do I." Some of the weariness had crept back into his eyes.

"I know it'll be hard for you to get away, but I'll be here every afternoon, so just come when you can."

Instead of looking pleased by what I'd said, Elias looked troubled. "I don't know that I feel right about you spending so much time down here just waiting."

"I don't mind. Really."

Elias shook his head. "I know you don't. But I do. And there is your mother, after all."

"Like she's ever around or wants to talk." I couldn't help the bitterness in my voice.

"But don't you want to be there if she ever is?" His question stung me into silence. "And surely you have made a friend or two at your school?" I thought of Derek and hoped Elias couldn't see my face flush. "Your silence speaks for itself," he said when I remained quiet. He sighed heavily. "Look, Julia, I would very much like to see you as much as possible, but I don't wish to do it at the expense of the rest of your life. And I need to be with my brother as much as I can."

"I know that."

"Then let's just choose a few specific times to meet, and if it doesn't work the first time, we plan on the next. But no waiting every day for hours."

"Okay, fine. I'll be here every other day for just the afternoon. And then Saturday at our usual hour." My tone must have made it clear I wasn't going to agree to anything less, because Elias smiled and tipped an imaginary hat to me.

"Yes, ma'am. I will come during those times whenever it is possible." We both stood. "Be well, Julia."

"You too. And for God's sake, eat something," I called after him as he moved toward the stairs. "You're looking a little skinny." I caught a glimpse of a rueful smile, and then he was gone.

⇢⊨◉ ◉⊨⇠

With Elias's words in mind, I decided to make more of an effort with my mother. At supper that evening, I suggested going out the next day.

"To do what?" my mother asked, looking surprised. Her question only emphasized how distanced we'd become.

"I don't know. Maybe a little Christmas shopping." Seeing my mother frown, I added, "Or we could go see a movie."

My mother studied her wine glass for a moment, then gave a small shrug. "Sure, why not?" It was all I could do not to roll my eyes at her seeming indifference. *Spend time with my daughter? Eh.* But at least it was something. She'd agreed to go out and do something other than mope around in the library.

But being with my mother didn't mean my mother was with me, something that was painfully obvious on our movie outing. After asking me a dutiful question or two about school on the drive to the theater, my mother lapsed into an absorbed silence, answering my own questions with only the briefest responses. It was like she had a word limit of only ten per hour and wanted to keep a few in reserve. During the movie, she had the same impassive and dull expression every time I snuck a glance at her. It was an eerie contrast to the loud hilarity of the comedy on screen and the laughter of everyone around us. I couldn't wait for the movie to end.

When we were home again and my mother had disappeared into her bedroom, I wrapped myself in a quilt on the couch and opened a novel I'd been reading, but I found it impossible to concentrate. What was Elias doing right now? How was his brother? What if my mother was a zombie forever? And what about Derek? I could only avoid him for so long.

My phone buzzed against my hip. "Hello?"

"Hi, Tink."

"Hi, Dad."

"How are you?"

"Fine."

"How's your mom?"

"Not fine." I heard my father exhale sharply.

"So no change?"

"Nope. It's pretty much the same thing every day. Lots of dazed depression stewed in gallons of wine." I didn't bother lowering my voice. I doubted my mother could hear me, but if she did, so what? It was true. My father, however, didn't appreciate my description.

"Show a little respect, Julia. She's still your mother."

"I know. I don't mean to be disrespectful. I'm just trying to, I don't know, balance out all the drama. It gets to be a bit much."

"I don't like how this is affecting you. It's changing you." When I didn't respond, my father said, "Christmas is coming up."

"Yep."

"Have you given it any thought?"

"Of course."

"And?" I could tell my brevity was irritating my father. Apparently I had taken on my mother's word-rationing. I didn't like her using it on me, but I could see the appeal.

"I don't know yet. I want to give things with Mom a little more time."

"Julia, be realistic. Do you really think things are going to get better at this point?"

"Just give it some more time," I repeated. "She took a real hit on your visit, you know."

"I know this is a waste of breath, but don't get your hopes up, Julia."

"So you're just giving up, is that it?"

"I've called her four times this past week, but she doesn't answer and she doesn't call back. I'm not giving up, Julia. I'm facing reality. And so should you." I thought of Elias and his impossible journey to bring his brother home, of Samuel's precarious hold on life, and how this had all somehow become part of my own life, just as my life had become part of his.

"But reality can change," I said. "I know what the reality is with Mom right now, but I can't be sure about it tomorrow or next week. Not yet."

I wasn't sure if I was telling my father or myself.

Chapter 17

THE NEXT MORNING, Samira cornered me in P.E. We were doing stretches and she plopped down next to me.

"So why've you been avoiding Derek?"

"What, no polite questions about my weekend?"

"Which is an avoiding kind of answer. Besides, why waste time saying other things when this is what I really want to say?" Samira's directness made me laugh, which, because we were standing on one leg doing a quad stretch, also made me wobble.

"Good point."

"And you still haven't answered my question." We were instructed to raise our arms over our heads and lean to the side for the next stretch, and I used this interruption to decide what to say to Samira. Since there was no good way out of this, I decided to try her own directness.

"Derek kissed me last week."

"Really?" Now we leaned to the other side.

"Yup."

"And this is a bad thing?"

"Sort of. I mean, it's not bad like he did anything wrong."

"But you didn't want him to?" We had finally straightened up again and were shaking out our arms.

"Not exactly."

"So you did want him to kiss you?"

"I don't know. It's kind of confusing."

"Why, don't you like him?"

"Geez, you are relentless. The Spanish Inquisition would have loved you."

"I doubt that, considering I'm a Muslim."

"You know what I mean." I sighed. I couldn't any more explain this situation to her than I could to Derek. I couldn't tell her that while I might have some feelings for Derek, even though I still wasn't sure what those feelings were, I was pretty sure I was in love with a boy from the 1860s who hung out in my cellar. I decided on a partial truth.

"I'm just not sure how I feel about Derek. I like him, but I don't know that I want to be more than friends."

"That makes sense. But why is everything so cold between you now? Did he not understand that?"

"That's kind of my own fault. I was a little harsh with him, and I guess I'm just not that comfortable talking about it."

"You can't avoid him forever."

"Can't I?" I said this half-joking, but Samira's expression remained solemn.

"Not if you want to be fair to him. Not if you care about him at all."

I knew she meant well, but Samira's words still irked me. "I know. I just need to figure things out first." We joined the tide of girls in blue sweats heading for the locker room.

"And you think you have to have everything figured out before you can talk to him again?"

"Well, yeah. Don't you?" We had reached the locker room and the other girls brushed past us, eager to change into their own clothes, but Samira and I stood in the doorway.

"No, I don't. I've never had a boyfriend, so maybe I don't know what I'm talking about, but it makes sense to me that working out what your relationship with someone is should involve talking to them. I mean, it's a relationship, right?" She smiled at me and gave my cheek a small, motherly pat before disappearing into the noisy chaos of the locker room. I shook my head and wove my way toward my own locker. *She* doesn't *know what she's talking about*, I thought. But her words sparked an uneasiness I couldn't quite shake.

That afternoon, Elias appeared just moments after I had sat down in the cellar.

"I can only stay a few minutes," he warned before he had even set his lantern down.

"That's okay. How's Samuel?"

"Not well. He still has a fever and my father fears infection has set in."

"Oh no." The pallor of his skin and the dark circles under his eyes were vividly clear. I wanted to say something helpful or comforting. "So your father is taking care of him? That should help, right?" I winced at how weak that sounded, and Elias frowned.

"Yes and no. Obviously, that my father is a doctor is some help, but even with his knowledge and skill, there is only so much he can do with a severe injury."

"But the time he's spending with Samuel—is there any improvement in their relationship at least?"

Elias sighed. "Not that I can tell. Samuel is mostly unaware of what's going on around him, and my father...well, he treats Samuel just like any other patient I've seen him with. His manner is completely detached. While my mother sits and weeps, my father simply sits in his chair and reads." His mouth twisted. "It's unnatural."

"I guess. But it could also be his way of coping. Maybe he's trying to keep strong for Samuel and the rest of you."

"I suppose. But I can't help getting angry sometimes—really angry, to the point where I have to leave the room because I can't bear it. My mother knows, and I feel terrible for causing her any additional pain or worry, but I can't help it."

"Of course you can't. I'm sure she understands. Just think about how much you've been through in the last few weeks." Elias shook his head, and I couldn't tell if it was in denial or just a way of clearing it. He then studied me for a moment.

"How are you? You don't look well."

"Thanks a lot."

"You know my intent," he responded quietly, making me ashamed of my sarcasm.

"I do. Sorry. It's still bad. I got her to go out with me this weekend, but it was horrible. She's so wrapped up in her depression. And like you, I start getting really mad at her. I mean, at what point does grief become pure self-pity? At what point are they *making* themselves sad? It's just so hard to tell, and I keep going around and around with feeling sorry for her, then feeling frustrated with her, and then feeling guilty that I get frustrated. It's kind of exhausting." I let out a deep sigh and then found myself smiling.

"What?" Elias asked.

"Is it just me or do we sound like a couple of old people? All this worry about our families. It's ridiculous. We're seventeen."

"I suppose. Although it's not written anywhere that hardship and distress can't occur before one is old."

"It should be. I should be worrying about clothes and dances and dumb stuff like that. And you should be worrying about…I don't know. What should you be worrying about?"

Elias smiled. "I would say my studies. And perhaps about the next dance as well. Before the war started, the Sloane family used to live in the largest house in the area and host an enormous Christmas party. They'd hire musicians and there'd be dancing. It was always an event everyone around here looked forward to for months."

"Where are the Sloanes now?"

"They moved further south in hopes of avoiding the worst of the conflict. A lot of families moved, actually."

"And who would you have taken to the dance?" I asked, trying to sound casual. One of Elias's eyebrows quirked up.

"Most likely my parents, since families usually attended together."

"Any particular girls you'd look forward to dancing with?"

Elias was grinning now. "Do I detect a bit of jealousy if there were?"

"Maybe a tiny bit."

"Then I will admit that there is no one in particular I would look forward to dancing with. What about you? Who would you dance with?"

"Oh, no one," I answered quickly, even as I thought of Derek. Elias looked at me curiously and I glanced away, clearing my throat.

"I'm sure there would be no shortage of suitors wanting to escort you." His compliment made me feel even more guilty.

"Well, I wouldn't say yes to them." I swallowed hard, gathering my courage. "But I would to you if it were possible for you to take me."

Elias smiled and pushed his dark hair back. "I'm pleased to hear that. If it were possible, I would be the first to ask." What would it be like to dance with Elias? I let myself imagine it for just a moment. "I'm afraid I must go now," Elias said, standing.

"Thanks for coming down here. I know it's not easy with everything going on."

"No, it's not. And yet even this short time together somehow makes everything else more bearable." He picked up his lantern and gave me one final, long look. "Be well," he said finally.

"You too." We exchanged a smile and then he was gone. I shivered in the cold air. Winter was definitely on its way, something I had forgotten, at least for a little while.

Chapter 18

As it turned out, Elias might have been on to something when he said I didn't look well, because I woke up the next morning with a dull ache in my head and neck, and the feeling that someone had scrubbed my throat with sandpaper. After making quick use of the bathroom, I returned to my bed, rolled myself up in my blankets, and went back to sleep. It seemed only minutes later that my mother was waking me up.

"Why aren't you at school?"

"I'm sick," I said, my hoarse voice confirming my claim. My mother put her hand on my forehead.

"You do feel a little hot. Are you achy?"

"Yes." My mother sighed, and I wondered briefly if it was because she felt bad for me or if she was disappointed her alone time was being disrupted.

"I'll get you some water and a Tylenol." I heard her rummaging around in the bathroom and sat up as she came back in. "We don't have any chicken soup, but I can go get some."

"Thanks." I handed her back the empty water glass and slid back under the covers. She tucked them around me and smoothed my hair back, making me feel bad about my earlier suspicion.

"Get some sleep." She closed the door behind her with a soft click, and I gratefully followed orders. I slept for most of the day, waking only to use the bathroom and ingest the soup and other liquids my mother brought up periodically.

The next morning, I woke up feeling better but still too weak and lethargic to go back to school. I felt a small prick of anxiety as I lay on the couch watching soap operas and sipping mugs of tea. I had a chemistry test coming up and was missing key review days. And then I remembered Samira had chemistry too, just in a different period. She was the kind of student who would take good notes. I could just borrow hers.

When the afternoon rolled around, I made sure my mother was safely shut away in the library and then crept out the back door, a quilt wrapped tightly around me. I waited twenty minutes for Elias to show, then headed back upstairs, a wave of tiredness making my legs weak. I fell back into bed, still wrapped in the quilt. "Hope everything's okay, Elias," I whispered as I drifted off to sleep.

↦═◎ ◎═↤

"Julia! Where have you been?" Samira waved at me from her desk in homeroom and I went straight over.

"I got sick. Some kind of cold."

"That's a bummer."

"Yeah. Listen, I was wondering if I could borrow your chemistry notes? I'll get them back to you by the end of the day."

"Of course." She dug through her backpack and pulled out a notebook. "This is what we covered in the last couple days. It's not too bad."

"Thanks." The bell rang, and as I turned to go back to my seat, my gaze caught Derek's and he quickly looked away. I sat down, feeling heavy in a way that had nothing to do with having been sick. I wished there were a way to erase that afternoon, to go back to how things used to be between us. But there wasn't time to think of that now. I opened my notebook to a blank page and started copying Samira's notes. There wasn't enough time to finish in homeroom, so I took her notebook with me to lunch.

Samira and I got separated into two different groups during P.E., and it wasn't until I was nearly to the highway on my way home that I realized I'd forgotten to return her notes. I looked back across the long stretch of field I had just walked across, reluctant to have to go all the way back and try to chase her down, but it wasn't fair for her not to have her notes all weekend when she'd been doing me a favor. I began a half walk, half jog in the direction of the gym. I didn't know exactly where Samira lived, but I remembered seeing her go in the opposite direction from me after school. Hopefully, I'd be able to catch up with her in time. The cold temperature and the darkening sky encouraged me to pick up my pace. Freezing rain had been predicted for the late afternoon and there was no way I wanted to walk home in that.

I rounded the corner of the gym and crossed the blacktop toward the trees at the border, scanning for any sign of her. I saw a flash of color toward the right and headed in that direction. As I got closer, I recognized the blue jacket Samira had been wearing today.

She seemed to just be standing there, which was a little strange, but I was relieved I had caught up with her.

"Samira!" I called, but she didn't turn. As I got closer, I could see why she seemed frozen in place. Hidden by the trees and bushes bordering the school property were Donny and Phil, who stood blocking her. When she made a move to walk past them, Donny grabbed her headscarf and yanked it off. I broke into a run.

"Samira!" I yelled again, and this time all three of them heard me and turned. "What the hell do you guys think you're doing?" My question came out breathless and weak. Being sick had really done a number on me. Phil laughed.

"Nothing. We're just making friends. So shoo—run along now, little doggy."

"Give her back her scarf." I took a step toward Samira and the boys immediately stepped in front of her, blocking me. They were both about a foot taller than I was, and I had to crick my neck to look up at them. This only added to the slow burn that had started in my stomach.

"We told you to leave." Phil poked me in the shoulder, hard. I saw Samira try to duck around Donny, but he blocked her again.

"Are you really such chickenshits that you're going to pick on a couple of girls?" Both boys moved toward me, their faces dark with anger.

"Shut your mouth, you little bitch, or I'll shut it for you," Phil snarled.

"Go ahead and try." The burn inside had become a raging inferno, part anger, part adrenaline. "Come on, Samira," I said. I moved to push past Phil, but he grabbed me and threw me to the ground.

"Julia!" Samira cried out. She hollered again as Donny grabbed her. "Stop it!" The impact of my fall had winded me and spilled my books out of my bag.

"Not so tough now, are you?" Phil's taunt came from behind me, and just as I was able to gasp in my first deep breath, he picked me up from behind and lifted me off the ground. When I was twelve, Uncle Denny had taken me to the local gym and signed me up for a self-defense class. I could hear his voice now in my head. *Kick down. Aim for the kneecaps.* I kicked my feet back and down with all of my force. When I felt my right heel make contact, I yanked it up and drove it down a second time. Phil howled in pain and dropped me. I landed on my hands and knees next to my bag. Samira was struggling in Donny's grasp. Her hair was spilling around her face, and Donny was laughing.

I felt like a bottle of soda that had been shaken one too many times, and all the frustration and anger that had been building up for so long at everything—at my mother, at my father, at all the circumstances beyond my power to change and control—shot up like a geyser. My fingers wrapped around my chemistry book, and in one swift motion I turned and smashed it into Phil's face. He was hunched over, holding his injured knee, and the book caught him head-on. There was a sickening *crack* as it made contact. Phil howled again, bringing his hands up to his face, which was now streaming blood.

"You stupid bitch!" Donny flung Samira to the side and came at me. I flipped the chemistry book sideways and jabbed its edge into the center of his chest as he lunged forward. He gasped a small *oof* and fell back a step. Still riding the swift tide of my fury, I raised the book again and swung it against the side of his head as hard as I could, knocking him to the ground. When it seemed certain that neither boy was going to come at us again, I dropped the book to the ground, shaking and panting. I looked over at Samira.

"You okay?"

"Yes." Her eyes were wide with shock as her hair blew against her face.

"Your scarf." I pointed.

"Oh, yes." She picked it up from where it had fallen and tied it around her hair, her wide eyes still fixed on my face. It almost looked like she was afraid of me.

At the sound of someone shouting, I turned to see a group of people running toward us. Most of them were students, who all stopped at some unseen border about a dozen feet away and stood with their mouths hanging open at the sight of Phil behind me. I turned and felt my own small jolt of shock at how he looked. His hands, face, and the front of his jacket were smeared with blood. Sitting against a tree with his legs sprawled in front of him, he looked like a large, broken doll. Donny had just rolled up into a sitting position and was clutching his head. His left eye and cheek were red and beginning to swell. My anger left me as suddenly as it had come, and I was left weak and jelly-legged.

"What's going on here?" Two assistant principals briskly pushed their way through the students and surveyed the situation. "What's your name?" one of them barked at me.

"J-Julia," I stammered.

"Julia what?"

"McKinley." I watched him write it down on a small notepad he had with him. The other AP was on her walkie-talkie, ordering someone to call the paramedics. The male AP, Mr. Carlton, went up to Samira and the boys and looked them over. Motioning me to stand next to Samira, he began firing questions at us.

"What happened?" I looked at Samira and she looked mutely back at me.

"I borrowed Samira's notes earlier today and forgot to give them back, so I was catching up to her and I saw Phil and Donny harassing her."

"How could you tell they were harassing her?"

"They were crowding her and wouldn't let her walk past them. Then Donny pulled her scarf off."

"Is this true?" He turned to Samira and she nodded.

"Yes." She cleared her throat. "I was walking home and they caught up to me and were trying to block my way and saying bad things to me."

"And then?" Mr. Carlton looked back at me.

"And then I confronted them and told them to leave her alone. When I tried to leave with her, Phil grabbed me and threw me on the ground, and Donny grabbed Samira. So I hit Phil with my book and then Donny came after me and I hit him too. It was self-defense," I added, my voice fading as we all looked back at the two boys on the ground, bloody and bruised. The wail of an approaching siren rose in the background.

"Mr. Carlton, she attacked us," Donny moaned. "We were just joking around and she went crazy. My parents are going to sue you, you—"

"That's enough, Donny," Mr. Carlton cut in. "The paramedics will take care of you and then you and Phil can tell me your side of the story and we'll figure out what's what after I've heard everything." He turned to the other AP. "Mrs. Jackson will escort you girls back to the office and call your parents. I'll be there as soon as I make sure these boys are taken care of." My stomach twisted as the implications of all of this began to sink in. These boys were going to the hospital. They were going to call my mother. I had never even gotten a detention before. How was she going to react?

Mrs. Jackson herded us through the now growing crowd of students gathering. When I looked over at Samira, she gave me a weak smile, her dark eyes still full of shock. Mrs. Jackson had us wait outside her office while she called our parents. Samira fidgeted with one of the loops on her backpack. "Are you okay?" I asked. Her hands stilled.

"Yes. Just kind of freaked out, I guess."

"Me too."

"Thanks for helping me. I'm glad you came and found me."

"Me too," I said again, which elicited a small smile. It faded a moment later and Samira cleared her throat.

"You hit those boys really hard."

"I guess." I couldn't quite tell if Samira's tone was admiring, condemning or just factual. "I just wanted to make sure they couldn't hurt us."

"Of course," Samira quickly agreed. "It's just…"

"What?"

"You were so…angry. I've never seen you like that before."

I stiffened. Was I imagining it or was there some criticism in her voice? "Well, of course I was angry, Samira. They were harassing you and they grabbed us. Was I just supposed to stand there and do nothing?"

Samira flinched at my own implied accusation. "No, that's not what I meant." I felt a rush of guilt for snapping at her, but my insides were churning with so much residual shock, anger, and anxiety about what would happen next that I didn't seem to have any control over myself. Before I could apologize, Mrs. Jackson opened her office door.

"All right, ladies. Your mothers are on their way. Samira, would you please come into my office?" Samira rose and Mrs. Jackson closed the door after them. I leaned back in my chair, resting my head against the wall behind me. Hadn't I done the right thing? I was just defending us. But that level of anger and how good it felt to smash my book into Phil's face—maybe that *had* gone a little too far. Samira came back out of the office.

"She wants to see you now."

"Okay." I stood up. "I'm sorry I snapped at you."

"That's all right." She offered me a small smile and sat back down. Mrs. Jackson had me repeat my account of what had happened, taking notes the entire time without comment. As we were finishing up, I heard new voices outside. Our mothers had arrived. I followed Mrs. Jackson out of her office and saw Samira's mother smoothing her scarf and speaking rapidly in a language I didn't recognize. While I couldn't understand what she was saying, her concern for her daughter was obvious. My own mother looked me up and down without a word, her face pale and pinched with tension. Mr. Carlton came in behind her.

"Mrs. Khan? Mrs. McKinley? Let's go into the conference room, shall we?" He motioned to a door on his left, and we all filed in and took a seat. He lingered outside for a few minutes, talking with Mrs. Jackson, before joining us. "Sorry to keep you waiting." He adjusted several sheets of paper in front of him and cleared his throat. "So, it appears that two male students were verbally harassing and physically blocking Samira on her way home from school. Julia came across them, there was an exchange of insults on both sides, and then things got physical, although there's some disagreement about who got physical first. Your daughter," he said, addressing my mother, "used a heavy textbook to hit both of the boys. She broke one boy's nose and gave the other one several contusions and a possible concussion. They've both been taken to the emergency room for further examination." Both mothers gasped.

"Is this…is she going to be in trouble? Surely this is a matter of self-defense," my mother said, her voice shaking. She looked terrible, and I wondered if she'd been in bed when the call came. Mr. Carlton leaned both elbows on the table and steepled his fingers.

"It's pretty clear that the boys were the aggressors in this situation, but what isn't quite clear as of yet is whether your daughter was overly aggressive in her response. Whether justified or not, we can't ignore the fact that she injured two other students whose parents are very upset."

"What was I supposed to do?" I broke in, unable to listen quietly any longer. My mother shot me a warning look, but I ignored her.

"For one thing, the minute you saw something was going on, you should have run to tell a teacher or one of us and let us handle it," said Mr. Calrton.

"There wasn't time for that. I would have had to come all the way back over the field."

"Julia." My mother's voice was sharp. Mr. Carlton shrugged.

"Possibly. But the reality is that you took matters into your own hands and there are consequences to that. Samira," he said, turning to face her and her mother. "From all accounts it's clear that you are not at fault in this incident. You are free to go. I hope, though, that in the future you will alert a teacher or one of us administrators immediately if there is any future harassment. It sounds like there's been a history of this. If you'd let us know earlier, we might have avoided this situation."

Samira bit her lip and nodded. "Yes, sir." She and her mother stood up.

"Wait. Your notes." I leaned over to pull them out of my bag. "It would be pretty lame if I didn't return them after all of this, right?" I tried to smile as I handed them over to her, but my mouth didn't seem to be working properly. Samira took them and gave me a sympathetic look.

"Thank you. Mr. Carlton," she added, "Julia was just helping me."

"I'm aware of that, Samira. We will do our best to be fair in this situation." She nodded and threw me another sympathetic look before exiting with her mother. How bad *was* this? Could it jeopardize my college applications? The thought made me sick to my stomach.

My father would kill me if that were true. And/or kill my mother. Yet another thing to drive them apart.

"Is my daughter in trouble?" my mother was asking again.

"Yes and no. We are going to have to suspend her and the boys for at least a day or two, which is standard procedure whenever's there's a fight like this. It gives the kids a chance to cool off and us a chance to get all the details sorted and choose the best course of action. While your daughter seems to have been rather, shall we say, *aggressive* in this situation, she's had an unblemished record up until now and has an excellent academic history, which will count in her favor. Donny and Phil are doing everything they can to play the role of victims here, but those two boys have had less than stellar school careers. They've been in my office more than once for this type of thing." His manner turned brisk. "At any rate, take your daughter home and we'll call as soon as we've come to a decision about all of this." He pushed his papers back into a stack and stood up. My mother and I did the same.

"What about my schoolwork?" I asked.

"I'll let your teachers know that you've requested assignments. Your mother can pick them up at the end of the day on Monday." I nodded, my stomach dropping at the thought of all the tests and projects looming ahead of me that I would now fall behind on.

"Thank you, Mr. Carlton," my mother said, gripping my shoulder and steering me toward the door. We walked to the car in tense silence. The sky was dark from the late afternoon hour and a thick mass of storm clouds. The first icy pellets of rain began to fall as my mother unlocked the car, and as we climbed in, a sudden downpour hit the windshield with deafening force. My mother hadn't looked at me from the moment we'd left the office.

"Mom?" I said, my voice almost drowned out by the noise of the storm.

"Not now, Julia," she said tersely, turning on the ignition. I slumped in my seat and watched the grey rivulets streaming down my window. My mother drove carefully on the slick roads, but I could tell by the way she gripped the steering wheel that she was furious with me. Once home, we ran into the house and stood in the front hallway, shaking off the water and taking off our coats. My mother strode down the hallway to the kitchen and I followed. She banged the cupboard open for a glass and opened a bottle of wine.

"Mom," I started, but she held her hand up and shook her head.

"Don't even start, Julia." She took a long swallow and then it began. "How could you be so irresponsible? Did you think at all? This is your senior year! If this goes on your permanent record, it could jeopardize your applications and everything you've worked for." Her pale face was now flushed with anger. When I remained silent, she prodded, "Well? What do you have to say for yourself?"

"Samira was in trouble. What was I supposed to do?"

"You could have gone to get help, like Mr. Carlton said. You could have let the proper authorities handle this instead of running in there like some brawling maniac."

"There wasn't time. I saw a bad situation and I did what I thought was the right thing. I was helping a friend." My own voice rose as some of my earlier anger returned. *Brawling maniac?* My mother slammed her glass on the counter and it shattered. In the dim light, the wine spilling over the fragments of glass looked like blood. She stepped away from the mess and pushed her hair back with a shaking hand.

"How is it ever the right thing to fight like that? To smash someone's face in? What is wrong with you? Who taught you that?" Her face was flushed with anger and her chin jutted forward. Tears pricked my eyes, and suddenly I was shouting.

"Uncle Denny did! He taught me to fight and not be a victim. I know fighting just to fight is wrong, but it's not when you're fighting for something good. When you're fighting to protect what's important to you. I'm not just going to stand around and watch something bad happen to someone I care about." My mother flinched.

"You're talking about me, aren't you? That I'm a victim? That I just let bad things happen, is that it?"

My mouth dropped open in surprise. "No." My mother's mouth tightened at my denial. *Was* I talking about her? I hadn't meant that. And yet, it was true. "I don't know. Maybe." She turned away from me and my anger spilled out again. I was tired of her turning away, of never being able to really talk about things honestly. "Okay, yes. Yes!" Her shoulders stiffened and I moved a step closer. "I know Uncle Denny's death has been awful for you. I miss him too. We all do. But it feels like you've given up on everything. On all of us." I couldn't stop the tears any longer. "You've given up and you're not even trying."

My mother spun around. "I *am* trying," she hissed. "I am trying in the only way I know how."

"Which is what?" I shot back. "Running away? Cutting yourself off from your family? Drinking?" My mother's hand shot out and slapped me across the face. The sound of it seemed to echo in the kitchen as we stared at each other in shock. My mother's face crumpled and she reached out to touch my burning cheek.

"Oh my God. Julia."

I jerked away from her hand and walked out of the kitchen.

Chapter 19

THE SOUND OF the front door closing woke me the next morning. I rolled over and let out a sigh of relief that I wouldn't have to face my mother just yet. In fact, for once I hoped she'd be gone for a long time. I was just about to drift off to sleep again when my cell phone rang.

"Julia, what happened?" The tension in my father's voice made me jerk awake.

"Nothing, Dad."

"That's not the impression I got. Your mother left a message this morning while I was out on my run. She said you'd been suspended and to call you for the details. Is that true? You've been suspended?"

I put my hand over my face and squeezed hard. *Thanks a lot, Mom.* "Yes, but it's really not as bad as it sounds, Dad." I went on to explain the situation in as positive a light as I could, emphasizing the whole self-defense aspect.

"This is absolutely unacceptable, Julia. It should never have happened. It wouldn't have ever happened if you were still here. You don't belong at that school."

"Well, it did happen, Dad. I'm here and it happened."

"I obviously made a huge mistake in letting you stay there."

"What are you talking about? This was my choice. I'm not a child."

"You're getting into fights at school, and you're my daughter. I'm not going to let you self-destruct along with your mother."

"She's not self-destructing." My defense was automatic.

"Why do you keep defending her?"

"Because she's doing the best she can."

"I know she is. But what if that's not good enough? Why do you insist on staying there? On being apart from Matty and me? Why won't you face reality and come home?" *Because that means our family is broken forever. Because I don't want to let Elias down. Because giving up would make me just like her. Because letting her go would be letting Uncle Denny down.*

"I have to go, Dad. I just woke up and I really need to pee."

"Fine. But this conversation isn't over. Things are going to have to change."

"They already have," I said, but my father had hung up.

I went downstairs and settled on the couch to watch cartoons, a bowl of cereal balanced on my stomach. I could picture Matty doing the same on our couch in Brooklyn. Maybe my father was right. All this time, I'd thought leaving my mother would be abandoning her. But maybe I'd just abandoned Matty and my dad instead. Either way, someone was getting left behind. I wondered what Elias would think.

When I went down to the cellar, I was surprised to find Elias already there. "I'm sorry, Julia, but I can't stay today. My brother is much worse. I think he's…" His voice faded and he pushed a trembling hand through his hair. "I need to be with him and my parents."

"Of course. I understand." My own problems seemed insignificant compared to his. "I'm so sorry." He was more clear to me than ever. I could see the dark circles and the lines carving grooves in his face. I could see his eyelashes and the faint scattering of freckles across his cheeks. I could even see the texture of his shirt. I stepped even closer to him. "Elias," I whispered, reaching for his shoulder. I moved very slowly, focusing on trying to discern any sensation of contact. And then I felt it—a faint resistance against my fingertips. I looked up and found Elias's blue eyes fixed on me, wide with shock. We were both breathing shallowly, afraid to disturb the fragility of this moment. He slowly lifted his hand to my face, and a moment later I felt the brush of skin against my cheek and gasped.

"You felt that," he breathed.

"Yes." I slid my hand across his shoulder, up his neck, and brought it to rest against his cheek. The sensation of touching him was faint and somehow muffled—as if it were through a layer of cotton—but it was there. Elias closed his eyes and his mouth curved into a faint smile as he leaned into my hand.

"This is incredible."

"I know." Both of us were whispering. Elias drew me closer and I felt the faint pressure of his arm against my back. I threaded my own around his neck, and his forehead came to rest against mine. "What do you think is happening?" I asked. Elias lifted his head and studied my face, his thumb stroking my brow.

"Comfort," he said simply. I thought of his brother, possibly dying, and my family, possibly broken beyond repair, and I nodded. Not physics. Not molecular disruption. Comfort.

"I think you might be right." He smiled, and I could see that one of his teeth was just a tiny bit crooked. Then I felt his shoulders tense.

"My mother is calling me. Something must be wrong." We broke apart as he reached for his lantern.

"I'll be thinking of you," I called as he rushed toward the stairs. He nodded, his face full of fear, and then he was gone. I stood in the same place for several minutes, my eyes closed, trying to preserve the memory of his touch. Trying to keep it from fading away like an echo. *I'll be thinking of you.* That seemed so weak, so small considering what he was facing. But it was true. I would be thinking of him and hoping with all my heart that Samuel would get better. That had to count for something.

And then I remembered the file in the kitchen drawer. I could just look it up. I could look up the date that he died and know right then whether or not he made it. But something held me back. I didn't want to know before Elias did. I wanted to go through this with him. I wanted us to be in the same place of knowing.

⁂

My mother returned mid-afternoon. I was upstairs, stretched out on my bed reading a book, and I tensed, wondering if she'd come upstairs and try to talk to me. When I heard the library door shut, I didn't know if I was relieved or disappointed. Either way, I found it impossible to focus on my book anymore. I went downstairs, grabbed a soda from the refrigerator, and headed into the living room to watch some TV. Before I could get there, someone knocked on the front door. I opened it and found Derek standing on the front porch.

"Hey," he said, shoving his hands in his pockets.

"Hi." I tried for a friendly tone, but it came out sounding as surprised as I felt. What was he doing here? The library door clicked open and my mother stuck her head out. "It's someone from school," I said. She nodded and retreated again without a word.

"Can we talk for a minute?"

"Um, sure. You want to come in?" He stepped inside and unzipped his jacket but didn't take it off. I glanced at the library door. "Let's go back into the dining room," I suggested, leading the way. "Do you want something to drink? Or eat? I could make some popcorn." My nerves were making me babble. Derek shook his head.

"No, thanks." We pulled out chairs across the table from each other and sat down. Derek fidgeted with his hands for a moment. When he caught me watching them, he clasped them together on the table. "I heard about the fight and wanted to make sure you're okay."

"I'm fine," I said. Derek frowned. "I mean, I got a couple bruises, but that's it, and Mr. Carlton said the suspension might not even go on my record. They're still figuring things out. But it was self-defense, so it should be fine."

"So you're not upset or anything?"

"Not really." *It's nothing compared to everything else going on,* I thought.

"See, there you go." Derek's hands flattened on the table.

"What are you talking about?" I asked, surprised.

"It's like you're sitting with me, you're right there, but you go off somewhere else. You get this look on your face and I can tell there are things you're thinking about but you're not telling me." I felt my face flush.

"Well, sorry. I don't mean to."

"So what is it you're thinking about? What else is going on that getting in a huge fight and getting suspended don't seem to bother you all that much?" I felt a jolt of surprise at how closely his words echoed my own thought moments before.

"Well," I started, then stopped. What could I say? I couldn't talk about Elias, and everything with my mother just felt too complicated to get into. My thoughts were interrupted by Derek's sigh. His face was taut with frustration as he leaned across the table.

"What bothers you most about your mom?" he asked me, his voice hushed but intense. I glanced at the wall behind him, the only barrier between us and her. His question caught me off guard and I struggled to follow.

"I don't understand. What do you mean?"

"I mean, if you could change one thing about your mom right now, what would it be? Don't think about it, just answer. Just tell me now. What would it be?"

"I'd want her to be more open," I blurted, flustered by his questions. "I'd want her to talk about what she's going through with the rest of us instead of cutting herself off and running away." Derek smiled, but it was bitter.

"Isn't that interesting. Like mother, like daughter, I guess." He stood up, his chair grating on the wood floor. "You know, Julia, I don't know why, but I really like you. And for a little while, it seemed like you liked me back. And yeah, I kissed you, and maybe that went too fast or something, but it feels like you used that as an excuse to blow me off completely. You act pretty tough, but it seems to me that underneath it all, you might just be a big coward." I gasped but he didn't seem to hear me. He gave a quick glance at the wall behind him and looked back at me. "Seems like the women in your family don't handle problems very well." His dark eyes bore into mine. "I want to be in your life, Julia, but you're making it really hard. Maybe it's because you don't want that, but if you do, then you need to let me know. I'm not going to beat my head against a brick wall. That starts to hurt after awhile, you know." He zipped up his jacket and strode down the hallway. I was still sitting in my chair when I heard the front door slam, too stunned to move.

I felt as though he had punched me in the stomach. As his words replayed in my mind, I found myself shaking my head. I was not like my mother, and I certainly was not a coward. I *did* share. I told Elias everything.

That's not the same.

I didn't know where the thought came from, but I couldn't shake it once it was there. Why wasn't it the same? *Because he's not fully here. Because he's safe.*

Was Derek right? Was I really a coward? I shivered at the thought. I couldn't be. I needed to be the strong one. What hope was there for my mother if I wasn't? As if I had summoned her with my thought, she appeared in the doorway.

"So what did your friend want? Derek, right?"

"Yeah." I was surprised that she remembered his name. "He heard what happened and just wanted to see how I was doing."

"That was nice of him." I felt my mouth twist.

"Right, nice." *Like a kick in the head.* My mother cleared her throat.

"I was thinking maybe we could go out to dinner tonight." Her voice was casual, but I could see the tension in her shoulders. For a moment, it was like a film of her hand striking my face was playing in the space between us, and I felt the sting of my residual hurt and anger.

"I'm not really in the mood to go out," I said. Her shoulders slumped.

"I understand." Her defeat made my victory feel hollow.

"Maybe tomorrow night?"

"Sure." She gave me a small smile before going back down the hallway. I didn't care what Derek said. I wasn't running away. I just needed some time. There was a difference.

⤛═◉ ◉═⤜

I slept late the next morning, and given how cold the coffee was when I got downstairs, it was clear my mother had gotten up quite a bit earlier. Unsurprisingly, she was gone, a terse note taped to the fridge—*back this afternoon.*

By the time I was showered and dressed, it was close to 1:00. Even though I knew it was unlikely he would appear, I decided to go down in the cellar and wait for Elias. Just in case. I wanted so badly to see him, to know how his brother was doing. And, if I was honest, I wanted to see him for myself. Between what happened on Friday and Derek's visit, I was beginning to feel a vague sense of guilt, as though I were somehow at fault for something, and I hated feeling that way. I hated feeling that I had let someone down, especially when that was the opposite of what I was trying to do. But as the minutes passed and the cold began to creep in, there was no sign of Elias. I waited as long as I could stand it, then finally accepted the fact that he was not going to show and went back upstairs. I hoped it wasn't because things had gotten worse for Samuel.

I was making myself a sandwich in the kitchen when my mother came home. Instead of going straight into the library as I'd expected, she appeared in the doorway. Her face was drawn and pale, but there was a quiet determination in it that I hadn't seen for some time.

"Sandwich?" I offered, suddenly feeling nervous about what that look meant.

"No thanks. Julia, we need to talk."

"Okay." I picked up my plate and followed her into the dining room. Her hands were gripped tightly together and she looked down for a moment, seeming to gather herself. I hoped she wasn't about to tell me off like Derek had.

"I had a long talk with Susan this morning. I told her what's been going on, what happened with you." She took a deep breath and looked me squarely in the face. "I'm sorry I lost control like that, Julia. What you said made me very angry—it hurt me deeply—but that was no excuse." This time, I was the one to drop my gaze.

"It's okay. I shouldn't have said what I said." I pushed my plate aside, my appetite gone. My mother was shaking her head.

"Maybe not quite the way you did, no, but that doesn't mean what you said didn't have some truth. I've been pretty selfish in all of this—I know that—and I know I've hurt you and Matty and your father by running away. But you need to understand something, Julia," she said, her eyes dark with pain. Her mouth trembled, and she took another deep breath.

"It's okay, Mom. You can tell me." Her apology and vulnerability swept away the anger I'd been holding onto. I reached out to put my hand on one of hers and she squeezed it.

"I've never really talked much about my parents—your grandparents—to you. They both died when you were just a toddler." I nodded. It was true. She and Uncle Denny had almost never mentioned their parents and had been vague the few times Matty or I had ever asked about them. "The reason for that is that they were not very nice people. My father was abusive. Not physically, but emotionally. No one and nothing could measure up to his standards, and he hated any sign of what he considered weakness. If any of us cried, he'd just go after us even more. My mother dealt with it by drinking enough to keep herself in an unfeeling stupor most of the time." She still clung tightly to my hand, but her gaze was now fixed somewhere over my shoulder as she remembered. "I don't know how I would have survived without..." Her voice trailed away.

"Uncle Denny," I finished for her.

"Yes." She wiped away the tears that began to fall and continued in a shaky voice. "He was always there to protect and comfort me. He was only ten minutes older than I was, but it always felt like he was ten years older. He could always make me laugh and feel like there was something good to life, that something exciting was about to happen." She laughed, a small hiccupping sound, and I also smiled. Uncle Denny had done that for all of us. "He was the only one who ever really knew, Julia. About everything. He was the only one who really knew me. He was my rock, and when he died—" My mother choked on a sob and started again. "When he died, that was the hardest and worst thing that's ever happened to me, only he's not here to help me with it, and I don't know what to do. I don't know how to be in this world without him and I'm so afraid!" It was the wail of a little girl, and sobs engulfed her as the dam finally broke. I moved around the table and held her while she wept.

Eventually, she quieted, and I whispered, "What are you so afraid of?" She stilled and sat up again, her face ravaged.

"Of not being strong enough to get through this. Of being alone."

"But you're not alone," I said, smoothing her hair back from her face. "Uncle Denny might be gone, but the rest of us are still here. You've got me and Matty and Dad." My mother's eyes filled again at my words and she pulled away.

"Do I?" She covered her face with her hands. "God, I've made such a mess of things. When I first got pregnant with you, I vowed I'd never be like my parents. That I'd always be there for you and strong for you. But I've gone and done the opposite, and I'm so ashamed." Her voice cracked. "Can you ever forgive me?"

"Of course." I grabbed a napkin and handed it to her. She wiped her eyes and blew her nose. "Why haven't you ever told me any of this? Does Dad know?"

"He knows some of it, but not much. I don't like to talk about it. It's not pleasant to think about, and it's not your burden to carry."

I shook my head. "But it is. Mom, we're your family. We love you. And whether you've wanted it to or not, this *has* affected us. There's no way that it couldn't."

"I know. It's just hard for me to remember that. It's instinct to want to get myself together on my own. To not involve all of you."

I felt the sudden, disorienting lurch of déjà vu as I thought of Samira's comments and Derek's accusations, and I found myself saying, "But that's not how it works, Mom. We already *are* involved, and to keep pushing us away just makes everything worse. For all of us."

"I think I'm finally starting to get that."

"So what now?"

My mother squeezed my hand. "I need some more time." I opened my mouth to protest, but she cut me off. "No, please, Julia. Just listen for a minute." It took some effort, but I obeyed. "I don't mean more of the same. Susan gave me the name of a therapist she knows, and I'm calling her tomorrow to set up an appointment. I just need some more time to start working through all of this."

"Okay, good." And it was good. I was glad my mother would be getting some counseling. But what about Christmas? What about going back home? I wanted more than anything to ask these questions, but my mother looked exhausted. *One thing at a time.* We'd just had the most honest and open conversation we'd had since moving here. Maybe ever. I swallowed my questions and leaned over to hug her.

"I love you, Mom."

"I love you too."

Chapter 20

I SPENT MONDAY morning alternating between attempting to study and flipping restlessly between daytime television shows. Thoughts about Elias, my mother, and Derek swirled around in my head like an out-of-control carousel. My mother had gone out to get some groceries, and when I heard her at the door, I opened it and took one of the bags she was carrying.

"Mr. Carlton called just as I was leaving the store," she announced as we set the bags on the kitchen counter.

"And?"

"And you may return to school tomorrow."

"What about the rest of it? Is this going to go on my record?" As much as I hadn't wanted to admit this to my father or Derek, I had been a little worried about how this was going to affect me.

"Well, while Mr. Carlton wasn't exactly thrilled about the way you handled things, he and the rest of the administration agreed that it was self-defense. They thought today's suspension was enough consequence without it needing to go on your permanent record."

"What about Donny and Phil's parents?"

My mother's mouth curved in amusement. "Apparently, once the boys realized that making themselves the victims would mean publicly admitting they'd been beaten up by a girl, they retracted their accusations. I got the impression that Mr. Carlton helped them in this decision. He's assigned them to a new homeroom and gave strict instructions that if there is even a hint of trouble with either of them in the future, you're to take it to him immediately."

"Yeah, of course." My mother gave me a skeptical look. "I promise."

"I suggest you go thank Mr. Carlton, and while you're at it, you should also thank your friends Samira and Derek. From what I gather, they both spoke up for you today."

"Really?" I was surprised Derek had gone out of his way like that. He seemed pretty mad at me on Saturday.

"You need to call your father and let him know."

"Why don't—"

"Just call him, Julia," she said. She stopped halfway across the kitchen and turned around. "I made an appointment with the therapist for tomorrow," she said slowly. "You can tell him that too. If you want."

"Okay." I watched her go into the library, then headed up to my room and pulled out my cell phone.

"Hi, Dad."

"So what's happened? Are you still suspended?" I updated him and heard him sigh with relief.

"You got lucky. You know that, right? And if you do anything that could jeopardize your future like that again, you'll be straight on a plane back here, no discussion whatsoever."

"Okay," I answered, trying to sound meek. In my mind, this whole school fight thing was already old news. "I had a really good talk with Mom yesterday."

"Really?" It was hard to tell if my father was glad or skeptical about this.

"Yeah. She feels really bad about how she's been acting and how it's affected all of us. It's the first real conversation we've had in months. She's going to start counseling, Dad, and she specifically asked me to tell you."

"She did?"

"Yeah. I think she wants to work on things, but she's scared she's messed everything up with us." I could almost hear my father's thoughts swirling over the phone line as he took all of this in.

"That's great, Julia."

"You don't sound like you believe it."

"No, I just don't want you to get your hopes up too much."

"Which means you don't believe she's going to get better."

"Stop putting words in my mouth. Am I glad to hear your mom is getting help? Yes, absolutely. Am I sure this will make everything better? No, I'm not. We'll just have to wait and see. You understand that, right?"

"I guess. She already told me it's going to take time, and from what she told me this morning about her parents and everything, it makes sense. But I think it would help if we reminded her that we support her. That we love her." I stopped and took a breath. "Do you still love her, Dad?"

"Of course I do," my father's voice was quiet but firm. "I never wanted her to leave, you know."

"Yeah, but she did, and you didn't do anything about it."

"Because it was her choice. Look, Julia, I don't think we need to rehash this."

"Okay, fine. But she's making different choices now and you need to support her."

"What do you want me to do?"

My father's question caught me off guard. "Well, I don't know. Call her. Come for another visit. Maybe meet her therapist." Was I really giving my father relationship advice? My father mumbled something. "What?"

"I said 'we'll see.' I've got to go now, but keep me updated, okay?"

"Okay." I put my phone on the floor and rolled on my side to look out the window. The bare branches of the oak looked black against the overcast sky. My father might have his doubts, but I could tell things were different with my mother this time. He hadn't seen her face or heard her voice, but I had. I had been there. *What if I hadn't been? What if I hadn't come out here with her?* But I had, and I had met Elias and he had helped me stick things out. "Thank you," I whispered to the branches shifting in the wind. Hopefully, I'd get a chance to say it to Elias soon.

⤙⟶⊙ ⊙⟵⤚

Samira greeted me as soon as I walked into homeroom on Tuesday morning, waving a stack of papers in her hand.

"I copied my chemistry notes for you," she announced, handing them to me.

"Wow, thanks, Samira," I said, touched she had gone to such trouble.

"Our big test is on Thursday, so if you want to study together today or tomorrow, let me know."

"You're not afraid I'll beat someone up?"

Samira laughed. "No. In fact, when my father heard about what happened, he said I should have hit them too. My mother wasn't happy about that, but oh well. So when should we meet?"

"How about tomorrow before school?" I didn't want to miss a chance of seeing Elias in the afternoon.

"Okay, fine. How about we meet in the library at 7:15?" I stifled a groan at the early hour and nodded.

"Sure. Sounds good." The bell rang and we took our seats. As Derek slipped through the door and into his seat, he glanced back. I tried to smile at him, but he'd already turned around. At the end of the period, I hurried to catch up with him, but he slipped out the door.

"Derek!" I called when I saw him heading down the hall. He paused, turning around as I walked over. "Listen," I said, "I heard that you spoke up for me to Mr. Carlton, and I just wanted to say thanks."

He shrugged, his face impassive. "I just told him about how Donny and Phil have said some things to you and Samira in class. You know, facts to establish that there was prior harassment." I was taken aback by his formal tone.

"Well, that was very…lawyerly of you. Anyway, I appreciate it."

"No problem. See you later." He turned and headed up the stairs.

"Yeah, see you," I said, stung by his coolness. I thought thanking him might bring down some of the barrier that now stood between us, but apparently I was wrong. *Fine,* I thought. *I tried.* But that did nothing to ease the tightness in my chest.

⤝⊷⊷ ⊶⊷⤜

After a quick stop in Mr. Carlton's office after school, where I thanked him for his mercy and got another strong warning against ever taking matters into my own hands again, I headed home. I went into the kitchen for something to drink and saw a note on the fridge. I felt an automatic twinge of disappointment and frustration, but then I read it and found myself smiling. *At my appointment. See you at dinner.* She really was following through this time. I glanced at the clock and hurried out the back door.

Inside the cellar, I dropped my bag on the floor and took my usual seat. The minutes ticked by, and just as I was beginning to think he wouldn't show, I heard the sound of Elias coming down the stairs. He seemed to be out of breath.

"Elias!" As always, it was hard not to leap up and hug him. I strained to read his expression in the dim light. "How is Samuel?" I was almost afraid to ask.

"He is much improved. I think he's out of danger now, or at least my father seems to think so."

"What a relief. I'm so glad to hear that."

"I'm glad to be able to say it. It looked like it was going to be the opposite for a while. After our last meeting, he was having convulsions. That's why my mother was calling me. We were all certain it was the end." I leaned forward to touch Elias's hand and stopped. It didn't look as solid as before. He saw my movement and opened his hand. I brought mine to rest over his and lowered it. Nothing.

I pulled my hand away, trying not to think about what that meant, and asked, "So what happened?" Elias drew his own hand back to rest on his leg.

"His convulsions eventually stopped and we all sat with him for hours. Eventually my father sent my mother and me to go get some sleep. I dozed for a couple hours, but something woke me and I went back to Samuel's room." Elias paused for a moment, his throat working silently, and then he continued. "The noise that had woken me was my father weeping. He was laying across my brother, weeping as I have never seen him weep before, begging God to have mercy on his son. To not take another one from him." Elias paled at the memory, and I found myself shaken by his description.

"Did you say anything?"

Elias shook his head. "No. What I witnessed was something private, and I knew my father would not have welcomed such an intrusion. So I went back to my room. When the sun came up again, my mother and I went in to find my father asleep in the chair, and when we checked Samuel, his sheets were soaked. His fever had finally broken."

"That's...wow. That's incredible." I didn't know what to say. Elias smiled.

"He woke up yesterday and was able to eat some soup. And he and my father exchanged words for the first time in nearly two years." His smile turned wry. "Granted, it was only about how he was feeling and drinking fluids, but at least it was something."

"That's great. I'm so happy for you that Samuel's going to be okay and that your father is, well, being more open."

"As am I. Last night was the first night I've slept well in at least a month." He shifted in his seat and gave me a penetrating look. "And how have you been, Julia? And your mother?" I gave Elias an edited version of what happened at school, my mother's reaction, and then, in more detail, a summary of our talk on Sunday. His eyes widened at the first part, and it occurred to me that maybe I hadn't edited it quite enough.

"I've shocked you," I said after a minute of silence passed.

"No, not at all. Well, I suppose a bit," he amended when he saw my skepticism.

"Your ideal of me and my ladylike character must be completely shattered."

"I can't say it's not a difficult thing for me to picture, but I have always known you were not a typical girl." My face must have betrayed some of my disappointment because he quickly added, "In a good way, of course. You fight for what you care about and that is an admirable thing."

"I'm glad you think so. If I'm honest, though, it wasn't completely noble," I confessed. "I might have been defending my friend and myself, but when I was in the middle of it, I was so angry—at them and so many other things—I wasn't even really thinking anymore. It just felt good to hit someone." I braced myself for a look of disapproval, but Elias merely looked thoughtful.

"It makes sense you would have felt that way. Think how much hardship you've endured and how unable to express what you've really been thinking and feeling. And here was a chance to let it all out on someone who deserved it. Or at least some of it." He grinned. "Trust me, there's an enormous pile of firewood upstairs that's the result of my own frustration."

"Yeah, chopping things up with an axe isn't exactly an option for me," I said, also grinning. I sobered at the next thought. "I must admit that I didn't like being on the receiving end of it, although it did lead to my mother finally talking to me." I thought of Elias's father weeping over Samuel. "Kind of pathetic that it takes such terrible things to make people finally talk to each other."

"Yes. We seem to lack a fair amount of wisdom about the most important things." We were quiet for a moment, and then I found myself voicing what I had noticed when he first came in.

"You're fainter again."

"So are you," said Elias slowly. "I was hoping I was imagining things." I shook my head.

"No." I felt my throat close with sudden dread. "It's going to happen, isn't it?"

"What's going to happen?"

"We're going to lose each other." I choked on the words, but there they were anyway in the space between us. Elias bowed his head and was quiet. Then he looked up again, his face grave.

"It is possible. Perhaps even likely."

"Because things are getting better for us." I couldn't help the bitterness in my voice.

"We can't know that for certain. But if that were true, wouldn't you be glad to have your mother get better? To have your family reunited?"

"Of course." It was hard to speak. "But I don't want to have to leave you behind. I don't want to lose you."

"You haven't, though. Not yet. We have each other now." He smiled at me but his eyes were sad. I did my best to smile back.

"Right. We have each other now."

"I must stay with Samuel tomorrow as my father will be riding out to visit patients, but shall we meet again Thursday?"

"Yes, Thursday would be great," I said, as though being able to meet Thursday was something we could take for granted. "You know I really am glad for you and your family. I want that for you, for everything to work out, even if it means…you know." I couldn't bear to say it aloud again.

"And I want the same for you." He stood up and his face was shadowed as he looked down at me. "I will always want that for you."

--->=◎ ◎=<---

Elias's words and the reality of our increased faintness to each other haunted me over the next day and a half. The thought of losing him brought back the unbearable weight pressing down on my chest. At the same time, I couldn't help my excitement when my mother returned from her counseling session tired but cautiously hopeful. "I like her," my mother said of the therapist. She had also agreed to join a support group her therapist recommended. All these conflicting emotions made me grateful for the amount of schoolwork I had to catch up on. None of that required any emotion, just my complete concentration, which gave me a small break from everything else.

I met Samira in the morning to study for chemistry and worked on a history paper after school until the librarian flicked the lights to signal closing. When I got home, I was surprised to see the library door ajar and light spilling down the hallway from the kitchen. I found my mother taking the kettle off the stove.

"Hi," she said, glancing over her shoulder at me. "Want some tea?"

"Sure." I got myself a mug and leaned against the counter. She busied herself with teabags and pouring the water for a minute, then leaned against the opposite counter and faced me.

"Your father called this morning. We had," she paused for a moment, "a long talk."

"You did?" It was hard for me to read my mother's expression.

"He offered to bring Matty here for Christmas and to spend a few days with us here."

"Really? Mom, that's great!" It was better than I ever expected. My dad was actually making compromises. I didn't have to make a choice between them. We would all be together.

"And then you're going back home with them, Julia." My mother's quiet statement burst my bubble of joy.

"What? Mom…"

"It's what your father and I both want."

"You don't want me here?" I was stunned. It was one thing for my father to urge me home, but quite another for my mother to say she wanted me to leave.

"Sweetheart, it's not like that. Look, you've been a trooper to come out here with me and stick it out as long as you have. But this is your senior year. You need to be home with your dad and Matty. You need to be back at your old school."

"What about you?"

"I'm going to stay here for a while. Susan asked if I'd help oversee the kitchen renovation, so I'll be keeping busy, and I'll be going to counseling. It'll be okay." She gave me a small smile, but I was far from reassured.

"But I can stay and help you. I really don't mind, Mom. I can't just leave you behind."

"You wouldn't be leaving me behind. You'd be giving me the space I need to work through things. To get better. I love you, Julia, and I love that you've been so loyal to me. But it's going to take time and it's just too hard for me to do this when I feel like I'm keeping you from living your own life."

I stared down at my mug, fingering a small chip on the rim. Did I even want to go back anymore? I was starting to like my life here. And how could I leave Elias? But I did miss my father and Matty, and it would be nice to graduate with the friends I'd known since elementary school. I heard my mother set down her own mug, and then she was lifting my face and smoothing my hair back. "I hope you can understand." She drew me into a hug and we held each other quietly for a moment.

"Do you think you'll ever come back?" I whispered.

"I don't know. I hope so. I'd like to be able to, but I just don't know. Is that okay?"

I nodded slowly. "I guess. I just have to get used to the idea." The idea that things could be okay even when nothing was clear. When they weren't what I hoped they would be. And especially when I was powerless to change them.

Chapter 21

THE NEXT DAY, Samira caught up with me as we were walking back into the locker room.

"So how do you think you did on the test?" she asked.

"All right, I guess. I felt pretty good about the first part, but I definitely struggled on the second. How about you?"

"About the same. It was a hard test." I had to bite my lip to keep from smiling. Samira was a whiz at chemistry. Most of our "study" time had consisted of her tutoring me. She'd probably aced the test.

"Thanks again for helping me. I think I would've done a lot worse without it," I said. She shrugged.

"Any time. We can make it a regular thing, if you'd like. Maybe study together once a week?"

"That sounds great. Only," I hesitated and she looked at me enquiringly. "It looks like I might be back in New York for second semester."

"Oh." Samira frowned, then seemed to catch herself and smiled. "Well, sad for me, but you must be happy." It was my turn to shrug.

"I don't know. It will be nice to be back at my old school and graduate with my friends, and of course I'll love being with my dad and brother again. But my mother's still going to stay here for awhile. And I'll miss you."

"I'll miss you too. What about Derek?"

"What about him?"

"Are you going to miss him?" *I already do*, I thought. When I didn't respond, Samira said, "You should talk to him."

"Maybe." I looked at my watch. It was almost 3:00. "Listen, I have to get home. I'll see you tomorrow."

"Okay, see you."

I wrapped my scarf as tightly as I could without choking myself and braced myself against the icy wind kicking up on the walk home. My thoughts turned immediately to Elias. *Would he be fainter than the last time? How much time did we have left? Would he even be there? How could I tell him I was leaving? How could I bear to actually leave?* The questions swirled around in my head with no answers to stem them.

When I got to the cellar, my hands were stiff and cold, making me fumble with the lock. I had barely turned on the light when I heard the sound of footsteps behind me. Elias appeared behind the glow of his lantern and I found myself squinting, trying to see him more clearly. He came to stand directly in front of me and held his lantern near my face, and as he studied me, it was as though someone had thrust their hand into my chest and was squeezing my heart. He had taken on the ghost-like, transparent quality he'd had when I first saw him. Was that only a few months ago? It seemed like so much longer. I could see from the sadness of his expression that I appeared the same to him.

"Hello, Julia."

"Hi, Elias." Neither of us was very successful at smiling, but we tried. As we sat down, I realized I could no longer see any part of the crate he sat on. He appeared to be sitting in the air. "How is Samuel?" I asked, striving for some normalcy. Elias seemed glad to follow my cue.

"He's doing well. His fever is completely gone and he's slowly gaining some strength now that he's able to eat some. He still sleeps a great deal, but my father said that's a good sign—that his body is recovering."

"You all must be sleeping better now."

"We are."

"And your father? How are he and Samuel doing now that Samuel's awake and everything?"

"It's difficult to say." Elias shifted in his seat. "They're both very stubborn men, which is why I think they've always clashed so much. But while neither will say so, I know they are both glad Samuel is home. They just talk about things like the weather and mud instead."

"Mud?"

"Well, you know how the roads get when there's been heavy rain." Elias grinned. "People around these parts can talk about mud for hours."

"I guess roads are a little better now than they used to be."

"And how are things with your mother?"

"Better. We had a big talk a couple days ago, and she shared some stuff about her parents and why losing Denny has been so hard for her."

"It must have felt good to speak of things honestly."

"It did. It felt really good."

"You sound troubled by that."

"Do I?" I sighed and pushed my hair back. "It's just, she's getting help and things are a little bit better, but she and my father have agreed that I should go home after Christmas. And she's going to stay here, for who knows how long."

"I'm sorry, Julia. I know that's not what you wanted."

"No, it's not. Although, I get it. Or I'm starting to. She wants me to go so she can focus on getting better. But it's hard to let go. And," I said, taking another breath, "I don't want to leave you." Elias bowed his head. There was a long silence, and I felt another squeeze in my chest at this now familiar trait of his—these long, thought-filled pauses.

"Perhaps that is why this is happening."

"What do you mean?"

"I mean, maybe our time together is drawing to a close so we don't have to be put in that position. Of leaving each other." His head lifted and he looked straight at me. "Saying goodbye would be hard enough against our will. Imagine if we had the choice not to." I pressed the palms of my hands against my eyes.

"I want a third option."

"I wish that were possible."

"This is awful."

"It is hard," Elias agreed. "But I can't imagine having never met you, and I can't ever be anything but grateful and glad that I did." This time I couldn't stop the tears.

"Why do you always say such beautiful things?" I asked, wiping my face with the cuff of my jacket. "I can't argue with that."

Elias smiled. "Do you want to argue?"

"No. I just don't want to turn into a giant puddle, which is what I'm about to do."

"I'm afraid I'm about to make it worse."

"How?"

Elias leaned forward. "You must know how much having you be a part of my life the last several months has meant to me."

"Why are you talking like we aren't going to see each other again?" I interrupted, panic flooding through me.

"Because." Elias took a deep breath and let it out again. "Because we don't know that we will, and I need to say these things to you while I can. And if we meet again on Saturday," he added in a lighter tone, "we'll find something else to talk about. Now, may I continue?"

I struggled to compose myself. "Okay." Elias's face grew solemn and he looked down. He stretched a hand toward me and I put out my own until they looked as though they were touching. His dark eyes met mine again.

"I most likely will never know how this was possible, but what I do know is that being able to meet with you and talk with you has encouraged and comforted me in a way nothing else has. You gave me the strength to confront my father and go get Samuel."

"I'm sure you would have done that anyway."

Elias shook his head. "I'm not so certain. Loss of hope can be crippling, as you well know." I nodded. I did know. "You helped keep that at bay for me. You, this," he said gesturing at me and then himself, "gave me hope. You've given me companionship and understanding when I needed it most, and I shall never forget you."

I didn't even try to stop the flow of tears at this point. "You've got it all wrong. You did all of that for me. I've had no one to talk to, or at least no one who understands like you do. Not about someone you love dying. Not about how it feels to be more adult than your parents. What am I supposed to do if I can't talk to you?"

"Oh, Julia." His hand curled and disappeared partway into mine. "Surely there are others you could confide in."

"It wouldn't be the same."

"No, it wouldn't. It can't be. But that doesn't mean it would be any less meaningful." My face must have shown my skepticism. "Please, Julia."

"Please what?"

"Please promise me you'll at least try. I don't want to worry about you." The concern on his face was real enough to make me feel a stab of guilt.

"Okay, I'll try."

"Good." Elias reached for his lantern. "I'd better go up now. It will be supper time soon."

"Can we try to meet again tomorrow?"

"My father needs me to get supplies from town and help him with some patient visits. He's gotten behind while caring for Samuel, so it will be a long day."

"Then Saturday?"

"Yes, Saturday. Can you come earlier in the day? Say eleven? Samuel likes for me to read to him after lunch."

"Sure. I'll be here."

"So will I." Elias stood still for a moment, seeming to struggle with something. "Julia," he said finally, "do you know if I have any descendents still living in the area?"

"You mean now, in my time?" I asked, surprised. Elias had always shied away from talking about the future before.

"Yes."

"Are you sure you want to know?"

"Yes," he repeated.

"Then yes, you do. In fact, I've met two of them. Some of your… family lived in this house until pretty recently. The last one who lived here moved in with his son's family across town." I cleared my throat. "I actually go to school with his grandson." Elias nodded and something in his expression stopped me from asking why he wanted to know.

"Thank you." He glanced toward the steps.

"Elias, wait." My heart was thrumming in my chest like the wings of a hummingbird, but I had to say it. "I love you." He stepped closer to me and his eyes moved over my face, taking in every detail.

"And I love you, Julia," he said, his voice hoarse. "You have been dearer to me than you can ever know." And in the next shuddering breath I took, he was gone. I stood there for several minutes, gasping the cold air into my lungs and fighting not to fall into the abyss that had just opened in front of me.

You will see him again, I told myself. *You will see him again.*

⭑⭑⭑

It was a struggle to focus on what my mother was saying at dinner that night, until I heard the word "Christmas."

"Sorry, what?" My mother gave me an exasperated look. She was still disappearing for long stretches of time, but she seemed to be paying more attention when she was around and she was drinking less.

"I said, your father called and said he's booked the tickets for him and Matty to come down here for Christmas. So we should probably go out and get a few things. I don't know if I'm up for a tree, but maybe we could get some lights and a few decorations. How does that sound?"

"That'd be fun." I didn't know how it was possible to feel so sad and so happy at the same time.

"All right." My mother looked down.

"What?" I could tell she wanted to say something else. She looked up again.

"It's just...I've started taking some medication. An antidepressant my therapist recommended. I just thought you should know."

"Okay."

"But it might take awhile for it to start working. And I've barely started to get into things with my therapist." Her hands were pleating her napkin into tiny folds.

"I know, Mom. It's okay. Really."

Her hands stilled.

⇥⇥● ●⇤⇤

Every teacher at school seemed to want to squeeze in one last project or exam before winter break, making Friday fly by. The next morning, I woke to the whistling rattle of a strong wind shaking my window in its frame. I burrowed deeper under the covers for a sleepy moment, savoring the warmth of my bed and the thought of seeing Elias in just a few hours. While it was hard to ignore the signs at our last meeting, it was still possible to believe that Elias would be there when I went down to the cellar. More than possible. *He will be there.*

I stretched, then in one quick motion threw back the covers and wrapped myself in the robe at the foot of my bed. It was a man's red plaid robe. Uncle Denny had given it to me for Christmas three years ago. When I'd opened it, my father had laughed and my mother, who was still trying to make me wear pajama sets with flowers on them, had frowned. But I had loved it and put it on immediately, disappearing into its folds. I was even more thankful for it now—it was like having a little bit of Uncle Denny wrapped around me.

My mother had taped a note to the coffee maker. *Out for a bit. Back after lunch to go shopping.* I filled a mug and tried to read the paper, but it was too hard to focus. All I could think about was Elias and whether I'd be able to see him and what he'd said the last time. About the choice being made for us. About reaching out to others and my promise to try. Just like I'd wanted my mother to. *Just like Derek said.* I folded the paper and stood up, unready to explore those thoughts.

When my watch finally read 10:40, I put on my jacket and went outside. My hands trembled as I unlocked the doors and my breaths were rapid and shallow. I turned on the light and sat in my chair, then looked at my watch again. 10:43. I took a deep breath and let it out, closing my eyes and resting my head against the wall behind me. I made myself wait until it became unbearable, then looked at my watch again. 10:51.

I sat gripping the edge of my chair, my gaze fixed on the stairs in front of me. The wind had died down a bit, but periodic gusts still made the cellar doors bump and groan. And then I heard it—a faint shuffle that was different from the wind and the doors. I stood up.

"Elias?" I called. I strained to see any hint of movement or light in front of me other than that cast by the dim bulb above my head, but there was nothing. I waited, every muscle taut with my listening. There was another rustle, and a breath of what sounded like my name. "Elias!" I shouted. "Elias, can you hear me? Can you see me?" *Was that a flash of white?* I waved my arms in the air, hoping he could see my movement. I knew he was there, that it wasn't the wind or some trick of light. I looked at my watch. It was 11:05. "Please," I said, my voice breaking. "Please let me see you." I waited in silence for several minutes, but there was nothing.

I dropped back into my chair and stared into the space in front of me. *Maybe he's late today. Maybe he got held up.* But as the minutes ticked by, I knew that wasn't true. I knew he had been there as he had promised, and I hadn't been able to see or hear him beyond those barely perceptible traces of sound of motion. It was just like it had been in the beginning, when I first started hearing things. *This can't be the end. Not yet. I'm not ready.* I dropped by head into my hands. "Elias," I said again. I imagined him sitting across from me, staring into the space where I sat and seeing the same emptiness, and the pain cut through me from throat to belly. I was a postmortem corpse, my skin peeled back and my ribs laid open.

I'm not sure how long I sat there. Long enough to know there was no point in waiting any longer. My mother would be home soon if she wasn't already. Somehow, I managed to stand up and force myself out of the cellar and into the house. When I heard my mother come in, I met her in the front hallway.

"Ready?" she asked.

"Yeah."

My mother's gaze sharpened on my face. "What's wrong?"

I concentrated on putting on my scarf and gloves, every motion seeming to take effort. When I looked up again, she was watching me with a concerned expression. "It's just…" I tried to come up with some kind of explanation but couldn't think of anything. I settled for the truth, or at least the part that mattered. "It's just really hard to lose someone you love, isn't it?" I finally choked out.

"Oh, baby." My mother wrapped me in her arms and hugged me tightly. One of her coat buttons was digging into my cheek, but I didn't care. She stroked my head and murmured soothing noises in my ear, and I gave myself up to it, pressing myself against her even more tightly as we rocked slowly back and forth.

Chapter 22

THE NEXT DAY, I took my schoolbag and made my way down into the cellar after breakfast. Part of me couldn't bear the thought of waiting again without seeing Elias, but a stronger part of me couldn't bear the thought of missing a chance to see him again if there still was one. But after almost three hours of hunching over my books and tensing every time I thought I heard any kind of noise only to have it turn out to be nothing, I was exhausted.

I went back up to the house, feeling like my body was filled with concrete, and found my mother in the kitchen. She opened her mouth and closed it without saying anything, which I was thankful for. I didn't have the energy to try to come up with an explanation for why I was spending hours in the cellar in the middle of December.

"I'm going to take a nap," I said. She nodded, and I trudged up the stairs and collapsed on my bed. It was strange how quickly we had changed places, my mother and I. The thought of it made me smile, but I was pierced by a stab of anguish when my next thought was to tell Elias about it. I buried my face in my pillow. *It's Uncle*

Denny all over again, I thought. Only it wasn't. Uncle Denny had been part of my whole life, and I had more memories of him than I could possibly add up. But I had only known Elias for a few months in a little cellar that I'd soon be leaving behind. What if I forgot? What if he just faded away? With Uncle Denny, there were pictures, videos, things connected to him like his mug and my robe, and a whole group of people I could remember him with. But I couldn't tell anyone about Elias, and I had nothing but my own memory of our talks together, which had already taken on a dream-like quality. *Please*, I thought. I don't know what or whom I was addressing, but it was all I could think and feel. *Please*.

⇒▷ ◁⇐

When I got home from school the next day, I found a note taped to the refrigerator. *At therapist's. Back by dinner.* I opened the refrigerator and closed it again without taking anything out. I didn't feel much like eating. I moved toward the back door and stood in front of it for several seconds. Did I really want to put myself through the heart-ache of waiting again? And yet, what if there was still a chance?

The sound of an unfamiliar car pulling up to the house interrupted my thoughts. I went down the hallway, opened the front door, and found myself staring at Derek's truck. But it wasn't Derek climbing out of it, slowly and stiffly, clinging to the side for a moment before walking toward me. It was Derek's grandfather.

"Mr. Gardner!" I started down the porch steps. "Do you need some help?" I asked, offering my arm. But he waved it away.

"No, no. I'm fine if you just give me half a minute. I'm not as fast as I used to be." We climbed the steps together, and when I motioned for him to come inside, he shook his head. "This won't take long. Why don't we just sit here," he said, pointing to the two chairs on the side of the porch. I hesitated. They were dirty and none too stable looking, and it couldn't have been more than forty-five degrees outside, but he was already grasping the arms of one of them and lowering himself into it. I sat down gingerly beside him and waited for him to explain his visit.

Despite his earlier assurance that this wouldn't take long, he seemed in no hurry to get started. "My wife and I bought these chairs at a yard sale for four dollars back in 1980," he said, his hands running lightly up and down the armrests.

"Is that so?" I murmured, trying to be polite. What was he doing here?

"I haven't been back to this house in nearly three years."

I shifted in my chair, unsure of what to say. "It's a nice house," I said finally.

"Yes," he replied. He gazed at some vague point in the distance, and I began to wonder if he was all there. Just as I was debating whether or not to call someone, Mr. Gardner turned and pinned me with a look that was anything by hazy. "Don't worry, young lady, I'm not soft in the head." I flushed guiltily and he snorted. "No, I'm not soft in the head," he repeated, "although what I'm about to give you sometimes makes me think I am." He reached into his jacket and pulled out an envelope. He didn't hand it to me right away but sat holding it for a long moment, staring down at it.

"What's that?" I couldn't contain my curiosity any longer. Mr. Gardner tapped it with his finger and sniffed.

"It's a letter for you," he said, looking up again and holding it toward me. *Derek sent me a letter through his Grandpa?* I thought. *How weird.* I took it from him, surprised by its heft and the condition of the envelope. It was browned and softened with age. I stared down at the old-fashioned script written across the front: "Please deliver this letter to Julia McKinley at the old Gardner home at the beginning of the third week of December, 2002." I gasped and looked up at Mr. Gardner, who was watching me.

"What is this?" My whole body began to tremble.

"I don't know what that is or *how* that is, and I don't want to. All I can tell you is that my grandfather gave it to me when I was a young man and firmly impressed its importance upon me, which had been passed along to him by his father. I can't even begin to fathom how any of this is possible. All I know is that you're supposed to have that letter on this day, so there you go."

"Does anyone else know about this?" I asked, trying to absorb the reality of what I was holding and what I was being told. Mr. Gardner shook his head and barked a dry, wheezy laugh.

"Hell, no. I already have enough trouble with them watching me all the time, asking me if I need help up the stairs and where I'm going when I just want to take a walk around the damn block. If I'd told them about this, they'd have locked me up in the loony bin."

"Does Derek know you took his truck to come see me?"

"No, I told him I had to get something at the store. He won't say anything about it to the others. He's a good kid."

"Yes," I said, looking back down at the letter in my lap and smoothing a trembling hand across its surface. Mr. Gardner stood up.

"Well, I'll leave you to it." When I made a move to get up as well, he held up his hand. "That's okay. I can get myself to the truck." He walked to the edge of the porch and stopped, turning to look back at me. "You know, you're the first girl Derek's ever talked to me about. I've never seen him so happy as when he was giving you those driving lessons. Or seen him so moody as when they stopped."

"I'm sorry," I said. "I didn't mean to…"

"Don't be sorry." Mr. Gardner waved a dismissive hand. "Love and disappointment are part of life. It's okay if you don't feel the same way he does." His gaze caught mine and held it. "But I will say this—don't give up the one who's here for someone who's not," he said, glancing down at the letter in my hand. I couldn't have spoken in that moment even if I'd wanted to, so I simply nodded. He nodded back. "Good. Well, that's that, I guess. Goodbye, Julia."

"Bye, Mr. Gardner," I managed to choke out. "Thanks." The truck started with a loud rumble and I watched as he backed out and drove down the street. I looked down at the letter again. There was only one place to read it. I went around the side of the house and performed the ritual of unlocking the cellar doors slowly and carefully, knowing that this would be the last time. I turned on the light, sat down in my chair, and studied the letters spelling out my name on the front of the envelope, tracing their curves and points with the tip of my finger. Then I closed my eyes and took a deep breath. It was time to read Elias's letter.

Using the key to the cellar lock, I carefully slit the envelope open and pulled out several thick sheets of paper. They were brighter than the envelope but still faintly yellowed and covered with the same script as the envelope. Drawing in another shuddering breath, I carefully unfolded the pages and began:

My Dear Julia,

This letter you are now reading, if in fact it has made its way through the years into your hands, has been written many times. The first one, written in the days just after our last meeting, was full of all the distress and sorrow you must be feeling right now. You should know that Thursday of the second week in December was our last meeting. I was there at our appointed time on Saturday and waited for nearly half an hour, but I was unable to see or hear you. I thought I heard something and perhaps saw a flash of light or movement at one point, but in retrospect it is hard to know if that was anything real or only my own longing. I was there again the next day for an hour, and many occasions after that—as often as I could slip away and go down—but you were never there. Or if you were, I was no longer able to sense you. As I said once before, I know you will probably either spend too much time waiting for me down in the cellar or tormenting yourself that you are not. I hope in telling you what I know, you will be spared some of that.

As you read this, you are still so young with so much life ahead of you. But as I write this, I am an old man with most of my life now behind me. I have thought of you often over the years. Sometimes my memory of you seemed to be a hazy dream, but at others, I'd go down into the cellar and you'd be as vivid and real to me as the jars I could pick up in my hands. I have searched all my days for the meaning of our time together and how it ever came to be, but even now in my old age I have no answer. I am beginning to realize that I do not need one. The experience of you and the comfort and help our meetings provided was enough. You were a light to me in a time of great darkness, and I have never forgotten you.

My one regret was that I wasn't able to give you anything tangible, to leave you with anything of substance or to have a last goodbye. And so I wrote you letters, pouring out my grief and love in the weeks after our final meeting, trying to communicate what I couldn't even properly understand myself. I came across them the other day, and when I read them, I realized they would do you no good because they cannot see beyond the pain of loss, perhaps much in the way you cannot right now. And it has occurred to me that perhaps I can leave you something after all— perhaps I can give you the gift of all my years of living and of seeing things from a larger perspective. Perhaps what I have learned and experienced might serve as stepping-stones across a river whose depths you might otherwise struggle through.

In the weeks and months after our last meeting, Samuel continued to recover and grow stronger. Though I don't think he and my father ever managed to speak about things directly, an unspoken forgiveness and peace developed between them, which made my mother and me profoundly glad. As Samuel grew stronger, however, he also grew more restless. Even with things improved between him and my father, there are some wounds so deep that they change things irrevocably. Samuel became uneasy living at home, and it was barely a year after he returned to us that he joined a group heading west. He ended up settling in Texas. It was hard to have him gone again, but in some ways it was perhaps for the best. He seemed, from his letters, content there in a way he had never been at home.

When I turned eighteen, I signed up with the Union army, which by then had gained greater control of northern Virginia. Given some of the training and knowledge my father had passed along to me, I was apprenticed to a field surgeon. I learned a great deal and we were able to help many, but the many we were not—the ones who died screaming in agony or calling for their mothers—shall haunt me until the day I die. When the war finally ended, I headed north to attend medical school like my father had before me. Perhaps predictably, I returned home to Virginia to take over his practice. The next part, my dear Julia, might cause you some pain, but I beg your forbearance and patience. I'm sure you must know that I married and had children since you've met my descendents, but it was never something we spoke of directly. A year after my return to Virginia, I married the daughter of a neighboring family. Her name was Susannah, and she was a lovely, gentle woman whom I loved dearly. I lost her last spring, and the days since have been long and lonely, though my children and grandchildren do their best to visit and cheer me.

I imagine it is not easy for you to read such things. During the months we met and for many months after, I would find myself full of jealousy at the thought of you sharing your life with someone else. I suppose I feared it would somehow diminish or take away from what we shared and the feelings you had for me. But now I know, and I hope you will also know, that this is not the case. When it comes to love, there is room for so much and so many different kinds. The heart is capable of expanding far beyond what we can ever imagine if only we will allow it. What I felt for you all those years ago as a boy struggling on the brink of manhood still resides in my heart, untouched by what I felt and still feel for my dear wife.

And now I ask you to take the years of my life and experience, Julia, that you might have the freedom to go forward in your own life, unafraid to love and unafraid to trust that there will always be things greater than we can ever comprehend that can come into our lives at any moment and be the greatest of blessings. You and I and our time together in the cellar are evidence of that, and it has been a comfort to me all of my life. I hope it will also be for you.

Who can know? Perhaps someday, in some other life, I shall see you again, and we will sit together and you will tell me the story of your own wonderful life, and I will be so very glad for you, my beautiful, strong, and loyal friend.

Elias

I read the letter through several times, holding it out so that the tears streaming down my face wouldn't fall on it and ruin it. I could hear his voice speaking to me out of the letter, and for a little while it was like being with him again. And yet, I knew now with certainty that I would never be with him again. His reference to another life where we could sit together and talk again was a beautiful fantasy he had concocted to comfort me. And yet, I couldn't help remembering the dream I'd had last month, where I'd sat at the table with my family and Uncle Denny and Elias. *Who can know?*

Coming to terms with the rest of it was a struggle between my heart and my mind. I understood and could even acknowledge some truth to what he was saying about love. I could even, on some level, be glad for him that he had found someone to love and marry and have a family with. I certainly wouldn't have wanted him to spend his life miserable and alone. But it still hurt that it couldn't have been me.

I wiped my face with my sleeve and carefully folded the letter back into its envelope. *There will always be things greater than we can ever comprehend that can come into our lives at any moment.* It was true, and this letter was further proof of that. The feel of it in my hands, coming to me after so many decades, filled me with a kind of humble awe. "Thank you," I whispered. And then I stood up, picked up my folding chair, and exited the cellar for the last time.

Chapter 23

I READ ELIAS'S letter so many times over the next two days that I pretty much had it memorized. Though I did my best to concentrate at school, different parts of the letter would come to mind at random moments, and I would find myself struggling not to tear up in the middle of a chemistry lab or a vocab quiz in Spanish.

I also found myself watching Derek in homeroom and thinking about our driving lessons and his visit after I got suspended. *Don't give up the one who's here for someone who's not.* His grandfather's words weren't very different from what I'd said to my mother. *Uncle Denny might be gone, but the rest of us are still here.* In some ways, both my mother and I had been acting like it was an either/or situation. My mother thought she had to stop being sad about Uncle Denny to move forward with us, and I thought loving Elias meant I couldn't have feelings for Derek. But there was no way my mother could love anyone and be herself without still loving and missing Uncle Denny. And the truth was that while I missed Elias, I missed Derek too. I missed the easy joking between us and the fun of being with him. I didn't want to lose him as a friend and, if I was honest, I also didn't want to lose the chance of him being more than a friend. *When it comes to love, there is room for so much and so many different kinds.* Words Elias knew I needed to hear because he loved me.

But was it too late? Had I let too much distance form between us? And was there really any point in trying when I'd be going back home so soon? I decided to confide in Samira when we got partnered in the weight room during P.E. I'd thought it would be hard to talk about things without mentioning Elias, but it was easier than I thought. Samira had been doing leg presses but slowed to a stop as I talked, listening intently.

"You need to talk to him," she said when I finally ran out of breath.

"Is it really worth it at this point?"

"Of course. It's obvious both of you aren't very happy about the way things are right now, and even if you're going back to New York, at least you can go back knowing that you tried instead of having to wonder about it forever. And you're going to be coming back to visit your mom, right? And you both applied to NYU. So, who knows?" *Who knows?* There it was again. I sighed. "What are you afraid of, anyway?" Samira pressed.

"Um, how about crushing humiliation and rejection? What if he blows me off when I try to talk to him like the last time?"

"That won't happen. I mean, not if you're really trying—which, by the way, I don't think you did the last time. Derek took a risk with you, coming to see you. Especially after he kissed you and you rejected him."

"I didn't reject him." Samira just gave me a look. "Okay, maybe a little. I didn't mean to, though."

"Well, maybe *he* didn't mean to. Anyway, if you're going to do something, you'd better do it soon. We go on break in a couple days and after that, you might as well forget about it. In fact, do it today before you chicken out."

I drew in a deep breath and let it out. "All right, I will. Man, you are bossy."

"I'm not bossy. I just know what's right." A shrill whistle signaled the end of the period. "Good luck!" Samira called as we parted in the locker room.

"Thanks." My hands began to tremble as I spun the combination on my locker. I was nervous, I realized as I changed back into my own clothes, but I was also excited. Samira was right. There was no reason to wait any longer. I wormed my way to the front of the girls clumped at the door, waiting for the bell to ring, and when it rang, I hurried toward the parking lot.

When I saw Derek's truck, I stopped. He was standing next to it talking to several friends. As I stood there, debating whether or not to try approaching him in front of the others—how humiliated was I willing to be?—he opened his door and climbed into the truck, waving a hand at his friends and firing up the engine. I broke out of my frozen state and ran toward the truck, but before I could reach him, he was already pulling out of the driveway. *Shit.*

I pulled my knit cap down over my ears, hunched my shoulders against the frigid air, and began my walk home. What should I do? Homeroom was hardly the place to have this conversation, and if I asked him to meet me after school, who was to say he wouldn't just take off again? Besides, like Samira said, I didn't want to give myself time to chicken out. Problem was, I couldn't call him on the phone since I'd never gotten his number. *Think.*

When I got to the house and saw my mother's car in the drive, I knew what I needed to do. I strode into the house and knocked on the library door, opening it even as my mother said, "Come in." She looked up at me, her hand poised in the air with a paintbrush. I hadn't been in this room in ages, but I barely took it in. "What's wrong?" she asked.

"I need to borrow the car."

My mother's mouth dropped open. "You can't drive."

"Yes I can. Derek taught me."

"But you don't have a license. And the roads could be icy." My mother was shaking her head. "No, absolutely not. If you need me to take you somewhere, I'd be happy to later on. I'm kind of in the middle of something here," she said.

I shook my head. "I need to go by myself, and I need to go now, before I lose my nerve. It's just a few miles and I promise I'll be super careful. I won't get in an accident and I won't get pulled over. I promise."

"How can you promise that? Don't be ridiculous, Julia. If it's that urgent, I guess I can take you now." I pictured my mother sitting in the car waiting for me like I was a kid at a birthday party. *No way.*

"Mom, please. I really need to do this on my own. It's important." She studied me for a long moment, and some of my desperation must have shown because I could see her starting to relent.

"Does this have anything to do with what you were so upset about the other day?"

"Sort of. Yes." It wasn't about Elias directly, but in some ways it was. I was trying to step across the stones he had put in place for me and keep my promise to reach out to others. My mother sighed and set down her brush.

"All right. This is probably the stupidest thing I've ever done and your father can never know about this, but all right." She fumbled in her pocket and pulled out her keys. "You'd better be careful or there'll be hell to pay."

"I will. I'll drive like an old lady." I grabbed the keys out of her hand before she could change her mind. "Thanks, Mom." I hurried out and slammed the front door behind me, then slowed as I went down the porch steps and approached the car, trying to look as deliberate and responsible as possible when I saw my mother peering anxiously out the window at me. I gave her a small wave and climbed in.

As promised, I drove slowly and carefully, zigzagging my way across town to Derek's neighborhood. I could have made it there in a fraction of the time if I'd taken the main highway, but I knew that would be too risky seeing as I'd never driven over 35 miles an hour and it was way too visible. A light drizzle had begun to fall when I pulled up to his house, making me glad I'd worn my cap. At least I wouldn't look like a drowned rat.

I knocked on the front door and, after a moment, heard the sound of slow footsteps. Mr. Gardner opened the door. "Huh," he greeted me as I stared at him in surprise. *What were you expecting? He lives here too*, I reminded myself.

"Is Derek home?"

"Yeah, he's in the kitchen. Come in." Mr. Gardner pulled the door open. "Through there," he said pointing, then shuffled down the hall.

"Thanks." I took a deep breath and stepped through the kitchen door. Derek was standing over the sink with a piece of pizza in his hand. "Hi," I said, my voice coming out in a nervous croak. The pizza froze mid-way to Derek's mouth and his head whipped around.

"Julia? What are you doing here?" He frowned, making my heart drop like a stone. I guess joy at the sight of me was a little too much to hope for on his part. I was tempted to run out of the house, but forced myself to speak instead.

"I wanted to talk to you. I tried catching you after school, but I wasn't able to get to your truck in time. And since we're about to go on break, I thought I'd just come over. I hope that's okay." He just stared at me, still holding his pizza. I shoved my hands in my pockets. "You can go ahead and eat that if you want," I said, nodding at his hand.

"Oh." Derek looked at the pizza like he'd forgotten it and set it on the counter. "That's okay. I'll eat it later. How'd you get here?"

"I drove."

"You drove," he repeated.

"Yes."

"But you don't have a license. You've never even gone more than 35 miles an hour."

"I took side streets."

"Does your mom know?"

"Of course. I had to get the keys from her."

"And she let you?" His voice was incredulous. I blew out a sigh of frustration. This was not going the way I'd hoped it would.

"Yes, I told her how important it was to me and she said okay. Just this one time. Are you satisfied? I didn't steal my mom's car and I got here in one piece. Do we need to keep talking about this?"

"I guess not." Derek shrugged. "Sorry. It just surprised me is all." He glanced up at the ceiling where the faint sounds of music drifted down. "My brother and sister are both home on break. Why don't we go out here?" he suggested, and I followed him out to an enclosed back porch. He sat down on a cushioned wicker sofa and I perched on the edge of a rocker. He stared at me expectantly and I swallowed hard. Now that he was ready to listen, I wasn't quite sure what to say.

"So, I just wanted to tell you…" I stopped and started again. "You should know that…" I sputtered to a halt.

"Would you just spit it out already, McKinley? I'd like to eat that pizza before it's actually dinner time." Derek's complaint jolted me out of nervousness.

"Fine," I snapped. "This isn't easy, you know."

"Yeah, I *do* know," he said, an edge to his voice.

"Well, that's what I wanted to talk to you about. I didn't like it at first, but I wanted to thank you for what you said when you came over, and to tell you that you were right." His eyebrows went up, but I ignored that and charged on. "I *have* been pulling away, and I was doing it because I was scared. And it wasn't fair to you. It's just not that easy for me to open up to people, and with things already so emotional with my mom, it was easier to shut down. I don't like getting all messy with other people."

Derek was shaking his head. "But life is messy. People are messy. You can't avoid it. No one can. So you're not Little Miss Perfect who's in control all the time. Who cares?" He saw me wince and said, "I didn't mean it like that. I just mean perfect is boring and you're not. You're complex. Frustrating as hell, maybe, but way more interesting than most of the girls around here."

"If you say so." I felt a small fraction of relief at his comments.

"I do." Derek seemed to remember that I was the one who was supposed to be opening up and he sat back, folding his arms across his chest. "So is that all?"

"No." I looked down at my hands. "I also came here because you said that if I wanted you in my life, I needed to show you." I lifted my head and focused on a point just above his shoulder. "I do. Want you in my life." He made a faint sound in his throat and I met his gaze fully. "I've missed you, Derek. I know I haven't treated you very well lately, but I'm going to do my best to be more open with you. If it's not too late, that is," I finished, looking back down at my hands. There was an agonizing pause, and then Derek's hand covered my own and squeezed it.

"No, it's not too late. Although," he added, leaning back into the couch and grinning, "you sure took your time about it." My body went slack with relief and I found myself smiling back.

"Good thing I'm worth the wait." My smile faded as I remembered something. "You should know that I won't be here much longer, though."

"Why not?"

"Well, the short version is that my mom wants me to go home. But it's okay," I said when Derek started to frown. "She's getting help now, and my dad and brother are coming here for Christmas. And I'll definitely be coming back to visit a lot. So, you know."

"That's great, Julia," he said, his voice quiet and sincere. For a brief second, it reminded me of Elias.

"Thanks."

"I mean, it works out well for me too. I'm going to need somewhere to stay when I visit NYU in the spring." He was grinning again.

"I'm glad you're not too crushed about my leaving."

"Nah, we'll see each other plenty. You can teach me to ride the subway."

"Right." I stood up. "Well, I'd better get going before my mom starts thinking I've crashed the car." Derek stood up as well, towering over me as usual.

"I'm glad you came over, Julia."

"Me too." I smiled up at him and he lifted me off my feet in a bear hug complete with growling.

"What would you say to one more driving lesson tomorrow after school?" he asked, still holding me in mid-air.

"I'd say that's a great idea." My voice was muffled against his neck.

"Cool." He set me down and opened the door to the kitchen. "See you tomorrow."

⟶▬◉ ◉▬⟵

It was nearly dark when I pulled into the driveway at the house, and my mother's face appeared at the window. She called out as I came in the front door, and I went into the library.

"Everything all right?" My mother was rubbing paint off her hands with rag. I looked at the canvases propped around the room and the mess of partially squeezed paint tubes on the desk beside her and nodded slowly.

"I think so. Or at least I think it will be."

"Glad to hear it." She put the rag down, and as I stepped forward to hug her, I couldn't help thinking of the first time I'd hugged her in this house. The loss was still there. It would always be there. But there was room for love and gladness too.

"Me too."